## *Girl, 20*

Kingsley Amis (1922–1995) was born in South London and educated at the City of London School and St John's College, Oxford. He began his literary career as a poet but shot to fame on the publication of his first novel *Lucky Jim* in 1954. He wrote over twenty novels including *That Uncertain Feeling*, *Take a Girl like You*, *One Fat Englishman*, *The Green Man* and *Stanley and the Women*. He was nominated for the Booker Prize for *Ending Up* (1974) and again for *Jake's Thing* (1978) and he won it for *The Old Devils* in 1986. Amis also published six volumes of poetry and many works of non-fiction including his *Memoirs*, in 1991. He wrote widely on science fiction, politics, education, language, films, television, eating and drinking. He was appointed CBE in 1981 and was knighted in 1990.

Howard Jacobson, novelist and critic, was born in Manchester and studied at Cambridge under F. R. Leavis. Author of eleven novels, including *Coming From Behind*, *The Mighty Walzer* and *Kalooki Nights*, he is also the author of several works of non-fiction, including *Roots Schmoots* and *Seriously Funny*, both of which were made into television series. He writes a weekly column for the *Independent*. In 2010 he won the Man Booker Prize for *The Finkler Question*.

# KINGSLEY AMIS

## *Girl, 20*

*With an introduction by Howard Jacobson*

PENGUIN BOOKS

PENGUIN CLASSICS

Published by the Penguin Group
Penguin Books Ltd, 80 Strand, London WC2R ORL, England
Penguin Group (USA) Inc., 375 Hudson Street, New York, New York 10014, USA
Penguin Group (Canada), 90 Eglinton Avenue East, Suite 700, Toronto, Ontario, Canada M4P 2Y3
(a division of Pearson Penguin Canada Inc.)
Penguin Ireland, 25 St Stephen's Green, Dublin 2, Ireland (a division of Penguin Books Ltd)
Penguin Group (Australia), 250 Camberwell Road, Camberwell, Victoria 3124, Australia
(a division of Pearson Australia Group Pty Ltd)
Penguin Books India Pvt Ltd, 11 Community Centre, Panchsheel Park, New Delhi – 110 017, India
Penguin Group (NZ), 67 Apollo Drive, Rosedale, Auckland 0632, New Zealand
(a division of Pearson New Zealand Ltd)
Penguin Books (South Africa) (Pty) Ltd, 24 Sturdee Avenue, Rosebank, Johannesburg 2196, South Africa

Penguin Books Ltd, Registered Offices: 80 Strand, London WC2R ORL, England

www.penguin.com

First published in Great Britain by Jonathan Cape 1971
Published in Penguin Books in Great Britain 1980
Published in Penguin Classics 2011

1

Set in 10.5/13 pt Dante MT Std
Typeset by Palimpsest Book Production Limited, Falkirk, Stirlingshire
Printed in Great Britain by Clays Ltd, St Ives plc

ISBN: 978-0-141-19424-0

www.greenpenguin.co.uk

*To Mary and Mike Keeley*

# Contents

# Introduction

Girl, 20, Kingsley Amis's ninth novel, was published in 1971, seventeen years after Lucky Jim, his first. In that time, by his own admission – in 1967 he published an essay entitled 'Why Lucky Jim Turned Right' – Amis appeared to change from being a sharp-tongued radical, who enjoyed scuttling British dufferdom in all its forms, to being an even sharper-tongued satirizer of progressiveness. It's easy to see this as a familiar descent (or ascent, depending where you're coming from) from idealism into disillusionment, but one shouldn't make too much of it politically, even if Amis himself decided to. In the first place, his radicalism was always soft and commonsensical, rooted in Anglo-Saxon decency, wary of too much change and suspicious of grandiosity. That almost goes without saying in a comic writer, for whom the fashionably new will always look as absurd as the unfashionably old. And, secondly, something happened between Lucky Jim and Girl, 20 that had nothing to do with Amis's own temperament. That something was the 60s.

The year before the publication of Girl, 20, the American hyper-journalist Tom Wolfe coined the phrase 'radical chic' to pillory the new sentimentalizing of extremist groups – in this instance the Black Panthers – by America's white and wealthy intellectual elite. At the start of an essay for New York magazine, Wolfe wickedly imagines the great composer and conductor 'Lenny' Bernstein waking up in the early morning of his 48th birthday 'in a state of wild alarm'. Groggy, he rises from his bed. Then, suddenly, he has a vision. He sees himself walking out on stage in white tie and tails and delivering an anti-war message to the adoring 'starched white-throated audience'. He sits in a chair and picks up a guitar – that symbol of populism. 'I love,' he tells the concert hall.

Any connection between Lenny Bernstein and Sir Roy Vandervane, the eminent composer-conductor, whose descent into voguish politics and youth-crazed philistinism *Girl, 20* mercilessly charts, is probably coincidental; but they are both archetypal figures of the time or, to put that another way, they are both conjured out of the same nightmare – that, after the capitulation of educated men to the child-speak of the 60s, we will never inhabit a serious culture again. In this way, Amis's novel and Tom Wolfe's extended essay – it was reprinted in *Radical Chic & Mau-Mauing the Flak Catchers* – deserve to be read in tandem, as twin comic indictments of the failure of the 60s intelligentsia to remember its function, its honour and its dignity.

Running through the erotic possibilities that might still be left to him as a sexually incontinent, ageing man – homosexuality, beyond younger women, flagellation, etc. – Sir Roy Vandervane crosses 'those other capers', necrophilia and bestiality, off the list too. 'No point in even discussing any of them,' he says. 'It would just be flogging a dead horse.'

It's one of those good, snortingly bad bar-room jokes you expect from Kingsley Amis. But that's not quite the end of it. Amis is a novelist, not a comedian, which means that the jokes, when they come, are all about who makes them. This one is very much Roy Vandervane's; we don't doubt he has made it before and will make it again. As a serial philanderer and plunderer, everything he does, he does again, and everything he does, however questionable, he takes pride in. 'Surely you got that?' he says, wanting to be certain that the person to whom he has made the joke this time is alive to it. 'Oh yes, I got it all right,' that person replies. 'I just wanted to make sure you had.'

It's all very childish and rude in the way that clever men who are friends and on the half-loose will be childish and rude with one another – straight-faced and quick, and no limits placed on subject matter, but with an undertow of undeclared seriousness. The recipient of Sir Roy Vandervane's preposterous speculations about the nature of desire is the music critic Douglas Yandell, the novel's narrator, a bachelor at a bit of a sexual dead-end himself, and a friend and admirer of Sir Roy's, called in by the composer's wife to dissuade him from his latest escapade, which, while it does not embrace necrophilia or bestiality, does entail a younger woman – not Girl, 20 but Girl, Something Even Worse: Girl, 17. What Douglas wants to make sure Roy has 'got' is not only his own good bad joke but the dire consequences, to all parties, of dating Girl, 17 when you're Man, A Hell of a Lot Older Than That. The joke, in other words, is no joke at all.

That essentially – the joke of Sir Roy Vandervane's incorrigibility turning out to be unfunny and even tragic – is the story, and it's plenty to be going on with. Kingsley Amis can make a lot happen with moral indignation. 'Irresponsibility', he once said in an interview, 'is what *Girl, 20* is about.' That's a heroically plain, not to say solemn statement for a comic novelist to make. But then, from his very first novel, *Lucky Jim*, Kingsley Amis always did operate at the more homespun, moralizing end of the comic-writing spectrum, his satire a check on humanity's outlandishness, a defence of fair play and honourableness, rather than a revelling in selfish appetite and disorder – more Fielding, in other words, than Rabelais.

Which is not to say that taking on irresponsibility as a subject precludes having fun with it. Sir Roy Vandervane's irresponsibility is of monstrous proportions, and not a single murky alley-way of the deviousness he employs to get his way is left unexplored: the 'favours' he exacts from his friend Douglas, to whom he as good as pimps his daughter; the egregious language of self-justification he employs; his energy for deception; his 'arse-creeping to youth'; his raging at 'absent or largely imaginary foes'; the slurring of his speech on political and arse-creeping grounds ('Spot of corm beef,' he orders faux-democratically for lunch, and 'some tin pineapple'); not to mention the baffling charm of the man, that 'system of total permissiveness towards himself that made him such agreeable company' – all this is rendered with so good an ear for his idiosyncrasies, and such fondness-in-disgust, that we feel we know what it's like just to cross the street with him, never mind to become complicit, as Douglas allows himself to be, in his affairs.

And if he is (at times lumberingly) witty in himself, he is also, like Falstaff, the cause that wit is in others.

'I don't know anything at all about her,' his wife says of the new girl in her husband's life – she was, of course, the new girl herself in her time – 'but they've been running at about twenty to twenty-two over the last three years or so. Tending to go down. Getting younger at something like half the rate he gets older. When he's seventy-three they'll be ten.'

The fact that these calculations point to an eventual criminality, if Sir Roy keeps going long enough, doesn't make them any the less absurd. Fascinated by the grotesque mathematical trajectory, Douglas Yandell keeps up the game: 'And when he's eighty-three,' he throws in, experimentally, 'they'll be five.'

Sir Roy Vandervane has done the sums himself, but that doesn't stop him deciding to leave his wife and family for Girl, 17, a decision which Douglas Yandell tries to counter with some unblinkingly cynical advice: 'Why can't you just stay put officially and see a lot of Sylvia on the side?'

Not just *see* her, notice, but see *a lot* of her. How much fairer can one be?

'No,' says the besotted Vandervane. 'I've had enough of that. So's she.'

Which is the cue for the great 'decency' speech one expects in every Kingsley Amis novel, the moment when the comic gloves come off and the necessary home-truths are delivered with a plainness that seems to belong to a different sort of work.

If you've had enough of it, then pack it in. And how do you mean, had enough? You talk as if you've the spent the last couple of years fighting in the jungle. What you've had getting on for enough of, no doubt, is making other people's lives a misery while you're watching . . . Do you understand what I'm saying?

That's Douglas telling it like it is, but Amis is too good a novelist not to allow Vandervane a biting riposte. 'I'll take criticism', he answers, 'from chaps who've been in my situation and chosen differently. No one else.'

What's at stake, though, in the great musician's arse-creeping after youth is more than an infatuation with a fool of a girl for whom he is prepared to ditch his family, there is also the small matter of *Elevations 9* (grossly echoing *Girl, 20*), a chamber concerto for violin, sitar, bass guitar and bongoes that Sir Roy has written in a parallel attempt to get the young to love him. And it is here that Douglas Yandell's speeches on behalf of decency take on a wider cultural application and grow more bitter. As Vandervane descends into a farcical musical underworld, it occurs to Douglas that he has finally lost him, that he no longer 'cares', that he has made his peace with a culture that positively dislikes 'the idea of the difficult being made to seem easy', a culture that doesn't care about the difficult seeming anything at all, come to that, that likes, in so far as it knows what it likes, 'the easy seeming easy'.

That, in the end, is the indictment that really matters – not Sir Roy Vandervane's misjudged passion for a near-minor, but his defection from the difficult to the easy, from accomplishment to celebrity. He was a serious musician and now he isn't. You'll . . . be helping to make music look like just another fun thing and now thing,' Douglas tells him. 'And that's a disgraceful thing to do.'

There are times when Amis's attacks on the culture of the young, the music they like to hear and the places they like to hear it in – 'ruffianly ululation' in 'abodes of muck' – feel distinctly Bufton-Tuftonish. That particular battle has been fought too many times, and forty years after *Girl, 20*, has been well lost. But the picture of a cultivated man and his family going to the dogs remains powerful, because of the novel's gathering moral and intellectual bleakness, expressed through Douglas Yandell's own unravelling. His decency, too, is lacklustre; his downward spiral into a sort of slack permissiveness, hating what Vandervane is doing to himself but always half conniving in it, is described in almost comic Dantesque imagery, as Vandervane, like an anti-Virgil, takes him down into a succession of deep, dark, hateful cellars and disused warehouses dedicated to what's 'fun' and what's 'now'. Douglas Yandell doesn't lose grip on his indignation, but the claustrophobic sense of hellish pointlessness that seizes him is of another order of distress. The final chapter is entitled 'All Free Now'. Never has the word 'free' been made to sound so desolate.

Howard Jacobson, 2011

*Girl, 20*

# One

## Imperialist Racist Fascist

'Is this chap really as good as you say?' asked Harold Meers.

'Well yes. He may be even better. In the sense that it's a bit early to tell. At his stage you can't be sure whether—'

'You mean technique and that sort of thing.'

'More than that,' I said. 'It's . . . He understands the music he plays. You'll see there that I've—'

'I should have thought they all did that.'

'They all don't, believe me.'

'By definition.' Harold added suddenly, as if in simple wonderment, 'He's from East Germany.'

'That's it.'

'One of the most backward and corrupt and tyrannical regimes in the world. Outside black Africa, of course.'

'No doubt. It hasn't stopped Kohler being a cracking good pianist. Perhaps it should have done, but it hasn't.'

'As you know, I had reservations about running a music column in the first place. People don't go to concerts any more, they buy records. All part of the stay-at-home culture. We deal with them already. And the whole thing goes on here, anyway. Manchester. Birmingham. Once in a blue moon. You've heard me say this isn't a London news-paper, it's a national newspaper. Is he a Jew?'

Harold said all this at his usual regular pace and level pitch, his small hands (joined on to small arms and by way of them to small shoulders) loose and palm upwards on his desk, the weak sunshine gleaming tranquilly on his nearly bald head. His style of discourse, with the mild strain it laid on his hearer's attention and powers of recall, was as usual too. One item, indeed, had strained my lot to

3

breaking-point. I had not known that he had had reservations about my having become, a few months previously, the paper's music critic, or rather musical-events reporter. He had told me then that this inno-vation, dreamed up by him alone as the first blow in a campaign to raise cultural standards in journalism generally, had been fought through by him alone in the teeth of opposition from his proprietor, his features editor and perhaps the liftman. Facing him now in his large, modern and shabby office, I answered his question truthfully.

'I don't know,' I said.

'Do we need to advertise these bastards? What about the do where there was that dust-up, you know, that Bolivian song-and-dance lot last Friday? People read about the hooligans busting in and being arrested and so on, but what about the actual stuff? A bit less esoteric than Telemann and Prokofiev and who's this other chap?'

'There was Beethoven too. I heard the Bolivians rehearsing, and I didn't think they really—'

'A critic ought to go easy with his superlatives.' Harold dropped his lustrous brown eyes to my copy that lay before him, and for a moment I thought he was reading it. 'We didn't put politics into art,' he went on very soon. 'They did. You do realize, don't you, that this chap's only allowed abroad because he's a loyal and trusted servant of that bloody awful regime? A walking advertisement for it?'

'Whether I do or I don't doesn't come into what I'm supposed to be at. The job you hired me for was to cover the most important musical events, and important judged by musical standards, not by any . . .'

One of Harold's telephones had started an enfeebled rattling, and he picked it up with one small hand while waving me down with the other.

'Yes,' he said on a high note. 'Yes. Who? Get her number.' He replaced the telephone and said to me, 'All right, what do you feel about just scrubbing where he comes from?'

'Just saying he's German, you mean?'

'Not saying he's anything. We're not handing out publicity mat-erial.'

'But Harold, if you're against the Eastern lot, then surely you—'

'All right,' he said again, neither impatiently nor coaxingly, in fact in not much of a way at all, 'all right. We'll leave it. But, as I say, you must let up a little on these technical terms. Remember, you're not writing for the profession.'

'Apart from one reference to a slow movement and another to a theme and variations, which ought to be elementary enough even for—'

'Fine. Give Features a ring about five thirty as usual, would you, in case we have to lose an inch or so? Right. That call was for you.'

'Who was it?'

'Kitty Vandersomething. Not Mrs Sir Roy Vandervane?'

'Sounds like it.'

'He must be worse than ever with that knighthood. Services to music, Services to the Prime Minister's backside more like.'

'He's better than that, Harold.'

'Yes, you used to work for him, didn't you?'

'For his orchestra.'

'Fine. See you.'

Along the corridor in Features I got the switchboard to put me through to the number Kitty had left there, realizing or remembering now that the Vandervanes had moved some miles north of Hampstead, where I had last visited them a year or more earlier, to a reputedly rather grand establishment on the fringes of the Hertfordshire countryside. After half a minute of ringing tone the distant receiver was lifted, but at first nobody addressed me. Instead, I heard a wordless yelling, loud but some way from the instrument, and a man's muffled voice saying he would go mad if that noise were not stopped. When the yelling had a little receded, I got my turn.

'Hallo, yes, who is it, please?' asked the same man's voice crossly. It sounded coloured.

'This is Douglas Yandell. Lady Vandervane wanted to speak to me.'

There followed no indication whether these facts had been absorbed, but at the end of another interval, during which the yelling changed to a vague shouting that faded out, Kitty came on the line.

'Is that you, Douglas?'

'Yes, Kitty.'

5

'Oh, thank God, thank *God* you're safe, my darling, my love, and I can start to live my life again' would not really have been an excessively emotional follow-up to the tone of heroically controlled hysteria in her opening question. But I knew Kitty always talked at that level, and all she actually said, with a mixture of dignified reprobation and a sorrow too deep for any mere words to be adequate, was, 'It seems ages since we saw you.'

I agreed, and in no time at all, without any formalistic nonsense about how I might have been intending to spend the rest of my day, I was listening to a fully researched account of how to get from where I was to where she was. She said she absolutely did most desperately need to see me, meaning she wanted to see me and took it for granted that I would come belting up to be seen by her as soon as so informed. Well, presumably there was the chance of seeing Roy as well.

'Is Roy round the place?' I asked as soon as I could.

'No, he's not, not at the moment. Actually, it was . . .' – I had no trouble visualizing the dignified furtiveness of her glance over her shoulder – 'it's him I so terribly urgently have to see you about. He's getting ready for another of his goes, Douglas. He may even have started.'

'Has he told you?'

'I just know.'

'Not the pants again?'

'*Yes*. How incredible of you to remember.'

'I've never forgotten.'

Who could? Though no stinker, Roy had never been one of the most fanatically cleanly of men except when building up to, or embarked on at any rate the pristine stage of, one of his 'goes', as Kitty called his affairs. Over the period since their marriage in 1961, she had learnt to recognize this situation by the stockpiling of pants in his underclothes drawer. Sudden rapid diminution of the pile, accompanied by an equally sudden flurry of oddly timed off-the-premises interviews with foreign journalists, abortive get-togethers with recording-company executives, etc., was the signal that the go was off the ground. Kitty had told me this years before, when I was still working as secretary of the orchestra of which Roy was then resident conductor. On ordinary male-trade-union grounds, I had promptly warned him about this dead give-away, but it seemed that he, unlike myself, had forgotten. Or had he? How could he have?

I had been considering matters while I listened and talked. It was exactly midday. What I had planned was a walk up Fleet Street for a couple of smoked-salmon sandwiches and glasses of hock at El Vino, a nice noisy afternoon in the flat going through some of the new discs I had to review in *The Record-Player*, an early dinner at Biagi's and a trip to the South Bank for a rather routine Bach-Handel concert. And there was always, or rather never, my book on Weber to be hauled past the Early Years phase. But I experienced no real inner struggle. Curiosity, always a powerful motive in matters Vandervanean, won hands down, though I had the sense not to indulge it for the moment. Asking Kitty over the telephone how I could help would have earned me twenty minutes of impassioned and impermeable hints. I said I would come straight away and added, out of more curiosity,

'How did you know where to find me?'

'Oh, that was Gilbert. He's marvellous at things like that.'

'Who's Gilbert?'

'You'll see.'

I was turning to go when the features editor, a fat man called Coates with a terrible cough, said to me,

'How was the great man?'

'Don't you know?'

'Sure I know. I was just wondering how you found him.'

I thought for a moment. 'What word would you use to describe being very decent about not paying attention to anything and not caring about nobody being any good?'

'I'd settle for shitty, but then I've got a simple mind. Did he cut you?'

'Not yet. He turned political again.'

Coates drew at his cigarette and coughed terribly. He seemed unaware of any link between these two actions. When he had finished coughing he said,

'Can't you get the Greek colonels to form a symphony orchestra and come over? It'd kill him. See you next week, if I'm spared.'

I took an 11 bus along the Strand and got on to the North-Western Line. As the train clattered out of the tunnel beyond Golders Green, and the April sunshine, stronger now, lit up an arbitrary mixture of cut-back greenery and what looked like emergency housing, I pondered Roy's goes.

The current crop of them must have started about four years after his marriage, itself product of an ancient go, for it had followed upon his divorce by a first wife. On my last meeting with Kitty, she had said that they were getting worse, in the sense that the girls seemed younger and more awful each time and Roy's involvement became successively deeper, and I had felt she was right. At that stage he had just come back from an actual week-end – the first such since their marriage – spent with somebody who called herself an actress and singer, but had never been seen or heard performing in either capacity. Kitty had said that she lived in acute hourly dread of some sort of final walk-out, and that she was plunged in despair, and I would have believed her easily if all her worries were not represented as acute dreads, and the tardy arrival of her cleaning lady did not regularly plunge her into despair. Anyway, I felt I could understand how Kitty, at forty-six or seven, must feel, and could not understand why Roy, at nearly fifty-four (twenty years my senior to within a week), should have to grow sillier as he grew older, except that his growing wiser would have been unbelievable.

The train stopped at the end of the line, and I and not many other people got out. Following instructions, I telephoned from a box near the station entrance and gave some either female or effeminate person the news that I had arrived. I was told to start walking and to expect to be picked up by a car. Asked what I looked like, I said – quite truthfully – that I was six foot three with red hair and glasses. I started walking, first up a stiff slope and then down a suburban road, past a garden with an artificial pond and a lot of painted plaster ducks in it.

Presently a large, new-looking car approached and pulled up rather violently alongside me. I saw that its driver was a young black man, conventionally dressed in dark jacket, white shirt and striped tie, and knew at once that this was Gilbert, as well as being the owner of the voice I had first heard over the telephone. I climbed in beside him.

Without looking at me or answering my greeting, he turned the car round and drove off, accelerating fiercely.

'What a nice car,' I said. 'Is it yours?'

'You think a stupid nigger could never make the bread to buy himself a status symbol like this.'

'Well, since you mention it, it would be remarkable, certainly.'

'It's Roy's car, if you've got to know.'

'He is doing nicely for himself.'

We turned off, climbed a long hill and emerged into an impressive thoroughfare with a wood and then a common on one side and infrequent large houses on the other.

'Where do you come from?' I asked.

'London.'

'Oh, I see.'

'You don't care anyway.'

A pond, a real one this time, came into view on the common, and the car pulled off the road at one end of a considerable dwelling with plaster urns and large rhododendron bushes in front of it. I remembered Roy telling me he had got the place for a song: yes, a song with mixed choir, double orchestra, brass band and organ. Then I realized that the car had stopped in front of some blue-painted wooden gates, and that my companion was sitting motionless beside me.

'Would you like me to open those?'

'If you think it won't soil your fine hands.'

'I'll risk it.'

I opened the gates and walked into a paved courtyard adorned with small trees in a sickly or dead condition. As I did so, a ferocious barking, diversified at times with a kind of slipping-ratchet effect, broke out within the house. I recognized the voice of the Furry Barrel, the Vandervanes' red cavalier-spaniel bitch. I had always thought it slightly odd that someone with Roy's political views should tolerate, let alone adore, as he did, such a reactionary little dog: authoritarian, hierarchical, snobbish, with strong views on the primacy of the family, the maintenance of order, the avoidance of change, the sanctity of private property and, as I was soon to discover, the preservation of barriers between the races.

The immediate focus of this last prejudice had driven the car in at speed and stopped it as if he had noticed a crevasse a yard in front. He slammed his door, came up to me and said,

'You are an imperialist racist fascist.'

'But how on earth did you know?'

He referred to my job on the newspaper whose offices I had recently left.

'What about it?'

'It's a white supremacist colonialist organization.'

'Of course, but I'm not an employee of theirs, I just do regular pieces for them. And colonialist music is rather hard to—'

'While you're still working on behalf of such an organization, you must expect yourself to be called a fascist and so on.'

'Yes, I suppose I'll just have to.'

Despite what he had been saying, Gilbert's tone had so far been remarkably free of hostility. His last remark, in particular, seemed to have been intended as a piece of moral suasion. But his face, which I now noticed was of European rather than African cast, and his voice, pleasing in the abstract, turned quite angry when he said,

'Don't you think that's a bloody serious accusation, to call you a fascist?'

'No I don't. Nor a communist or a bourgeois or anything else. I just don't care about any of that, you see.'

He looked at me in pure amazement. 'But these are some of the great issues of our time.'

'Of your time, you mean. The great issue of my time is me and my interests, chiefly musical. Can we go indoors now?'

With Gilbert following in defeated silence, I went through a glass porch of recent addition where there were a lot of very old coats on an old coat-stand and a lot of empty whisky- and wine-bottles. A further door gave on to a passage. I saw a near and a distant staircase and, fixed to the wall, an empty Perspex box labelled 'Anti-apartheid Fund'. Preceded, then accompanied, by tremendous barking and growling, the Furry Barrel pattered round a corner and danced about in our way. I bent over her, noting that she had grown still more like a furry barrel (with appendages) since our last meeting. She either recognized me or saw that I was admissible under her pass laws, for she moved on to Gilbert, showing a tooth or two. I could have told him that although her bark might be bad her bite was non-existent, but, no doubt still reeling under my revelations of a moment before, he seemed a good deal daunted by her. At this point Kitty appeared, greeted me and drove the dog away out of sight more or less simultaneously. We entered a drawing-room with a large bow-window at the farther end and Roy's splendid old Schwander-action concert Blüthner slightly off centre. A young man and a girl were sitting on a couch muttering together. He looked up at my entry, jerked his head and neck in salutation or suppression of a belch, and looked down again, but not before I had recognized him as Roy's twenty-or-so-year-old son Christopher. The girl, who was dressed like – rather than as, I suppose – a Victorian governess, kept her face lowered.

'Christopher, you remember Douglas Yandell,' said Kitty. 'Douglas, this is Ruth Ericson.'

This time there was no doubt about it: the lad distinctly nodded. The girl glanced at him, me and him again in what might have been sleepy consternation. Kitty's demeanour overflowed with mute appeal to me not to despise them utterly on such brief exposure.

'Hallo,' I said. 'How's Northampton?' I alluded to the university there, impressed at having performed the feat of recall needed.

'Oh, you know, usual crap. Nothing really gives.'

'What are you reading?'

'I'm doing sociology, politics, economics and sociology. I mean anthropology.'

'Ah. Sounds a pretty, uh, all-embracing course.' I battled to keep out of my voice the senile tremolo I imagined the pair were willing me to put into it. 'Are you there too?'

Christopher answered the question I had put to Ruth Ericson. 'No,' he said.

'I see.'

'Darling, if you're going to show Ruth the garden before lunch I really do think you ought to start soon,' said Kitty, smiling and blinking.

'Soon, yeah.'

The two resumed their muttering. Kitty drew me over to the window, from which there was a view of descending lawns, a sunlit wall with trees fastened to it, and some much bigger trees, cedars of different types, farther down. Much farther still were the roofs of the town, looking rather serious over the distant treetops, as if someone in particular had once been beheaded outside its church or unique glassware formerly made there. Nearby, some croquet debris was lying about.

'Where's Gilbert?' I asked idly.

'He doesn't really mean all that, you know,' said Kitty, illuminating the truth that not all types of egotist are unobservant. 'He feels he has to say things. His friends go on at him so if he doesn't. The white ones more than the black ones. He's terribly nice when you get to know him.'

'Oh, good.'

'He'll have gone back up to Penny and Ashley. They're absolutely marvellous with him, both of them.'

I retained a very clear picture of Penny, Roy's other and elder child by his first marriage; indeed, if possessed of the least graphic skill I could that moment have dashed off a rough scale-drawing of the outward semblance of her breasts, which I had once unsuccessfully tried to fondle in a taxi between a concert of Roy's and the subsequent party at Hampstead. Ashley Vandervane was an altogether different case, the comparatively recent joint issue of Roy and Kitty, whom I had barely seen at any time and had quite forgotten about. I tried to conceal this.

'He's what, he must be four now?'

'Just turned six.' She gazed at me with rather too rich a mixture of emotions, so that I hardly knew whether she regarded her only child with pride-plus-grateful-humility or with apologetic horror. Then she said very eagerly, 'Would you like to see the house?'

'Later on, perhaps,' I said, in the hope of avoiding such an ordeal. 'But it, uh, it looks jolly nice. Must cost a packet to run, though.'

'We're managing. You know, Douglas, it's quite frightening how much Roy earns now. He's really arrived. Oh, we know he's had the respect of the musical world for years and years, but these days he's a national figure, in the top bracket. And without lowering his artistic standards.'

At this opportune point, the couple on the couch, probably feeling that enough time had elapsed for them not to be thought to be leaving because they had been asked to leave, left. Kitty at once turned an overmasteringly urgent face on me, but switched it off again as fast and told me to have a drink. When I demurred, she pleaded that she must have a drink herself to talk to me properly and could not drink alone, or should not, or would not, or one of those. I mentioned beer and she went out.

I was glad to see and hear that Roy was doing well. He deserved to be, in a 'musical world' in which so few people deserved to earn literally as much as their daily bread. It was more doubtful whether that world had ever accorded him its highest respect, but he had always been more or less grudgingly admitted to be well trained and conscientious. He could get a better performance out of the average orchestra than some conductors who perhaps surpassed him in musicianship, by means of charm, or alternatively by means of doing a certain amount of comradely swearing at rehearsal, buying drinks for the section leaders, and similar stratagems. His career as a solo violinist, never very distinguished, had ended early, though not so long ago he had still been quite creditably taking on a Vivaldi or a Mozart concerto at charity jamborees and the like. He had been, possibly still was, a composer too, of what I had heard unkindly described as a sub-Rachmaninov persuasion, to be sub-whom was not, to me, any sort of disgrace. His pieces were not often performed, apart from an early and sugary *Nocturne* for fiddle and strings, plus a xylophone and one or two other novelties of that period, or the one just before. This had been turned into a popular song about 1950, and had recently enjoyed a fresh lease of life, or somnambulism, as that sadly different thing from a popular song, a pop song. As the latter, it must have contributed not a little to the frightening amount he was alleged to be now earning.

It was as a composer, of the most serious sort, that Roy had tried to see himself in the days when I had known him better. But it was evident even then that he had come along a bit late in the day to make

the best creative use of his taste and talent. Somebody called Vandervane would have fitted fairly neatly – by more than coincidence, I had
always thought – into the era in which it had evidently been compul-
sory for English composers to be called something non-English:
Delius, Holst, van Dieren, Moeran, Rubbra. But he had turned up a
good half-generation after it ended, and, again somehow character-
istically, would not have fitted into it with total neatness because of
the anglicization of his surname, imposed by grandfather van der
Veen upon arrival from Rotterdam a century ago. (Roy would sometimes warmly defend the change, at other times deplore and threaten
to reverse it, depending simply on how he felt, not on how his coun-
trymen seemed to be treating him.)

Before I could start speculating on the current level of his artistic
standards, Kitty came back with some beer for me and almost as much
of what looked like sketchily diluted gin for her. I thought on a second
view that, while still attractive in a plump, florid, not-my-cup-of-tea
way, she had aged since I had last seen her. Or perhaps she was just
tired and strung-up – strung-up higher and tighter than she habitually
was. Certainly her torn, faded check shirt and stained jeans were indi-
cations – in one whose breakfast wear was likely to recall Mary Queen
of Scots – of lowered morale. But the dry, scoured look of the skin at
the outer corners of her eyes pointed to something more permanent.

We settled down side by side on the couch vacated by Christopher
and the female mute. Turned towards me with arched back, and drink
and cigarette held before her in a sort of low boxer's-guard position,
Kitty started.

'I checked on the pants after you telephoned. There are definitely
three fewer than there were last week-end. What's so utterly terrify-
ing is the openness of it. He knows I deal with all the laundry and
things. He must realize . . . It's not even that he doesn't mind if I know.
He wants me to know. Flaunting it. Throwing it in my face. Using it
to show how he hates me,' she shrieked quietly, giving her usual
treatment to an earlier thought of mine.

'I doubt it. He's just careless.'

'Why can't he buy a pair and change somewhere? Just answer me
that – if you can,' she challenged me challengingly. 'What's to stop

him buying a brand-new pair at a shop and changing at his club, for instance? Come on, what's to stop him?'

'I don't know, Kitty. Well, he just doesn't think of it. He wouldn't.'

'I wish to God I knew who it was. Or rather I don't. Not after that one who designed jewellery.'

'Oh, there's been one who designed jewellery, has there?'

'Belts and bracelets and things. You must have heard about it. He took her to Glyndebourne and Covent Garden and Aldeburgh and everywhere. That was the only thing that saved me. It was all fixed up for them to go to Bayreuth and at the last moment she found out what it was.'

'What it was about what?'

'Bayreuth. Wagner. Opera. Music. Weeks of it. Really, Douglas.'

'Sorry. Where is he now?'

'You may well ask.' Showing all her command of oral italics, ditto inverted commas, black-letter and illuminated capitals, she said, 'Having a working lunch he's not sure where because the chap hadn't made up his mind with a chap whose name he can't remember because it's so unpronounceable who's got some very vague ideas about fixing up a tour of Brazil which he thinks probably almost certainly would be a bad idea but he might as well find out more and anyway it's a free lunch and he's no idea how long it'll go on.'

'I see. It does rather sound like a—'

'I don't mind him just having a go occasionally. He probably needs it. Or he thinks he does. It isn't really him taking them to bed.'

'Isn't it?' I asked as required.

'Well yes of course it is. I mean I hate that like bloody poison, but I can put up with it. It's the going off altogether thing that petrifies me.'

'But there's no sign of that at the moment, surely. This Brazilian lunch. He's doing his best to cover up. Doing something towards it, anyway. Not like trying to take her to Bayreuth.'

'That'll come. I know the pattern, Douglas dear. I've been through it all myself, you see. I know it from the inside.'

'Did he take you to Bayreuth?'

'That kind of thing. Anyway, I went. That was how I scored. I was the best one he'd met at being told about music since his first wife. I can remember so clearly him playing the tunes over on the piano and then bits of the record, so I could follow the themes and recapitulations and things when he took me to the concert. Still, why shouldn't I be able to remember it clearly? It's only about ten years ago.'

There were tears in her eyes, but then there so often were. Had Roy really married her for her docility as an audience? I said, 'But you really do like it, don't you, Kitty? Music, I mean.'

'Oh yes, I like it all right,' she said, making her moderate statement of the month. 'I'm very fond of music. Always have been.'

'Well, then . . . Look, what do you know about this girl? How old is she?'

'I don't know anything at all about her, but they've been running at about twenty to twenty-two over the last three years or so. Tending to go down. Getting younger at something like half the rate he gets older. When he's seventy-three they'll be ten.'

I checked the last bit mentally and found it to be correct, given the assumptions. It seemed to me extraordinary that anyone capable of making these in the first place, and then of following them through to their 'logical' conclusion, should (as Kitty clearly did) see the final picture presented as nothing but tragic or repulsive. 'And when he's eighty-three they'll be five,' I said experimentally.

'*Yes*,' she agreed, glad that I had followed her reasoning.

I gave it up. 'Well, I was going to say, if he wants a music pupil he's looking in the wrong place. Nobody in that sort of generation cares at all about any sort of music. Except very sober types with horses and lists of who to send Christmas cards to. Not Roy's speed at all.'

'At his age he may have decided the music-pupil thing isn't so important,' she said, and added incuriously, 'Isn't pop music music?'

'No. Anyway, what can I do to help? I do want to, but I can't see quite—'

'Dearest Douglas. First find out who she is . . .'

'But you said—'

'. . . and how far it's gone, and then we can sort of make a plan.'

'But that's spying. And what kind of plan?'

'I don't mind you telling him I've asked you to have a word with him about it. And surely you'd do anything to stop him from, that is surely you'd agree he mustn't throw himself away on some filthy little barbarian of a teenager? It would be such a crime, so awful for everybody, for me and the children, and for him too of course when he gets fed up with her, and for people like this young 'cellist boy he's encouraging, and there are so many people who depend on him, everybody he's got obligations to . . .'

Not to mention the chaps at the nuclear-disarmament talks. 'I suppose it would. I mean of course it would, I quite see that. But I still don't see what you or I or anyone else can do to stop him if he's made up his mind.'

'But if you found out something about it, then at least we could . . .'

A distant but rapidly approaching disturbance had broken out on an upper floor, constituted of the wordless yelling I had heard over the wires, the Furry Barrel's tones with full slipping-ratchet effect, Gilbert sounding annoyed, traces of a fourth voice, and variegated footfalls. Kitty got up and behaved for a few seconds like somebody about to be machine-gunned from the air, then moved as if to a prearranged spot. Here a fearful small boy in a smart suit of bottle-green velvet, after blundering through the doorway and starting to yell louder and at a higher pitch, threw himself into her arms: Ashley Vandervane, I judged. Gilbert was not far behind, and an altercation ensued. It was soon clear that Ashley had not been fleeing from Gilbert so much as coming to enlist his mother's support in gaining possession of some object, like his eleventh chocolate bar of the day or a bottle of hydrochloric acid, which Gilbert had perversely denied him. But I paid little attention, because I was looking so closely at Penny Vandervane, now also of the company, and most closely of all at her breasts.

This was not difficult, in the sense that a good half of their total was directly visible in the wide V of a dark-brown Paisley-patterned blouse or shirt or, just as possibly, pyjama-top. They struck me as not so much large as tremendously prominent, that and high, yes, and somehow immovable, giving the impression that poking at them with a finger, say, would have no more effect than poking at somebody's knee-caps. That was it: they were like a pair of knee-caps carefully sculpted and re-covered in Grade A skin. I saw now that they were attached to a rather tall, long-limbed frame, and finally surmounted by a shapely shorn head that included a face remarkable for the width and blueness of its eyes.

These last turned towards me as I reached them with mine, and I got a very brief stare, with no recognition in it and slightly less curiosity than one passenger in a lift will normally show another. Never mind: I had realized that I was in the presence of the reason for my ready yielding to curiosity when Kitty had asked me to come up that day. But I was clearly going to have to wait quite a long time, if not for ever, before I would be in any position to start explaining to Penny Vandervane about her breasts.

Ashley, twisted round in his mother's arms, had one thumb in his mouth and the extended first two fingers of the other hand going up and down in the air, a manual combination I could not remember having seen before. He removed the thumb for a space in order to accuse Gilbert of having hit him. Gilbert denied it, and I believed him, but the Furry Barrel, growling near his ankles, took the other view. Kitty solved the matter by carrying her son from the room, the dog bustling officiously behind them.

'The way you bring up that boy is decadent,' said Gilbert.

'It's nothing to do with me how he's brought up,' said Penny in her classless accent, or one combining the ugliest features of at least two dialects.

'It seems nothing to do with anybody. Toys, presents, candies, ice-creams. Why isn't he at school today?'

'He didn't feel like it.'

'He should be forced to go. At six years of age he can't be blamed. What do you expect of a boy who's allowed to sleep in his parents' bed?'

Penny shrugged her shoulders, a movement which had good results lower down, and started to turn in my direction, but stopped and turned back again.

'I'm Douglas Yandell,' I said thinking it safest to start from scratch.

She grinned slightly and said, 'I know.'

Gilbert frowned at her, holding it until she had noticed. Then he said to me, 'I'm Gilbert Alexander', and held out his hand, which I shook.

After a moment's inner toil, I said, 'How's your father?'

'Blind drunk. Oh, don't be a sodding idiot, Gilbert, it's an old music-hall gag thing. He's no more blind drunk than he always is. Quite fit, actually. Going after the birds always tones him up.'

Gilbert made a disgusted noise and went out.

'Dead funny, aren't they?' Penny began giving me quite a lot of her attention. 'You know, Victorian. He's even a bit Victorian in bed. He was when I first met him, anyway. Speeded up a lot since. Well, he's got the equipment, you see. That's all true, all that.'

It interested me a little that she had taken the trouble to drive Gilbert from the room and then at once switched to what was, for someone like myself, an in-depth anti-pass move, though I quite saw that another might take it as a come-on. I wondered whether chance or a sure instinct had guided her. A look at the width of those blue eyes firmly decided me for instinct.

'Jolly good for you,' I said heartily. 'What sort of bird is it this time?'

'No idea. Young. She got you up here to, you know, get on to him about it?'

I took this to refer to Kitty. 'She's worried.'

'Listen, did you ever see her when she wasn't worried? It's her life. Her bloody life, mate. I think she had sodding Ashley to give herself something new to go on about. Crisis on tap. No wonder he does all this bird stuff,' she went on in her pronominal style. 'But then he lets her know about it and we're off again. You needn't think it's any different from today. This is pretty quiet, actually.'

'Do you live here?'

'It's free,' she said, answering my thought.

'What about Gilbert? Is he a resident, or just passing through?'

'Oh, he thinks he's a resident.'

'What do you think?'

She gave another shrug, saw my look, and came an inch or two nearer. 'Where do you live, then?'

'Maida Vale. I've got a flat there.'

'Anyone else in it?'

'Not at the moment, I'm sorry to say.'

'Oh.' She lowered her green-painted eyelids.

Even without taking into account her earlier praise of Gilbert's physique, I knew what I was in for at this stage, but there are situations in which a lancer must charge an armoured car. I could hear somebody approaching the doorway across the uncarpeted wooden floor of the hall. 'Can I show you the place some time?' I asked.

'No,' she said, grinning and shaking her head. 'No,' she added.

Kitty came in with the face and carriage and then voice of one just released after a secret-police interrogation. She told us we might as well have lunch now, and we trooped off. I wondered why Penny should dislike me so much: not, surely, because of my breasts-fumble of a couple of years previously. She, or they, must long have been hardened to that kind of thing. And I sensed there was more to it than simple suspicion of any presumptive ally of her stepmother. Perhaps it was just the sight and sound of me she found unpleasant. Then I cheered myself up by reflecting that it was overridingly important to have renewed my assault, even verbally and vainly, on the tested principle that every minute a girl is allowed to spend in official ignorance of a man's intentions means two extra minutes of build-up when the time comes.

I followed the women through a small room full of boilers, tanks, pipes and associated machinery, and into another doorway. 'Mind your head, Douglas,' said Kitty as I gave myself a smart crack across the hairline with the edge of the lintel. It hurt like hell. I stumbled down two or three steps into what I came by degrees to see was a large, lofty kitchen looking on to the courtyard. Most of those present reacted to my misfortune, Kitty by repeatedly crying out and pressing a wet tea-towel against the place, Gilbert by sending me glances of satisfaction while he transferred a number of bottles of sauce and jars of chutney and pickles from a wall-cupboard to a laid dining-table, an elderly domestic with sympathetic concern, Ruth and Penny with smothered and open laughter respectively. Only Christopher was unmoved, going on rapidly and noisily loading a tray with materials for two. This, a minute later, he carried out of the room, followed by Ruth, and the domestic soon went too, urged on with some dismissive gratitude from Kitty. So it was only she and I and Gilbert and Penny who sat down at table.

Gilbert took charge, doling out bowls of soup, distributing cold meats and salad, fetching tinned beer from a larder that diffused an Arctic breath. He asked the women whether they wanted this or that by the use of words, me by raising his eyebrows or chin, sometimes both. Ordered by Kitty to tell me what he did, he conceded with what in the circumstances was quite good grace that he was connected with the stage (by moving pieces of scenery on to and off it, I guessed) and had nearly finished a book about West Indians in London.

'A novel?' I asked.

'No, no. The culture that produced it is dying. Something much freer from narrow traditions, more adventurous altogether in form. It bears analogies to music and the visual arts. I've got into the habit of thinking of it as my *London Suite* in three movements and three colours.'

This, if indeed an ingrained habit, was one I considered he should set about breaking while there was still time, but did not like to say so. 'Is it very autobiographical?'

'That question has no meaning. We can all only re-create what we have felt and experienced and suffered in our lives.'

While I tried, not very conscientiously, to apply his dictum to Suppé's *Poet and Peasant* overture, Kitty asked, 'But it's got a story?'

'Story. Rhythm. Characters. Plasticity. Shape. Melody. Frame. Plot,' said Gilbert, so oratorically that I could not tell whether he was ridiculing these concepts or claiming that the *London Suite* had as much of all of them as anybody could possibly want. Kitty seemed to be in a similar difficulty. At my other side, Penny showed no sign of ever having been in a difficulty in all her born days.

'And what are you doing these days,' I said heavily, 'Penny?'

'I wish you could see what you look like with that bloody great egg on your head.' Her laughter sounded quite unforced, even engagingly naive. 'It's overdone. You know, like a false nose. As if you're not meant to believe it.'

Gilbert clicked his tongue and Kitty said, 'Penny', in torpid reproof, going on to add, 'She's at a domestic science college in—

'I am not at any sodding domestic science college. I've left it, see? I don't go there any more. I am eh drop out. Not that it's very far to drop. I am completely idle. I . . . don't . . . do . . . anything.'

Her tone could have been described without either trouble or inex- actitude as one of cold anger. The eyes were working hard too, though they were not looking at anybody. I decided I was not whole-heartedly enjoying my lunch, always having preferred something quick and light midday, and started to plan my leave-taking. Then I saw someone finish passing the window and go in at the glass porch, but could not make out who it was. After a moment, a man's voice began loudly singing somewhere inside the house, the throat muscles tensed to produce the plummy effect often used in imitations of Welsh people, though this last was not evidently part of the singer's intention.

> 'Ah-ee last mah-ee hawrt een ahn Angleesh gawr-dan,
> Jost whahr thah rawzaz ahv Anglahnd graw . . .'

Most musicians have a poor ear for linguistic or verbal nuances, and many for musical ones too, come to that, but it was like Roy, whom I had heard singing this song in this style more than once before, to take the trouble to substitute 'Angleesh' for the 'Eengleesh' that might have been expected, thus subtly hitting at persons who pronounce the name of our nationality as it is spelt. Indeed, the tone of the whole performance, which continued and drew nearer as we all listened at the table, was hostile, wounding, designed to humiliate, though Roy could hardly have supposed that some individual or group keen on the vocal manner he was caricaturing had stolen into the house while his back was turned. Rage at absent or largely imaginary foes, however, was a part of his life-style. A more obvious explanation of his behaviour was, of course, that he was trying to be funny, to which the objection was that he often did quite closely similar things that nobody, not even he, could have intended to be funny. Just the same cycle of reasoning applied to the notion that he was showing off. More likely, this was nothing more than a way of entertaining himself, something he might often have had to do in youth, as the child of middle-aged parents whose earlier progeny were well into their teens by the time he came on the scene. And why was he singing about Angleesh gawrdans at the present moment? To give the fact of his unexpectedly early return a chance to sink in before he actually appeared, rather as Jonas Chuzzlewit had once done after much more serious delinquency than anything Roy would have been up to.

The door into the kitchen opened and Roy came in, a bulky figure in a wide-lapelled double-breasted jacket that, after a then recent fashion, set up uneasiness in the beholder by looking very, very nearly as much like a short overcoat, a glistening two-tone shirt and hairy trousers with widely separated stripes on them. His face was unchanged, a unified whole, I had always thought, with prominent straight nose, full lips, and pointed, slightly receding chin, a physiognomy I had often come across in photographs of public figures of the 1930s, especially actresses – a resemblance now underlined, I noticed with some concern, by the rough bob in which his thick, dark, ungreying hair had been done. There could never be anything actressy about Roy, that sort of behaviour being heavily over-subscribed hereabouts as it was, and in general he was uneffeminate to a fault; but at the sight of him today I felt a twinge of a kind of discomfort that I would have sworn he could never arouse in me. In his hand was a large brown drink.

He, at least, seemed unreservedly glad to see me, and a moment later very, if briefly, concerned about the state of my head, though he might have been piling it on a bit as a diversion from his present moral disadvantage. Kitty and Penny heard out in staring silence his detailed account of the Brazilian's sudden indisposition owing to an attack, he said with a wondering laugh, of some tropical bug the chap had picked up on a trip up the Amazon, of all things and rivers. I asked myself sadly if he would ever learn that to think an explanation convincing because it sounded too obvious and uninventive to be invented was the sort of typically male error most males discarded before they left school. The reappearance of Ashley, now in pyjamas and escorted by the Furry Barrel, saved him from public rout. Father and son went into a reunion scene of Neapolitan warmth, on father's side at least; son soon started wriggling and asking about his present. This was quickly produced from one of the immense patch-pockets of the jacket-overcoat, a miniature fire-engine with, as we soon discovered, a hee-haw siren on it. The lad began playing with it on the floor under the table and round our feet. Gilbert, who had duly shown his disapproval of the fire-engine, asked Roy if he had had lunch.

'Of course not; I rushed back here as soon as I could,' he said seriously. 'But don't bother about me – anything'll do.'

'How did you get here from the station?' asked Kitty, speaking for the first time since his arrival. Her tone was distant, about ten yards more distant than where she sat.

'What?'

'*How* . . . did you *get* . . . *here* . . . from the *station*.' This came out in chewy, easy-to-lip-read chunks, with churchyard-pigeon head-effects.

'I walked. Glorious day. Whatever's easiest, Gilbert, thank you. Spot of corm beef'll do me fine. And some tim pineapple or tim peaches to follow, if they're there. Great.'

When I first met him, Roy had had a sort of Northern accent that disappeared into public-school English at all his frequent moments of excitement. No doubt recognizing, at some intermediate level of self-consciousness, that the disparity was too obvious even to the uncritical ears of the other prosperous socialists he spent most of his time with, he must have decided on the new slurring policy as more adaptable, better politically and like young people talked, too. I thought I saw him wondering whether I had noticed the change.

Having said no more, the women left the room, followed, after he had laid in front of us a piece of board with cheeses on it, by Gilbert. Roy ate meat and salad with studied ferocity. Presently he said,

'Can you stick around for a bit? Something I want to talk to you about. There's, uh, a favour I'd like you to do for me if you possibly could.'

'I'm already supposed to be starting on some sort of aid programme for Kitty.'

His chair juddered as the fire-engine crashed into it. 'Christ. Sharp,' he seemed to say, sounding a note of warning over the bray of the siren and the Furry Barrel's outraged barking.

I nodded. 'I don't want you to think I've sort of come up here behind your back.'

'Certainly not. Anyway, I heard you were going to be asked. Everybody knows what everybody else is doing around here, though they don't always admit it. That didn't go down too well, did it? That stuff about the Amazon and so on.'

'Not too well, no.'

'I thought it was bloody good myself. But I'm no judge. They never give you credit for anything, do they? You'd suppose that a chap who'd winged his way back to the nest for a late lunch of corm beef and the rest of the rubbish instead of stuffing himself with delicacies at his club or in Soho somewhere and rolling up pissed at half past five would thereby ingratiate himself slightly with the women. Not a bloody bit of it. I'd have been better off all round doing the other thing. You're looking well, Duggers. Apart from that head. Nasty. Anyway, how's your life?'

'Moderate. Pushed for cash as usual.'

'Someone told me you and Anne had broken up.'

'She went back to her husband. For the sake of the children.'

'Oh balls, I do wish people wouldn't behave like that. So stuffy. Boring beyond words. It's the books they read, and all these television series. Nobody would dream of "going back" if they hadn't been told for years that it's what you do – not even what you should do, just what you do. Most depressing. Still. Got anyone to replace her?'

'Only part-time.' I considered whether it would be in order to reach down and cuff or pinch Ashley, who was making a number of runs with his fire-engine on one of the front legs of my chair. 'A girl who lives on the other side of the river, so I do a fair amount of commuting.'

'Ashley, stop that.'

'Shut your trap, you fucking monkey-face.'

I heard this remark with hidden pleasure and anticipation. Roy was rightly famous for his way with every grade of defiance, whether offered by a world-renowned soloist with strong unacceptable ideas about *rubato* or by a surly waiter. But the shocking event was that he told Ashley in the mildest of tones to come and sit on his knee and

25

be given some special chocolate he had brought for him. This order was obeyed. The Furry Barrel, now directing sultry looks at me from a nearby chair, yapped peremptorily.

'You are a silly old His Majesty King Charles the Second cavalier-spaniel dog,' said Roy, and added to me, 'You've got the cheese by you, you see. Could you give her some of that Cheddar? Not too much and cut up small and see that she sits when you give it to her. You ridiculous old hound.'

The dog ate with head nodding and eyes still fixed on mine, the child like a gluttonous ogre. After some suspiciously paraded rumination, Roy said,

'Of course, you and I have always differed fundamentally about, uh, well, people like Anne and so on. You never get invawved, do you?' (This is as near as I can get to representing the curious gliding sound he made, a valuable and popular accent-worsener of the period.)

'You mean you are involved.'

'He's always invawved with somebody,' said Ashley thickly. 'Mummy says she'd give a hundred quid to know who it is this time.'

'I was talking about Mr Yandell, darling.'

'Yeah.' The boy said it as his half-sister might have done.

'Perhaps we'd better—' I began.

'No no, it's all right. Anyway, you don't, do you? Get invawved.'

I wanted to say that, whether through natural virtue, constitutional prudence, coldness of heart, cowardice or luck, I felt I had so far managed to avoid some of the grosser symptoms, at any rate, of invawvement. But Roy was pushing on regardless, still ruminatively.

'I've never been able to make out what chaps like you are really looking for.'

'I'm not looking for anything. At least, nothing that can't be fairly easily found if you're a bachelor with a bit of energy and a place of your own.'

'You don't want to get married.'

'No. Not at the moment, anyway.'

'Perhaps not ever.'

'I don't know.'

'Don't want the responsibility.'

'If you like. It's expensive, too.'

'Perhaps it's just a matter of a physical type.'

'What is?'

'That you're looking for.'

Still talking, he grasped both of Ashley's wrists in one hand, just in time to prevent a lot of chocolate being wiped on to his clothing, and bore him off to the kitchen sink, where he set to work on him with the very tea-towel used earlier on my head. Doing all this, he was under no obligation to meet my eye.

'I mean, Duggers, it's always struck me that you do seem to cast about pretty bloody widely in your choice of, you know. Moce people—'

'You talk as if I collect them like butterflies. I just grab what's going past. It's all luck, availability . . .'

'I know, I know. I only meant what you'll admit is true if you'll just bring yourself to consider it for a moment, that *moce chaps* seem to *prefer* one particular *type* of . . .'

'*Bird*,' said Ashley, efficiently maintaining tempo and sound-quality.

'Belt up, you little bastard,' said Roy, restoring something of the respect he had lost. 'No, uh, you know perfectly well that some chaps go for tall ones or short-arsed ones or blondes or . . . you know. But you don't. I've never been able to see any consistency in your tastes at all.' He made it sound grave, and looked it himself. 'I don't even know what your sort of basic standard is, absolutely basic.' He finished polishing Ashley's mouth with a preoccupied flourish. 'For instance, how would you rate, say, well, young Penny? I mean, she's—'

'No, Roy. I've no idea what it is, but no. Whatever it is, no.'

'I don't know what you're talking about,' he said coldly. 'I asked you a simple question. However. Well, my little tough guy' – he swept his son up into his arms – 'my little bruiser, what are we going to do with you, eh? Let's go and find your mummy, shall we?'

Mummy was easily found in the drawing-room, listening to, or apparently keeping quiet during, a Miles Davis record. Gilbert presided at the gramophone, which faithfully rendered that tiny, elementary universe of despair and hatred. Penny was eating chocolates, a good antiquarian touch, and reading a paperback book of what looked like poems, or at least non-prose. Roy dumped Ashley, who seemed drugged with chocolate to the point at which he had forgotten about his fire-engine for the time being, and took me and the Furry Barrel out into the garden.

'Changing-huts,' he said, gesturing towards some loose-boxes.

'When you build the swimming-pool.'

'Right.'

'Roy, what's this favour?'

'Favour?'

'You said you wanted me to do you a favour.'

'Oh. Oh, just bearing with me when I maunder on. Sympathetic ear. There's nobody much round the place I can talk to.'

'I see. Not a very arduous favour.'

He led me into a barn full of empty cardboard boxes and pieces of wood shaped for some now superseded purpose. 'I was thinking of turning this shack into a music laboratory.'

'Before or after the swimming-pool?'

'Oh, Duggers, I do wish you'd try not to be such an ole square. Times are changing whether you like it or not. Weber's bloody good, I agree, but he's hardly as relevant as Webern. That chap might have produced something that would make even you sit up if the Yanks hadn't murdered him.'

'To hell with relevance, and it was an accident, and he was sixty-three, and sit up—'

'Verdi was over eighty when he—'

'And sit up and lean over slightly to one side in order to fart briefly. Don't let's go into all that again, Roy.'

'No, sorry.'

We came out of the gloom of the barn and walked down a modest avenue littered with fallen wood. Bars of soft shadow lay across it. The Furry Barrel, nose to the ground and tail wagging at half tempo but full stretch, hurried aside into some laurel bushes.

'How are you on the ivories these days?' asked Roy.

'Hardly concert standard, but I usually spend most of one day a week at the instrument.'

'I thought we might tackle a snarter together later on.'

'Tackle . . . Oh, yes. Yes, that would be fine.'

'Do you feel up to the Brahms D minor?'

'You'd have to be in a pretty tolerant mood.'

'In thack case we might be better advised to go for something a little less demanding. Any objection to Mozart?'

'On the contrary. While I remember, for God's sake let up on those pants of yours', and I went on to explain at once and in full to save the time he would have wasted on very slowly dawning comprehension and the rest of it.

'Bloody Gestapo,' he said when I had finished.

'Kitty wonders why you don't buy a pair somewhere and I must say I agree with her. You could save yourself so much—'

'Yeah, and have the bloody shopman say, "And will there be anything further, Sir Roy? Some deodorant, or a packet of horn pills?" It's that bastard telly. Honestly, half my troubles come from never knowing when some bugger isn't going to recognize me. Only the other evening I was sneaking into a block of flats in, well, never mind where, and the bloody porter stuck his head out of his window and yelled, "The lift's not working, Sir Roy, I'm afraid you'll have to use the stairs." If you don't bleeding well mind. It was those concerts I did last year for LCM Television. Them and that ballocking silly panel game. I wish I'd never let them talk me into it.'

I wished the same thing, though for different and perhaps priggish reasons, but I said, 'If you think buying one pair's such a give-away, and I can't see it matters, buy a dozen. Or are you afraid the bloke'd think you were taking on a dozen birds one after the other? What if he did? I can't understand why you're so sensitive about it.'

'I'm not going to carry a dozen pairs of pants with me everywhere I go.'

'No need to. Leave them at your club.'

'Out of the question.'

'But just by—'

'I don't want to discuss it any further.'

The avenue petered out at a five-barred gate, beyond which was a field with two inexpensive-looking horses in it. Roy seemed to think it would diminish him politically if I were allowed to take away the impression that the animals belonged to him. He explained at length that they did not and whose they were. I was wondering whether Kitty's flaunting theory about the pants might not have something in it after all. Guilty alarm lightly dusted with embarrassment was what anybody who knew him would have predicted as his response to my warning, the dead opposite of the evasive-defiant mixture I had been handed. The thought of the favour, too, was worrying me. Presumably I was not at the moment in a fit state of mind for its nature to be broached, and Roy was waiting for my wits to become impaired by lust, alcohol or fear of imminent extinction, especially lust: it must be here that the Penny thing fitted in. I decided to try to take him near enough to the favour for him not to be able to resist asking it, and pushed forward my first pawn.

'If buying a pair of underpants makes you want to wear a false beard, how do you manage when you take her out somewhere?'

'I don't. Take her out anywhere. Do you think I'm a bloody fool?'

'What do you do, then?' I asked, hoping he would not insist on an answer to his question.

'Stay under cover. Occasionally I go to her flat, though there's a lot of room-mate trouble there. On the up-grade, too. Or I borrow a flat off someone. But that's tricky in a different way. I only know a few people with flats well enough to ask them, and most of those know Kitty too, and go British on me if I do ask them. And then the ones I can ask are always the ones who'd talk about it. It's odd how strictly that rule applies.'

With an air of philosophic gloom, he led off down an overgrown path that proved to be two or three inches deep in rotting leaves. My forebodings, however, had vanished.

'If that's all you – I mean, you're welcome to my place any time with a bit of warning. And I can keep my mouth shut, as you know.'

'Thanks a lot, Duggers, I'll take you up on that,' he said, making it as clear that this was not the favour as turning round and bawling the news in my face would have done, and feeding my forebodings back to me in mint condition.

'How old is she?'

'Nineteen.'

'Good God,' I said, largely out of respect for the accuracy of Kitty's observation.

'What's wrong with that?'

'Well, nothing at all really, I suppose, though it did strike me that it's somehow a bit young.'

'What's wrong with that? I do wish you'd make an effort to get out of this habit of thinking in categories all the time. The whole generation-gap idea's just an invention of the media and the Yanks. You obviously don't know the first thing about youth in the true sense. You've no conception what it's like, what it knows, what it can do.'

The path had turned a corner and begun to climb back towards the house. We moved on to the lowest of a series of lawns, rather squashy underfoot. I was enjoying the garden and the air and sun, but was clearly getting nowhere with the favour. I plunged on nevertheless.

'Is it just youth you're talking about, or this lot of youth?'

'The whole bit. She's shown me so much I'd never even suspected the existence of before.'

'Really? What sort of thing do you mean?'

'Oh, everything – ways of feeling, ways of seeing.'

'Not ways of hearing too, I hope.'

'Oh, bugger off, Douglas. Of course she likes pop; they all do. And if you look into it at all, I mean the good stuff, Led Zeppelin, say, not Herman's Hermits, you'll come across a surprising amount of real music. But I suppose you wouldn't accept that.'

'No.'

'School of thought!'

This phrase I recognized as one of Roy's obscenity-savers, or fuckettes, to which he was prone in moments of stress. His use of much greater amounts of genuine obscenities alongside them, whatever his company, inclined me to feel that here was no outcropping of prudery, more likely just the relic of a childish habit, originally taken up as a way of observing the letter of some law of home or institution. To qualify as a fuckette, a phrase had to have annoyed him at some stage of his life, and this in some cases could be fairly positively identified. School of thought itself, for instance, might spring from some middle-period academic experience; sporting spirit, another favourite, from a slightly earlier epoch. Christian gentleman, I had established through research, had been an admiring description of General Franco at the time of the Spanish Civil War, and I had often imagined Roy, baulked of any more active form of defiance, growling it out from the Barcelona hospital bed where he had lain with appendicitis and its aftermath during the autumn of 1937 – all but the first few and last few hours, in fact, of his stay in the country.

After a silence, Roy was going on, 'She likes jazz too. She hears different things in it from what we hear, but she likes it.'

'Good for her. Who is she?'

'Nobody you know,' he said, spelling out by his tone the fact that who she was was important.

'Anyway, I've got to give you one thing. It's good going for a man, uh, of your general—'

'An old shag like me to have it off and go on having it off with a kid of nineteen.'

'Yes. But I meant more than that. Not just the having it off, but keeping her happy with never going out with you, no parties or flash restaurants, none of the perks of being Sir Roy Vandervane's bit of stuff. That's new with you, isn't it, by the way, Roy, keeping the whole thing dark, except from the family? Kitty was telling me—'

'There are special circumstances.'

'No doubt. But she must be an unusual kid of nineteen, especially by today's standards, to put up with being kept indoors like that. Or has she got another bloke who does take her about?'

We had reached the top lawn and were moving across it to the courtyard. Now, abruptly but abstractedly, Roy turned and began pacing back the way we had come. I joined him, certain that the favour was about to declare itself.

'She's not putting up with it. Every time I see her she spends longer complaining about being hidden away. Any moment now she'll refuse to come to bed with me unless we go out in public. And I can't have that. Not just the two of us on our own.'

'So it'll have to be the four of us, you and she and Penny and I disguised as you and your daughter's girl-friend and your daughter and her girl-friend's boy-friend who also by a happy coincidence turns out to be an old friend of yours. Very neat. Cosy, too.'

He showed no appreciation of my acumen. 'It's the only thing I can think of. I was at my wits' end until you happened to turn up today. Her putting me off this morning was all part of it, you see. Bloody war of nerves.'

'It strikes me that Gilbert would be far more your man. Penny likes him. Presumably. And then he's, uh, he's more the right age and everything.'

'I've already asked him.'

'And he turned you down.'

'Flat. These . . . chaps can be very puritanical, you know. Result of all the bloody Nonconformist propaganda we pumped into them to keep them quiet while we were exploiting them.'

'There's quite a few it hasn't rubbed off on so's you'd notice, from what I hear.'

'Well, it's rubbed off on him. He won't do it.'

Roy kicked savagely at an already disintegrating croquet ball and waited for me to make a start on the huge list of objections to his proposal.

'It's grotesque.'

'It may sound a bit on the grotesque side to you at this stage. When you've thought about it, which I want you to do before you decide, then you'll see it won't look in the least grotesque when we do it, not even to people who know us, assuming there are any of those round the place.'

'It would feel grotesque.'

'You'll get into the way of it.'

'Gilbert wouldn't like me taking his girl out on expeditions he already thinks would be immoral.'

'One expedition. No, really, Duggers, I promise you that. Just to give me time. And what can he do? Go for you or Penny with a knife? He's not that type.'

'No. Yes, there is that. But what about her? She can't stand me.'

'Oh, balls, that's all juss the way they go on. You know, cool. I suppose you know about cool? Of course you do. She'll come like a shot if I . . . put it to her in the right way.'

'You're proposing to bribe your own daughter to do camouflage duty so that you and your mistress can have an evening out against her boy-friend's wishes and behind her stepmother's back.'

'Mistress, eh? By gad, sir. Not bribe. And it'll do Gilbert good to have a bit of opposition. And the stepmother part's just what she'll like about it.'

'She oughtn't to, and you oughtn't to put her in that situation.'

'I see we've got more than one puritan round the place. No, honestly, I didn't mean it like that. I don't care for how she feels about Kitty either, believe me. It's a fact, that's all. And she's exactly the type, Penny is, to be much nicer to her after something of that sort. Anyway, I know all this makes me look a right shit, and probably be a right shit, and I don't want to, but I am in love with this curious little creature, and perhaps that doesn't justify anything, but you can't imagine how it makes me look forward to each day, and really want tremendously to work, which hasn't happened to me for years. I can assure you. You know, it's true the young deserve a bit of special tolerance and understanding, because they're young and in conflict and have this different vision, but poor old sods at my time of life deserve it too, or anyway we need it, just starting to shape up to the idea of being dead or ole men. It's all right for buggers like you. In the middle. That's the place to be, by Christ. Now let's drop it. What do you say to K.481?'

'Is that the one in E flat?' I asked torpidly.

'Yeah. Come along.'

He led me away and to the drawing-room. Christopher and Ruth got to their feet respectfully at the sight of us, and at once left. Only Penny remained, having finished the chocolates but continuing to read her book, or so it seemed while Roy and I tinkered about and finally got into our stride with the Mozart. Then, during an undemanding bit of accompaniment, I saw that she had not turned a page since we began. Very few women outside the profession take any kind of interest in music at all, and the idea that a girl like Penny might be a secret listener surprised me so much that I nearly muffed the passage of modest bravura that then confronted me. After that I played at my very best, and we rounded off the first movement really quite creditably.

'Bloody good,' said Roy. 'Nicely done, old lad. You certainly have been doing a bit of work.'

'So have you.'

'Oh, glad it shows. I've been reasonably hard at it for the last couple of months now. One of the results of, uh, feeling pleased with life.'

'Are you building up to something public?'

This plainly scored a hit, but his damage-control unit lumbered into action at once. 'Not really, no. More for the satisfaction than anything else. I may have some sort of charity do in the autumn, but it's all quite vague. I don't know where I might be by then.'

Penny turned a page of her book and caught his attention.

'I say, Pen, do try listening to this next bit. First-rate stuff. I can't think why it isn't better known. Quite short.'

As an eviction order, this could not have been surpassed. On her way to the door I heard Penny mutter something about having to help Kitty, which I thought was fulsome of her.

'Oh dear,' said Roy when she had gone. 'Touch me not, what? One simply can't reach thack girl.'

'Doesn't Gilbert reach her?'

'I suppose he must, here and there, but it doesn't seem to make her any easier to live with. Still, you can't blame her, can you?'

'Why can't I?'

'This bloody awful society. Simply doesn't offer anything to anybody with any kind of sensibility or creativity or . . . I know you think it's absolutely unimprovable, of course.'

'I don't think anything about it.'

'Precisely. Let's get on, shall we?'

The slow movement went rather less well, largely because, with Penny out of the room, I was free to think about the favour and whether to take it on. Curiosity, as always, said yes. What said no most loudly was the thought of what a fearful evening it would be. Penny's recent performance had amplified this objection. Halfway through the finale, the sight of Kitty coming into the room decided me. No.

Kitty was so good about not interrupting or distracting us, her mouth thinned and eyes narrowed with concentration as she fetched, opened, deployed and started on some sewing, that Roy and I had to work hard to prevent the closing pages from degenerating into chaos. We finished approximately together. Kitty hurled down her sewing and clapped in the childish mode, hands pointing the same way instead of across each other at right angles.

'I do wish I'd been able to be here for all of that,' she said in a faint voice designed to show something of what the frustration of this wish had cost her.

'What?' Roy cupped his hand behind his ear, either not having heard or countering the faint-voice tactic.

'I said I do wish I'd been able to be here for all of that,' shouted Kitty, no elaborate mouthing about it this time.

'Thanks.'

He put his Stradivarius back in its case. Kitty, her neck looking several inches longer than it had a moment before, picked up her sewing again. I got to my feet and looked round the room, which was furnished with a hi-fi set-up, a mahogany sideboard that had a marble top visible here and there among bottles, a science-fiction giant lily or two, some bloated china cats, and framed posters of Che Guevara, Ho Chi Minh, a nude couple making love and other key figures of the time.

Behind me, I (quite distinctly) heard Kitty say, 'Darling, I wonder if you'd have a word with Ashley about the bathroom.'

Roy answered, 'Have a word with him about what?'

'I wondered if you'd have a word with Ashley.'

'That was the bit I heard. Have a word with him about what? I heard the bit about having a word with him.'

'About the *bath . . . room.*'

'What about the bathroom?'

'Darling.' Kitty sounded relaxed to the point of imminent sleep. 'Would you have a word with Ashley about it?'

'I know! I know! I heard the bit about have a word with him about the bathroom. What about the bathroom? Christ – what is it about the bathroom that you want me to have a word with him, Ashley, about?'

'Really, darling. About *peeing* in the bathroom. That's what I want you to have a word with him about. If you would.'

He howled like a wolf, his usual method of indicating belated comprehension, and said, 'There at last. You want me to have a word with Ashley about peeing in the bathroom.'

'Yes,' said Kitty in a voice full of lines of strain and glazed eyes and skin stretched tightly over cheekbones.

There was a pause, during which Roy nodded his head a good deal and I began to wonder, for the first time in my life, whether the experience of listening to the whole of Bruckner's Eighth Symphony might not have something to be said for it after all. Then Roy asked,

'What about it?'

'*Oh!* Tell him *not* to!'

'I've done that and he goes on peeing.'

'Use your authority.'

'How? What authority? We agreed he's not to be punished and we can't go back on that. I'm not suggesting for a moment we go back on that. But what sort of word can I have with him? I'm not asking rhetorically, I can assure you. I really would like to know.'

'Could I make a telephone call?' I asked.

'Certainly, old lad.'

Roy took me across the hall to his study and departed. It was a small room on which some sound-proofing had been done, not enough to keep out the faint wails and solid thumps of pop from the floor above. Some thought, perhaps too much, had gone into the selection and arrangement of objects on view: photographs of Brahms and Castro, small busts of Beethoven and Mao, copies of Hutchings on Mozart's piano concertos and Marcuse on liberation, posters announcing a Nikisch concert in 1913 and an anti-American demonstration in 1969. I telephoned the airline office where somebody called Vivienne worked (where I had first met her, in fact) and arranged to pick her up at her flat for some supper after my concert, which was taking place conveniently close by. As I talked, I noticed a sheaf of music manuscript lying on a miniature upright piano across the room, and hurried to pick it up the moment I had rung off.

It was several pages long, unfinished, in Roy's hand: a quartet, or chamber concerto for violin, with parts for sitar, bass guitar and bongoes. Across the top of the first sheet *Elevations 9* was written, perhaps by way of title. I felt a particular loathing for that *9*: either there were eight other *Elevations* or the numeral was arbitrary, a piece of decor, which was nearly as bad. I studied the violin part for a few moments. As far as I could tell, which was probably far enough, it called for some virtuosity but not much – not too much, anyway, for a trendy old idiot of a fiddler who until quite recently would have had, not the sense, but the sense of style, to refrain from musical adventurisms like writing a sort of pop tune (as I now saw it to be) with a classical-type violin *obbligato* to be performed by himself – who else? A first-rate example of the not-lowering-artistic-standards Kitty had talked about.

Then I thought I must be going too fast and far. There was no real reason to suppose that *Elevations 9* was anything more than an exercise, an experiment, or even a parody, designed to raise a laugh or so as part of some cod mélange at a charity do. But, to a Roy who went on as he now did, that would be inadmissibly square. And an exercise for its own sake, with no thought of performance? Hardly Roy. And the amount of practising he had so clearly been doing. Then why had he . . . ?

I went quietly out into the hall and at once caught sight of what I had been certain would be there: a perfectly good telephone, in working order, as it proved. I returned to the study and stared at the pages of manuscript. Yes. By God. I (representing the orthodox musical public) and they were the artistic equivalent of Kitty and the pants. Flaunting it. I went on staring, mostly into space.

After a couple of minutes I looked at my watch. Five thirty exactly. I dialled the newspaper and soon got Coates's cough, then his voice.

'We've had to lose half an inch, Doug.'

'The half-inch about where Kohler comes from and where he studied and the rest of it.'

'That's the one. Reasons of space, of course.'

'You or him?'

'Well, both, in a way. He was in here when we were making up. Sorry, I didn't realize.'

'Is he in his office now?'

'He wasn't five minutes ago. Look, we can put it back if you want. We'll have to lose a half-inch somewhere else, though. Have you got a carbon there? What about this bit near the end about this fellow whose name begins with J's early style?'

'Janáček. No, I need that.'

'Well then . . . You can't pop in, can you?'

'No. Leave it. Leave it as it is.'

I rang off. Over the past few days I had been telling myself now and then that if Harold cut me materially, as he had done twice before, I would do no more work for the paper. But I knew now without thinking about it that I was going to carry on. Why not? Nothing said I had to inform five million readers that Heinrich Kohler was an East German; their continuing ignorance of this fact could not damage him, only, by remote extension, his country, and *it* could blow itself up tomorrow for all I cared either way, on the understanding that it sent its good musicians and singers and instruments abroad first. My sole concern had always been to promote the people and the works I admired and to demote the other sort. I must positively hang on to my job with Harold, then, if only to keep out the sort of little mountebank likely to do a turn at it between a spell on the books page and the real prize spot, the restaurant column.

Across the hall a door slammed and someone – Kitty – ran upstairs at a great rate. Another, more distant door slammed. I scratched my backside. Nothing said (did it?) that I must never do anything that those who behaved like Kitty would probably not like. Doing my best to block *Elevations 9* was a higher obligation. So I was changing my mind about Roy's favour, with its opportunities for exploration of his immediate musical intentions. That still left a problem about Penny, but I pushed it out of sight.

On the desk, the telephone bell pinged. I thought briefly, then went back into the hall. Roy was at the telephone there. When he saw me, he gave a glance and a nod that invited me over beside him; I went; he jabbed his finger at a dog-eared directory lying before him. Its cover bore what I had always felt was a dispensable slogan about its being a great place to look up people's telephone numbers in.

'I've been meaning to do this for a long time,' said Roy. He had a serious, dedicated look about him. 'They shouldn't be allowed to get away with this kind of . . . Inquiries? Good afternoon. I wonder if you can help me . . . I'm sure you will. Now: the other evening, last Thursday to be precise, I met a very nice chap and his wife at a party in Chelsea somewhere. He was about forty, forty-five, running a bit to fat, dark, hair receding rather, said he worked in public relations. Uh, smoked a pipe. She was a few years younger, on the thin side I think one would say . . . Do let me finish; there isn't much more. Yes, she was wearing a green dress with a wide belt, and earrings, they looked late eighteenth century to me, two children they had, a boy and a girl, both at school. That's about all I can remember. I do hope it's enough . . . For you to tell me their name, of course, so that I can look up their number in the directory. I want to telephone them, you see . . . But if I knew their *name*, I could look up their *number*, as the Post office so helpfully reminds me on the front of this foam book I have here. It's precisely because I don't know their name that I got on to you in the first place . . . You can't? What bloody use are you, then?'

He rang off with a triumphant crash. 'Pity in a way. She sounded quite a nice girl, actually. I should have got hold of the supervisor. I can do that tomorrow. Got to keep at them. What's the matter with you?'

'Nothing. I don't think that rubbish is on the latest directories.'

'That doesn't affect the principle. Like a drink?'

'No thanks. You have one.'

'I most assuredly will.'

He had walked me down the hall a few paces and now switched on a light (the house was generally rather dark), in an alcove where there was a squat refrigerator and a couple of shelves piled with glasses and bottles, most of them dirty and empty respectively. The ice compartment of the refrigerator looked like a small sample of a glacier, but Roy tugged an ice-tray out of it and put some of its contents into a presumably clean tumbler. After that he took me into the drawing-room, poured about a gill of Scotch on top of the ice, and drank a certain amount of it. He still had the intent air I had noticed at the telephone. We started speaking at the same time; he signed to me to go on.

'Sorry. Roy, I've changed my mind about that favour you wanted me to do for you. We can fix an evening whenever you say.'

He pointed his nose at me and did one of his rich, dependable-sounding laughs. 'I was just going to tell you I shan't be needing it now. The whole thing's off.'

'Off?'

'I'm giving her up. Cleam break. Best thing for everybody. You'd probably agree, wouldn't you? I had the whole thing out with Kitty just now.'

'It didn't sound as if it went down too well. I couldn't help hearing ...'

'Oh, that was just a minor point. I think I rather over-stressed the attractions of, uh, what I've been up to. It'll blow over in no time. The great stroke is that I've told her the full story from the word go.'

'With what object?'

'Oh, Christian gentleman! What object would you expect? So that I can stop feeling guilty and she can stop feeling insecure. You know.'

'And clear the air and wipe the slate and square the account. Yes, I know. You must be off your head. I thought you were supposed to be in love with this girl. Or have you wiped that clean too?'

'Do you imagine I can't see how difficult it's going to be?'

'Indeed I do, despite your past experience, and when you find you're starting again, or trying to, you'll realize that all you've done is create fresh difficulties for yourself. Once you start making with the pants again, Kitty's bound to—'

'Bugger the pants! You and Kitty are obsessed with the bloody things. She even brought them up just now. It seems such a trivial point to me.' He was quietening down, preparing to pull out of the whole topic. 'Why don't you stay to dinner, Duggers? We're having a few locals in, nothing very spectacular ...'

'Thanks, but I've got a concert. You've just erected a permanent obstacle in your own path without doing anybody else any good.'

'Oh, I don't know. What is your concert? I might come along.'

'But what about your ... ? Oh, London Handel Players under

Matheson. To have heard all the details isn't going to make Kitty the slightest bi—'

'It's not a formal party. People just drop in. They've come on a lot since Matheson took over. What are they playing?'

'Even if you never touch another girl in your life you'll suffer because of it. Bach and Handel. The First Suite. A concerto grosso, one of the op. 6, I forget which. Some other stuff. Why can't you ever keep it to yourself? You—'

'I can't get that kind of thing better performed on my hi-fi. No, I think I'll stay after all. Kitty would like me to be here.'

Having now to contend with Kitty herself, Ashley, the Furry Barrel, Gilbert and Penny, who had started infiltrating the room, as well as Roy in top evading trim, I gave up. A headache had spread out from the place I had hit on the door frame. The best part of an hour's journey by Tube lay ahead of me. I said my goodbyes, receiving from Penny a wordless grin and a glance at my forehead. Gilbert drove me to the station in unbroken silence. A train had just left. The one I took stopped for a quarter of an hour under the river. I hurried to the concert hall and arrived exactly on time. There was a ten-minute delay in starting. The concertino violin broke a string in the Handel. Afterwards I walked nearly a mile in a light drizzle before I reached shelter. Vivienne, at the best of times an undistinguished dresser, was wearing a fearful trouser-suit that looked as if it had been made out of the seat-covers of some excitingly new motor-coach. She was mildly sullen and preoccupied, but would not say about what. At the restaurant, her omelette was dry and too salt, and I spilled most of a glass of wine over the tablecloth. It was a little better in bed. Not much, not nearly as much as I had had solid grounds for expecting. I saw next morning that the paper had transposed two lines in my piece and misspelt Kohler's name. After such a promising plunge into the bush, life seemed to have returned to its old beaten path.

# Two

## Something Soft

I heard nothing of Roy for five or six weeks. Nothing direct, that is. But his name remained before me and the rest of the public. With others, he signed a letter to *The Times* calling for an ultimatum to the Smith Government in Rhodesia to hand over all power to black leaders within forty-eight hours or face an airborne invasion. He gave an interview to a Sunday newspaper, in which he developed the ideas about youth he had dimly outlined to me in his garden, saying, in part, that it – youth – was in the process of discovering something as momentous as Christianity, and that those who resisted the free sale of hashish and other drugs did so out of guilt. He appeared in a television discussion on the future of the arts, no doubt forgetting the troubles that such exposure had allegedly brought him not so long before. I missed the programme, but heard that it was political in tendency, the views represented ranging from Roy's to those of an American sculptor who, it seemed, had demanded an end to all art not directly destructive of society. I was relieved to see a paragraph on some cultural chit-chat page saying that ebullient conductor Sir Roy Vandervane was preparing with the New London Symphony Orchestra to give a series of concerts of the symphonies of Mahler. Trendy, true, I thought to myself, but far, far better that than such as *Elevations 9.*

Nothing much happened to me over this period. *The Record-Player,* having tried all the reviewers senior to me and been rebuffed, sent along a huge box with a couple of dozen early Haydn symphonies and a small library inside it: eight long-playing yards, or about ten hours, of perfunctory periwiggery, not to speak of all those words, which provided a frightening amount of information on the composer's life and times without descending to any particulars at all about the symphonies concerned. That week I had Haydn coming out of my ears, or rather out of the other ear than the one he went in at. Harold Meers behaved himself on the whole, vetoing only a passing reference to the successful tour a string quartet had had in Poland. I finally winkled Weber out of Salzburg and established him in Vienna. I got the laundry to render up a shirt of mine they had been sitting on, if not wearing, for a couple of months, and had my piano tuned. Vivienne's sullenness-cum-preoccupation, never so marked as to sour any occasion, continued to fluctuate in a regular pattern: deepening as the week-end approached, vanished by Saturday afternoon, when I usually drove her out somewhere in a hired car, beginning to stir faintly again by Sunday evening. It was one Sunday about eight o'clock that I decided to change my usual policy of sitting (or, in this case, lying) about and waiting for female moods to go away.

'Has this other bloke been acting up, or what?'

'No,' said Vivienne.

This reply illustrated one of the best things in her character. Although the other bloke had been on the scene since Christmas or so, and took up all her free time and half her bed every Tuesday and Friday, and although she knew I knew about him, he had not been made conversational flesh until now. It was a relief not to have to machete my way through a jungle of what-are-you-talking-aboutery before I could get at him. Admittedly, this readiness to concede facts went with a reluctance to volunteer them, so that the process of finding out from her what, for instance, her father did for a living (it transpired that he was the lay secretary of an ecclesiastical body) was too much like one of those yes-or-no guessing games. But one cannot, and in this sort of case probably should not, have everything.

'Is he rich?'

'No. About the same as you.'

'I see. Married?'

'No.' She spoke with some heat.

'Well, a lot of people are, you know. Is he nice?'

'I wouldn't go with him if he wasn't nice, would I? He's fairly nice. No, a bit nicer than that. Say about halfway between fairly nice and really nice. He's rather small, you see, only about an inch taller than me. And then he's got this beard. Without a moustache. It goes all the way round his face without him having a moustache.'

'He doesn't sound anything like as nice as me.'

'He isn't. Not in that sort of way. But he's very kind and thoughtful. Oh, I mean you're kind when you think of it, but he always is. It's a big thing with him. And he's dependable. I can rely on him no matter what it is.'

'Don't mind me saying it, will you? but I think you're making him out to be rather dull.'

'There is a touch of that,' said Vivienne.

After a pause, I said, 'Does he know about me?'

'Oh yes.'

'How did he find out?'

'He asked me and I told him.'

'Yes. Does he mind sharing you?'

'He'd far sooner not, but he says it's better than not having me at all, and it's up to me, he says. He leaves all that side of things up to me.'

'Do you mind being shared? Have you done it before?'

'I'm usually shared, actually, and once I tried three for a bit, so I suppose I can't really mind. And I know you don't mind, in fact you'd sooner, wouldn't you? because it means I can't get serious. It sort of looks as though it ought to be wrong, doesn't it, sharing? I mean it's just exactly the kind of thing that is. I can't see why it isn't, but I went over it all in my mind before I started it, and I couldn't find anything that said I shouldn't, as long as I stuck to the rules, telling the truth and no married men.'

'Why no married men?'

'Making someone else unhappy. Same with a man who's got a girl he'd marry if he could, but his wife won't divorce him. You don't mind, do you? Me quite liking being shared?'

'Fine with me.'

'Because it's so enjoyable. Oh, darling,' she said, moving up against me and in other directions as well, and immediately, in fact simultaneously, breathing hard. It was easy for me to do something about that, since we were in bed together in my flat at the time. Doing something adequate about it was, as always, a matter of a good deal more than a couple of minutes. Vivienne was quick off the mark all right, but she was equally quick off a more or less indefinite successive series of marks. It was really very practical of her, quite liking being shared.

There was a different side of things that I, and in all probability the other bloke too, left up to her: the moment when the gentleman should come into his own. That evening, as always, she picked it admirably. Very soon afterwards she said, 'Good heavens, is that really the time?', jumped out of bed and ran into the bathroom. I lay on my back, put my glasses on to aid thought, and decided slowly that the sullenness-cum-preoccupation must be derived from the unflattering uninterest I had formerly shown in the question of the other bloke. I would have to remember to inquire about his welfare every so often, without at the same time letting it be known what hell I thought he sounded.

When Vivienne came out of the bathroom I went in there, returning to find her dressing. She kept her back to me, but this was standard; indeed, I had only recently, and after constant pressure, been able to stop her going into the bathroom to dress. Her underclothes had their familiar look of being both new and old, as if she had that afternoon come across a hermetically sealed unused set from her mother's trousseau behind a secret panel. On top of them went a variegated shiny silk shirt in lilac, flame, mustard and navy blue, a thick, rather long skirt with a black hound's tooth pattern on pinkish beige, pale green stockings and brown shoes. A chain belt, amber beads, a charm bracelet constructed for maximum noise-level, and earrings featuring little gold birdcages with painted parrots inside – these were added as I put my clothes on. Apart from intrinsic qualities, the ensemble abolished the substantial breasts, narrow waist and curving hips beneath it. She had brought her abundant and (literally) coal-black hair into disservice by piling it up into a roughly rectangular wedge across the top of her head, and now smeared mauve grease-paint over the firm outlines of her lips. But even she had not been able to muddy the brown of her eyes, pock her skin, skew her nose, unwhiten or snaggle her teeth. These failures were what had led me to her that first morning in the airline office, together with what the olive uniform she wore there had not concealed. (She had told me once, without making any evident deduction from it, that it was funny how men only tried to pick her up in the office.)

'Would you like a drink?' I asked.

She looked at her watch, which had a spaceman's head depicted in pop-art style on its considerable face. 'We mustn't be too long, Doug. I don't want to be late back. Could I have a small bianco and soda?'

I prepared a couple of these, and we were drinking them in the sitting-room when the telephone rang. After the idiot periodic tweet, signalling a call from a public box, I heard Roy's voice.

'May I speak to Mr Yandell, please?' (He had not yet learnt to bring his telephone manners up to date by baldly naming the person he wanted.)

'Yes, Roy, speaking.'

'Duggers. Marvellous. How are you? Look, old lad, I'm clutching at straws. Have you got anybody with you?'

'Yes.'

'Oh, sporting spirit. Oh, that's it, then.' He sounded in some distress. 'Oh well, never—'

'We're going out soon to have dinner.'

'Oh. Oh, I see. Well, look, I've got somebody with me too. We've been sort of let down. I wonder if I could possibly—'

'Where are you now?'

High-pitched female giggling came from the other end, then some muffled words from Roy, remonstrative in tone. Soon he said, 'What? Just round the corner from you. Carlton Hill.'

'Come along straight away. I'll let you in and we'll disappear.'

'Are you sure?'

I convinced him I was, rang off, and did some explaining to Vivienne. Without surprise or delay, as expected, she took in the situation and agreed that, should it prove necessary, I could later share her bed, which she insisted on occupying on Sunday nights anyway, so as to begin her working week on her own ground, as she put it – and incidentally, as I had discovered, at six a.m. Then I told her which Roy it was who was coming.

'You mean *Sir* Roy Vandervane. Doesn't he go on television?'

'Frequently. And conducts orchestras. He's an old music friend of mine. You won't tell anyone, will you, Viv?'

'Of course not. Isn't he married, though?'

'Yes. It's all a—'

'What about his wife? Doesn't she mind or anything?'

'I suppose so. It's hard to be sure. She must. Or she would. She probably doesn't know. Almost certainly.'

'People always know.'

She stared at me accusingly, and I could find nothing to say, but at that moment my doorbell rang and I hurried downstairs. Of the two waiting figures I got a brief look at through the glass panel, one, which I took to be Roy, was so much larger than the other that I wondered for a moment whether, Kitty's forecasts having fallen short, he might not have reached the child-abduction stage already. When they stepped into the hall, I saw that matters had not yet reached that pass, but, in the spirit of a bibliophile taking his time about polishing his glasses before starting to peruse some rare tome, deferred a comprehensive survey until we were all four gathered in the sitting-room.

'This is Sylvia,' said Roy, leaving us in no doubt that he would much rather have introduced her as Miss X.

Not to be outdone in pointless mystification, I introduced Vivienne as Vivienne. The matter of the pants recurred to me as something more to the point than any number of suppressed surnames, and I felt very much like letting Roy know that, if he ever happened to take up espionage, he would in no time at all find himself asking a policeman the way to the bacterial-missile launching site. But he would have considered that fanciful, and it might have interfered with my scrutiny of Sylvia, so I kept my mouth shut while Vivienne, curiosity and disapproval bursting out of her eyes, exchanged amiabilities with him.

Was this Roy's great love of a few weeks back, or just something he had picked up at a party an hour before? The latter, I fervently hoped, studying face (pale, round, thin-lipped), hair (waist-length, lank), clothes (jeans, midget-fisherman's jersey, long sleeveless leather jacket), figure (none perceptible: Vivienne's get-up was shamelessly provocative by comparison). She exuded a curious smell, not unlike that of damp hay. I watched her looking round at the rows of books, the hi-fi, the piano, the record-racks, the typewriter, as if these objects were not only mildly strange but also virtually indistinguishable from one another. Every few seconds she scooped aside the two long hanks of hair that fell from a centre parting across most of her face, which they as regularly repossessed; troublesome for her, no doubt, but infinitely preferable to the gross humiliation of haircut or ribbon. Through it all, she put me in mind of somebody, or perhaps she had just had her picture in the papers, like most people under twenty-five.

'What a terribly nice fluht,' she said, using the then fashionable throaty vowel. Her voice was thin and clear, with the sort of accent that Roy tried to suppress in his own speech. 'Do you live here all on your own?'

'Most of the time I do.'

'You seem to have an awful lot of books and records and things like thuht.'

'I've sort of got to. It's to do with my job.'

'Roy was telling me,' she said. Then, just as I was beginning to settle down to nothing worse than a couple of minutes of boredom, she gave a loud snigger and looked not so much at me as at my face, as one in search of imperfections there; I immediately thought of the way Penny had reacted to the lump on my forehead, though it was not she of whom Sylvia had reminded me a moment before.

Roy broke in abruptly. 'I'm really moce grateful to you two for doing this for us.'

'Not at all. Right, Viv, let's be on our way.'

'Oh, don't rush off.' Roy sent me a private scowl of emphasis. 'You can spare ten minutes. Stay and have a quick drink with us.'

'What can I get you?' I asked Sylvia.

The girl had perhaps been doing her best to hold her mirth in check, but this last hilarity proved too much for her. She hunched her narrow shoulders and made a tearing, sneeze-like sound at the back of her nose. Repeating my question in shaking tones, she rotated slowly and unsteadily, her eyes coming to each of us in turn, but not in any very directed way. Tears or sweat lay on her pale cheeks.

'She'll have something soft,' said Roy, who seemed a little embarrassed. 'I don't suppose you've got a Coke or a Pepsi? Never mind, tonic, bitter lemon, dry ginger, anything.'

'Nothing for me, Douglas.' Vivienne clearly thought that her censorious looks at Sylvia looked like nothing more than looks.

'She'll have something soft,' quavered Sylvia. 'She'll have something soft.'

'I'll have a whisky if I may, Duggers. Let me give you a hand.'

'Is she always like that?' I asked Roy in the kitchen.

'No, only sometimes. Not often, really. You know, when she's high.'

'High? Do you mean on filthy hash? Pot?'

'My dear ole lad, I do wish you wouldn't always come up with the middle-class reaction. So predictable.'

'Well, she's not going to smoke it here. And what class are you?'

'Sorry. All right, I'll see she doesn't.'

With a show of irrevocable decision, he drank off about half the Scotch I had given him. Even in the days when his hair had been shorter and he would speak up occasionally against rock 'n' roll, Russia and the like, he had never diffused much confidence in any of his non-musical promises or decisions. It could do no good now to remind him that I would be breaking the law in my absence if he later failed to prevent his fearful little companion from lighting up a joint. I parenthetically wondered for a moment about the current state of his musical reliability.

'Is this the one, by the way?' I asked, pouring out a bottle of tonic water and wanting to top it up with dishwashing fluid.

'The one?'

'Roy. The one you said you were in love with up at your place.'

'Oh yes. Yes, this is the one. Of course, that was the day I decided to give her up, wasn't it? I remember now. Didn't last, as you see.'

'What changed your mind?'

'That I can't remember. Oh yes, Kitty put me in the wrong about something. Yes, it's all coming back to me now. I turned up sober for a dinner-party she was giving and she took it very well. Kitty did. Considering how pissed I'd been when one of the same chaps and his wife had come along the time before. Hungarian chap who settled here after the civil war there. Very reactionary. As a matter of fact I was very nice to them both, both times, as I recall. Couldn't have been sweeter.'

'What about the pants?'

'Oh, Puck-like theme! Have you been talking to Kitty again?'

'She rang me up the morning after that day and I told her I hadn't found out anything, which was true. Not a word since then.'

'I prefer to keep my underwear to myself, if you don't mind. No, actually I've been watching that. Laid in a whole stock of them, pants I mean, and vests and handkerchiefs as well. It would take a genius to keep track. Hang on for another few minutes if you can bear it, Duggers, to help me cool her down. Nice girl, that one of yours. What is she, twenty-eight? Do you mind if I top this up before we go back in?'

Back in, we found Vivienne not only still alive, but listening with apparently close attention to something being explained to her by Sylvia, who sat on the couch scooping her hair off her face with the regularity of a bodily exercise.

'We're not like that. We're different.' Without looking anywhere near me, she put her hand up and out in my direction, fingers and thumb spread, so that I was able to fit her glass of tonic into it with the minimum of trouble and delay. 'Uhbsolutely different. We reject money and making your way in the world and setting yourself up in life and rules. All the things they want us to use up our energies on so they can stay in power.'

'The structure,' said Roy encouragingly, and with an air of relief, sitting down next to her on the couch.

'Do you reject the fire-brigade when your house is on fire?' asked Vivienne.

Roy smiled indulgently and shook his head, so that his back hair waggled to and fro. 'That's not the same thing. Of course you use all this stuff. You use houses and telephones and shops and television sets and schools and so on. That's quite different from being dominated by them.'

'Who does the fire-brigade dominate?'

Boredom again seemed entrenched, so firmly that I felt I could well do with another bout of sniggers from Sylvia, now quite impassive apart from blinking hard and biting at her thin lower lip. Roy told Vivienne that she had chosen a bad example, and that he was talking about what lay behind the fire-brigade. Vivienne asked who the we was that rejected money and the fire-brigade, and, on learning from him that it was broadly speaking youth, said she considered herself still part of broadly speaking that, or had done until quite recently. At this, Sylvia sniggered in a way that showed how wrong I had been a moment before, and whispered into Roy's ear, putting one arm round his shoulders and the other hand on his knee.

'No no,' said Roy. 'No.'

Vivienne pursued her point. 'And you won't catch me doing any rejecting.'

'Why not,' said Sylvia, giggling hard, 'why not make a start with that blouse? If that's what you call it.'

'I beg your pardon?'

'Why do you wear such awful clothes? And so many of them. Doesn't *he* tell you? And those earrings. Are those birds in them?'

'That's enough, Sylvia,' said Roy without emphasis.

'Really, the things some people think they can say.' There was only a little indignation in Vivienne's tone and her cheek remained its usual light pink, unexpectedly in a girl who blushed almost as readily as she breathed.

Roy turned expository. 'I suppose the real division comes between those who want to have and those who want to be. What the have ones want to have can be a lot of different things, not all of them bad in themselves. Some are, of course, like power in all its forms, which is what politicians obviously exiss for, and I don't just mean fascist dictators, I mean anybody who wages politics. Then there are, well, businessmen and priests and administrators and all that lot, but I'm talking about personal power too, by one person over another person, like in most marriages and so on. Or it can be possessions, cars and washing-machines and furniture and collections of china and things. The people who want to be can be a lot of different things too, like artists and mystics and philosophers and revolutionaries, some sorts anyway, and just people who live and feel and see. You've got to make up your mind whether you're a have person or a be person.'

Outside the concert hall, I had never admired Roy more than during the couple of minutes it took him to get through to the end of this speech. As early as 'real division' Sylvia had started stroking the back of his neck; by 'politicians' she was stroking his thigh fairly near the knee and nuzzling his ear; at 'personal power' she fell to stroking one cheek and kissing the other. Up to this point Roy had pretended, carrying what conviction he could, that she was not there, but then he had changed his policy to one of non-violent resistance, crossing his legs and canting his head over as near as possible to his farther shoulder. When 'collections of china' saw her moving round towards his front, trying to undo a shirt button and pushing her hand between his thighs, he caught her by the wrists, and immediately after 'philosophers' had cast her at his feet, trying energetically to uncross his legs, he crossed them tighter and bent forward until belly met upper thigh, intensifying his grasp on her wrists. So matters stood for the moment.

'We really must be going,' I said.

There was a testing interval while Vivienne looked for and found her cigarettes and lighter and put them in her handbag, but the two of us had gained the door only an instant after hearing, from the direction of the couch, a double thud which told that the heels of the shoes on the feet at the end of Roy's finally uncrossed legs had struck the floor. I called to him over my shoulder that I would telephone in the morning.

'What was she going to do?' asked Vivienne during dinner at Biagi's.

I allowed time for the waiter to finish pouring out Valpolicella and go away before indicating what I had seen as the choice before Sylvia and saying which alternative I thought the more likely.

Vivienne blushed. 'Not with you and me there. She wouldn't have done that with us there.'

'Oh, I think especially with us there. That was the whole point. Or most of it. Demonstrating her liberation from such-and-such and her contempt for this, that and the other.'

'For what? Why?'

'Oh, God. To go against what she thinks we think is decent. To show she's a be person. It's not worth finding out. That girl's a puzzle you'd have to be out of your mind with curiosity even to consider finding the answer to. Viv, why weren't you cross when she . . . had a go at you?'

'Well, I was a bit, of course, but I know what you mean. I could see she was annoyed at your nice place and us getting on all right together. And it being all right for us to get on. Was she stoned? you know.'

'I think she must have been.'

'Well, you can't really be cross with someone in that state, can you? They're not themselves. At least, they're . . .'

'Yeah.'

After efficiently throwing down some more of her *escaloppe di vitello alla Biagis* for a minute or two, Vivienne said, 'Doug, is this blouse awful? And the earrings? You've got to say.'

'You dress in your own style. What you've chosen yourself. That's just the sort of thing she'd resent. Somebody who won't conform.'

'Conform? She doesn't exactly dress like they tell you.'

'No, well I don't mean what the magazines say. Her own crowd. All rejecting everything. Including very much King's Road or wherever the hell it is now.'

'But you do like the blouse? And the earrings?'

'You know I do.'

'She could talk, the way she'd flung on any old dirty thing she'd happened to pick up. All tatty.'

'She was awful.'

'I just hope your flat's all right,' said Vivienne.

So did I, especially when I telephoned Roy there the next morning as promised and found him vague, uncommunicative. Sylvia had left; he would wait until I returned; we might have a chat if I could spare the time. I said I could, even though I had used up a good deal of it already that day, notably between five thirty, when Vivienne had woken me, and six o'clock, when, right on schedule, she had got out of bed. More time had elapsed while she bustled about putting clothes into and taking other clothes out of cupboards and drawers, and more yet while she vacuum-cleaned the flat in its entirety, paying special attention, I thought, to the area immediately round the bed in which I still lay, but out of which she turned me soon after seven so that she could pack up the sheets for the laundry. A lot of bacon and eggs and coffee, prepared by me according to custom, acted as a temporary reviver; indeed, she looked so appealing in her office uniform that I would have been tempted to get her to take it off again, if time had not gone into short supply at that stage. We left and parted to our respective buses, having confirmed our usual arrangement to get in touch on Wednesday; Monday evening was the one on which she went to see her father in Highgate, and Tuesday was the property of the other bloke. There was a tinge of sullenness-cum-preoccupation in her farewell, rather less than normal for this point in the week. I dismissed it from my mind without trouble.

Smells of a strange breakfast hung about the Maida Vale building, or at least its ground floor, where there lived a Pakistani (employed, so he said, in some radio service of the BBC) and his fat Welsh wife. I climbed the stairs and confronted Roy, who appeared unshaven, though patches of dried blood on his cheeks and chin testified to some sort of struggle with my razor.

'You look a bit shagged,' he said.

'So would you if you'd been awake as long as I have. And so you do, anyway.'

'I bet I do. A heavy night, one way and another.'

'I can well imagine.'

'I doubt it, old lad.'

My eye fell on a patch of bare floor in front of the sitting-room couch. 'What's happened to my rug?'

'I'm sorry about that, Duggers. It had an accident.'

'Which destroyed every fibre of it.'

'No, I got Sylvia to take it away with her. That was no mean achievement on my part, I can assure you.'

'I'm convinced. What happened to it?'

'It wouldn't have been any use to you after, uh, what happened to it. I'll find you another one and have it sent up to you today.'

Roy's practice in matters of this sort was such that I knew a rug would indeed arrive and that it would be better than the one I had had, without being absurdly better. The rest of the sitting-room appeared unchanged. I wondered what the other rooms were like, especially the bedroom.

'There's nothing else much,' said Roy, who had followed my glance. 'A couple of plates and a cup. Also I gave your Scotch a bit of a pasting. I'll see to all that as well, of course.'

'No, the Scotch is on me.'

'Thank you, that's very nice of you. Look, I'm sorry about, uh, the way she went on last night. She's not as bad as that as a rule.'

'Oh, good. Never mind, it was a laugh of a sort. I'm going to shave now, if you've left me any blades. You put some more coffee on.'

The bedroom was in no worse a state than usual, the bed even rather carefully made: a waste of Roy's labour, because this bed was another bed that was going to have its sheets changed, not on his account. I deferred the operation, out of returning fatigue and the thought that to catch me in the act might dash him slightly.

Over coffee in the sitting-room, he asked, 'What are you up to this morning?'

'Well, it was supposed to have been Weber, really, followed by a recording at Broadcasting House at twelve fifteen – Music Diary.'

'Weber can hang on for a bit, can't he? How long is it till his bicentenary? Ten years?'

'Sixteen. At the present rate of progress I'm going to need all of them. What had you got in mind?'

'Oh, nothing in particular. I thought we might idle about for a spell, ending up at my club, where I could shoot a couple of glasses of champagne into you and send you off in top form to your recording.'

'After which we meet Sylvia and Penny for lunch at the Mirabelle.'

'No, honestly, nothing like that.' Roy looked neither transparently honest nor pained at having his honesty thrown in doubt, which meant he was being honest, or very, very nearly. 'How do you feel about Gilbert Alexander?' he went on. 'You remember, the chap who—'

'Yes, the black chap. I feel fine about him. Why?'

'He's bringing the car in for me. I said I'd give him a drink and show him the club. You wouldn't mind if he joined us?'

'Not in the least, but isn't he going to find things rather on the fascist racist side at Craggs's?'

'I don't think so, much. I've explained to him about it.'

'You mean that although it may look fascist and racist it isn't really?'

'He won't make any trouble,' said Roy confidently.

Acting as the Vandervane all-purpose social diluent had been no uncommon experience during our former association. Today's usage seemed unlikely, in prospect, to take much out of me, differing in this regard from the favour to which I had alluded a minute before. While Roy put the new Oistrakh on the hi-fi and I carried the rubbish bucket down to the dustbin, the full complexity of my intended role in the favour dawned on me: not only diluent, not just camouflage, but whipping-boy, bodyguard, odium-sharer, listener to tales of the have people and the be people, and probably getaway man, fetcher of police, ambulance, or the rejected fire-brigade. I went over my recording-script and set about hardening my heart against all talk of the favour.

'Are you ready, Duggers?'

'Bit early, isn't it? I can't drink champagne for an hour and a half and then go and work.'

'It's a bloody marvellous day. I thought we might walk down as far as the flyover, or anyway the canal.'

It was dusty, windy and noisy in the Edgware Road, but so sunny that even the tower blocks on the western side looked inhabitable, gave the illusion of being places where the good life, whatever that might be, was possible to pursue. The buses seemed unusually red and solid, the articulated lorries to be clattering and bouncing to some purpose. I said,

'What's special about her? I mean I can see she's young and all that, and you say she knows a lot about whatever it is, and I've only met her for a few minutes, but what's special about her?'

'The chief special thing about her as far as I'm concerned, and I'm the only one who is concerned, is that there she is. I met her and I started going to bed with her. It's Sylvia and not anybody else that I met and started going to bed with. Oh, the being young thing and knowing things is important, sure, but a lot of other kids have got that. Only I haven't met and gone to bed with them. Another point about her is that she isn't my wife.'

'True. Very few people are Kitty.'

'It isn't Kitty she isn't, you bloody fool. What she isn't is my wife. Not the same thing at all. As you get older you'll find that absolutely straight-down-the-middle sex doesn't strike you in quite the same way as it did when you started off. It *is* the same when you get to it, in fact it may be rather better, because you'll probably have picked up a few tips over the years, got better control and so on, but it doesn't strike you as the same. And there's no whacking fucking as a side of life where how things strike you matters at least as much as what the things are really like. Whatever they are really like. Everybody spends much more time being struck by it all than actually on the job. Not juss stuff like looking at tit magazines and pulling your wire, though you can't leave that out, and not just all the ground you cover in your mind from first catching sight of a bird to throwing the definitive pass, though there's a lot of that, too. No, it's looking at your wife in the bath, seeing a bird for a few seconds in the street and wondering how it would be, reading a sex scene in a novel and putting yourself in the chap's place, or not, and why not, and running into an ex-girl-friend and wondering about that, and wondering how you'll be functioning in ten years' time if you still are. All that. Anything to do with sex that isn't any kind of actual sexual activity, and there's a hell of a lot of it. Ah, now here's a bit of luck, by Christ.'

We had halted on the kerb at the corner of St John's Wood Road, waiting for a green light or a gap in the traffic. Near us there also waited a man of about thirty, wearing a sober dark suit and a large pair of dark sunglasses. Roy went over to this person and abruptly linked arms with him.

'Don't you worry, old lad,' I heard him say. 'I'll get you across. Mind you, if I may say so, I think it's a bit silly of you not to carry a white stick. And you really ought to go into the guide-dog question. I'm told they're absolutely marvellous. Transform your life.'

The flow of vehicles stopped for a few seconds, and before the man had thrown off his bewilderment Roy had conducted him to the opposite pavement. Here he shook himself free.

'What the devil are you playing at?'

'That's no way to talk to somebody who's juss seen a blime man across the street. Talk about ingratitude.'

'You crazy or what? I'm not blind.'

'Then why are you wearing dark glasses on a day like this? Any reasonable person would certainly assume that you were blind. Wasting my time. Pure bloody affectation.'

'Roy,' I said when we were side by side again, 'it is quite a sunny day, you must admit.'

'Not that sunny. This is England in May, not Italy in August.'

'Agreed, but some people have weak eyes.'

'That's not why that little turd was wearing his blinkers. Pure showing off. You can't let them get away with it all along the line. Got to keep at them. No, I quite see it would have been better if the sun hadn't been shining. The trouble is it's so rarely one's going to get the chance, with the chum there actually waiting to cross. I've been wanting to do that for two or three years, and this is the first time it's come up. I couldn't let it go, could I?'

After we had walked in silence for a time, I said, 'Go on about how sex strikes you.'

'Oh yes. Well, what I was really building up to saying was, you remember the chap in that Joyce book who went round the streets at night yelling out "Naked women!" to give himself a thrill. And there was some other chap, in some book by a Frenchman I seem to remember, who said he couldn't read "Girl, 20" in a small-ad column without getting the horn. Well, that was all very bloody well for them. We all went through that stage in our youth. Nowadays, as far as I'm concerned it's got to be something more. For sex to really strike me. More detailed and off the beaten track. I suppose in one sense it doesn't matter what it is as long as it's something. Take the chaps who after three-quarters of a lifetime of the most boring marital respectability start trying to bugger Boy Scouts, or flashing their hamptons at little girls in trains – I think Aldous Huxley's got a bit on that somewhere. It's not that they'd really rather have been doing that right from the start and finely decide they'd better get it done if they're going to, not just that, anyway. It's much more that Girl, 20 won't work any more as a thing to strike them. As a slogan, sort of. Girl, 20 as a reality might be fine for them, but that's different. Look, I don't know about you, but I'm pretty well knackered with all this walking. Let's get a taxi, for Christ's sake.'

'How does your own case fit into this?' I asked when we had done so.

'Yes, well I was coming to that, as you may well surmise. Sometimes, you know, you find yourself thinking things over as if you were well, deciding which country to emigrate to, climate versus cost of living, exetra. What about turning queer? you say to yourself. Plenty of facilities, these days highly respectable, pleasant companions, comparatively inexpensive. And a prick is a splendid thing, and a splendid *idea* as well. It strikes you. The trouble is that in every case it's got a man on the end of it. Which I'm afraid puts paid to it as far as I'm concerned. Then there's flagellation. I never even seriously considered that. It strikes you, sure, but what's it got to do with anything? You might as well play tennis or knit a pair of socks as a way of working up to a screw. And the same goes for those other capers like necrophily and bestiality. No point in even discussing any of them. It would just be flogging a dead horse.'

I turned in my seat and stared hard at Roy, who twitched a hand and a knee and a shoulder, and muttered to himself.

'Well . . . I mean, that's only a way of saying it's of no interest,' he said defensively. 'And flogging and dead and horse. Surely you got that?'

'Oh yes, I got it all right. I just wanted to make sure you had. Carry on.'

'Really, Christ . . . Anyway, I was knocking Girl, 20 just now, but it gets about fifteen per cent better as an idea if you can expand it to Girl, 20 and man just old enough to be her grandfather if you assume a soupçon of juvenile delinquency in both generations. And, uh, didn't I tell you it was Girl, 19? Yes, that's what I tell most people. I mean the people I have to tell something. Well, between ourselves, Duggers, it's actually Girl, 17. That jacks it up no end, I can assure you.'

'Good God.'

'Ageing shag tries to stimulate jaded appetite by recreating situation of days of firse discovery of sex plus whiff of illegality, corruption of youth, dirty ole man luring child into disused plate-layer's hut and plying her with wine-gums and dandelion-and-burdock to induce her to remove knickers and slake his vile lusts. That's it exactly. No better description possible. Hit the thing right on the nose.'

I was still a little shaken. 'Aren't you taking rather a risk?'

'Yes, there's that too. You can see why I've been keeping her out of sight to some extent. Actually I haven't been breaking the law much, as far as I know. She doesn't drink, and anyhow she'll be eighteen soon, I'm sorry to say.'

'How do her parents feel about this?'

I could see him start to take evasive action as plainly as if he had been a merchantman and I a U-boat. 'Well, they . . . give her a lot of freedom . . .'

'They seem to, certainly. Do they know about you?'

'No.' He laughed at the absurdity of this idea. 'They know she has men, of course, but, uh . . .'

'It might be awkward if they found out, mightn't it? Where had you been last night before you turned up at my place?'

'Some party. Friends of hers. Quite safe.'

'Who are her parents?'

'Oh, he's a . . . banker,' said Roy, eliminating at a stroke one category of employment tenable by Sylvia's father, and adding with dissimulated relief, 'Here we are.'

We descended at Craggs's Club. Roy shouldered me aside in order to pay, crying out like a man in a film falling off a high building when a florin rolled over the edge of his hand. The driver put his vehicle in gear, revved up and said in a high monotone,

'You Sir Roy Vandervane?'

'That's me.'

'Why don't you bugger off to Moscow if it's so bloody awful here?'

The cab shot away. Roy sighed heavily as we turned towards the steps.

'No use telling a chap like that I spoke out against the invasion of Czechoslovakia.'

'Not the slightest use. He'd think you ought to go just the same.'

'He's got his ideas laid out in blocks.'

'That must be it.'

We entered a lofty, squarish hall where a ticker-tape ticked, or rather chattered. Roy went over to a porter who was glaring at us from within a glass-and-mahogany emplacement. Another man, doubtless a member, but resembling a pop singer attired as a City gent, swung past with hanging jaw towards the street. I took in a small fraction of the scores of portraits and groups that covered the walls, feeling anew the shakiness of the whole concept of a population explosion, there having demonstrably been so many more people about a hundred years ago than now.

Roy rejoined me and we walked down a carpeted passage that crepitated very loudly underfoot. At its end there was an equally tall and much larger room with enough writing materials spread about to supply a hundred compulsive correspondents for the foreseeable future, and sheltering at the moment half a dozen solitary men in slightly different stages of torpor. Roy pushed a bell-push, a youthful white-jacketed waiter came and an order for champagne was given. I looked thoroughly round the room and then at Roy.

'It's convenient,' he said placatingly. 'Somewhere to be between appointments. Good food. It impresses Americans. And you can stay here.'

'With birds?'

'No, but you can cash cheques. And it's a good alibi spot. Of course I was here, dear. Asleep in the colour-television room. The porters are getting very slack. I'll have to have a word with the secretary. You know.'

'Speaking of alibis, where were you last night?'

'Here. Frugal, wholesome dinner and early bed. No phone calls; I checked.'

'That's all right, then. One thing you didn't go into was the business about you-know-who not being your wife. I can see that Girl, 20 or Girl, 17 don't come in as that anyway, but what about Girl, 28? I suppose she'd just be too—'

'Let's leave that until the drinks have come.'

When they had, we settled in a corner bounded by volumes of *Punch* and *Who Was Who*, and Roy began,

'There are two things really. The obvious one about anything up to about Girl, 45 being more striking than your wife, not better in fact, just—'

'I've got all that. Let's have the other thing.'

'Well, that's simply a matter of you wanting to get away from normal, decent, God-fearing sex and your wife being no good for that. The tone of the thing's all wrong, the whole context. It can't be done. Darling, here's a letter from the Toolboxes asking us down for Easter and you remember how you enjoyed it before when you, I don't know, uh, pissed in his rain-gauge so shall I accept? And would you give me my hambag off the dressing-table? And could you ring the bloody, oh, paraffin man as you promised and give him hell? And anything interesting in your post? Not really, dear, just the tickets for the Shitshitski recital and the BUM contract and a few clippings and have a look at this and what about going down?'

I sat on for a moment while a clock at the end of the room struck the half-hour. 'You mean it's all so routine, getting up and going down to breakfast and never getting the—'

'Oh, peace in our time, Duggers! Statesmanlike act! *Going . . . down.* Where have you been? She takes your—'

'Quiet. I know what she takes all right.'

'Allow me to present you with the information that these days it's called going down.'

'I know what it's called.'

'Well, you didn't seem to just now.'

'You threw the phrase at me without sufficient preparation.'

'Did I? Sorry. Let me top you up. Well, you get the point. Girl, anything will do that for you, and other things besides, whereas . . . It's not so much that she will as that you can ask her to. I suppose it is very much an age thing, too.' He turned judicial and wise, reminding me that a week or so previously I had read of his forthcoming contribution to a symposium, run by some churchman, on a sexual morality for our (or their) time. 'I think even somebody like you would admit that one solid, unarguably liberating gain from the new atmosphere of tolerance, among younger people at any rate, has been the admission of all that type of stuff to the, Christ, to the standard repertoire of what people get up to in bed.'

'So that everything becomes as natural as breathing.'

'Precisely. Where's Gilbert got to? Normally he's punctual to a fault. I hope nothing's wrong at home.'

'Might something be?'

'Something might always be.'

He looked at me assessingly, and I guessed he was trying to make up his mind whether to present domestic going-wrongness as an inevitable effect of the bourgeois social structure or, alternatively, as a healthy sign of a larger, higher going-rightness just round the corner. But, before he could decide, Gilbert came into the room. I had not noticed his slimness before, nor the ease of his movements. His face, however, was at the moment troubled. He addressed himself immediately to Roy.

'Penny's here.'

'What! She can't be. Women aren't allowed in before five.'

My immediate thought had been that here was one of the little prearranged surprises that had brought Roy a modest fame in the past, but it was soon clear that his wonder and apprehension were every bit as genuine as his feelings of outrage at such infringement of Club protocol. This, it was next revealed, had not actually been infringed after all, or not yet: Penny had been left sitting in the car, which Gilbert had parked in St James's Square. In admitting as much, he went out of his way not to offer the smallest comment or suggestion or comfort. Roy gave a sweeping gesture of anger and hopelessness which blended into a jab at the bell.

'What's she playing at?' he asked. 'What did she say?'

'She barely announced her intention to make the trip,' said Gilbert.

'Perhaps she felt like a bit of a jaunt, a look round the shops and lunch out somewhere,' I said, drawing upon myself remarkably similar glances of pitying contempt for such imaginative poverty.

'Come on, Gilbert, what's she up to? How's she been behaving? You must have some idea, surely to God.'

'She's been perfectly silent. It appears to me that she's bent on some destruction, as usual.'

'Yes, I'm afraid you're right. All part of the pattern.'

'What can she destroy from inside a parked car?' I was beginning to feel like one of three ennobled surgeons called in at short notice to advise on the lancing of a royal boil. 'I suppose she could work on the upholstery a bit with her nail-scissors, if she's got any.'

Gilbert ignored me. 'She must suspect you're engaged in some activity that she could somehow spoil with her presence, or the threat of her presence.'

'Like having it off with me, you mean, in the colour-television room.'

'Cut out your pawky, perky little sallies for the moment, Douglas, if you would.' Roy moved aside to talk to the returning waiter.

'Miss Vandervane,' said Gilbert to me, 'is totally unaware of your existence.'

'I should have thought that, if anything, that rather strengthened my point.'

'This is the kind of elitist environment in which one might expect to find someone of your basic attitudes.'

'Yes, or Roy's. It's his club.'

'You are against life.'

'Oh, wrap up.'

'Cool it, Duggers,' said Roy. 'We've got to think what's best to do.'

'No doubt you have.' I looked at my watch. 'I must go or I'll be late.'

'You've got over twenty minutes.' Roy gave me one of his person-to-person scowls. 'Hang on just a second and we'll drop you. Have some more shampers.'

'All right. Thanks.'

'Then we can all go off together and you and I can take her to the Savoy, Gilbert. She said once she liked it there. That's the thing.'

'What's the age of this building?' Gilbert spoke with an anthropologist's detachment.

Roy told him that and other things. A champagne glass arrived for Gilbert and a tumbler of Scotch for Roy. Both drank, while I thought about the problems of being a jobbing diluent, more vaguely about Penny, and then more specifically about how late I was going to be at the BBC. We left the Club at the point in time at which a brisk trot along King Street, followed by a rally team's type of progress up Regent Street, would forestall any reproaches on my arrival.

'What have you got on this afternoon?' I asked Roy as we walked.

'Whole pack of stuff. Buggering around here and there. One thing that should be fun. Telling a shag why I won't do *Harold in Italy* for him.'

'I suppose the viola part would be rather on the—'

'No no, this would have been waving the stick. Because of Byron.'

'What's he got to do with it?'

'Duggers, the music by Hector Berlioz, ob or dee 1869 as we both have cause to know, is based on a—'

'God. I'm with you. God.'

'Sorry, but these days you do rather seem to need to have stuff spelt out.'

'What's Byron got to do with it?'

'Christ, he's a Greek national hero. They're always going on about him.'

'So we refuse to perform a piece of music by a Frenchman inspired by a poem by an Englishman who died a hundred and fifty years ago in case it might get blokes to turn soft on the present government in Greece. I see.'

'You can't let it slip, you know. Got to keep at them.'

'I'm surprised you thought it was all right for you and me to play K.481 the other week. Wasn't Hitler an Austrian too?'

'That's a dead issue now. And the idea's too far-fetched.'

'Too what?'

'Far-fetched,' said Roy loudly. 'No flag-waving sentiment in Mozart.'

Gilbert, on Roy's other side, had been showing a respectful impatience, clearly resenting my readiness to waste Roy's time while rather admiring his lenity. Now he settled my hash by chiming in scornfully, 'Hell, I should just about say not.'

The car came into view, singling itself out from others by its size and splendour. Not at first sight the obvious choice for a be person, I reflected uncharitably, then considered the notion that Roy did not so much own it as fulfil his personality by means of it. Anyone else might be said to *have* it; it was his distinction to *be* the person it belonged to. Or perhaps it was just that he had not yet finished changing over from having to being.

A bowed shape inside revealed itself as Penny under a cartwheel-sized hat. She was in the back seat. Why? She had moved there after arrival so as to allow her father to take his place in front. Out of the question. She had spent the journey there so as to emphasize her disaffection from mankind, as personified by Gilbert. Much more like it. But it touched the edge of my mind that she might have wanted to diffuse the impression (among a limited audience, admittedly) that the flagrantly progressive Sir Roy Vandervane kept a coloured chauffeur: a part that Gilbert, with his dark-blue suit, pale-blue shirt and black-knitted-silk tie, could plausibly have filled. To have thought of this at all made me feel humiliated in some way.

'Right, into the car with you,' said Roy in grim, riot-squad tones. 'You in the back, Douglas.'

Penny moved a few inches away from me like somebody in a bus making room for a not necessarily very drunken stranger, a relatively effusive greeting. Roy half turned in the passenger's seat in front and was very bald about dropping me at the studios and going on to the Savoy, while she looked out of the window at some nearby railings. What with this and the hat I could not see much of her, but even so I caught a strong physical reminder of Sylvia. It was gone before I could do more than decide tentatively where it had not originated: face, hair, figure, clothes, smell. In the last-named department Penny was offering a good deal of, though nothing more than, the consequences of warm female flesh; perhaps she was a secret washer as well as a secret listener to music. Excellent, but if I had glimpsed a resemblance elsewhere between the two girls, it was likely, or possible, or conceivable, that Roy had too. Perhaps an incestuous fixation had been transformed into a . . .

Vowing weakly to dig out the popular-psychology paperback I was nearly sure I still had in a cupboard at the flat, and to drop the volume unopened into the Regent's Canal at an early opportunity, I prepared for a closer look at Penny, but had to defer this for the time being when Gilbert drove out of the parking area like an international ace leaving the pits at Le Mans (or somewhere) and snapped my head back against the cushions. More delay supervened while he took us into a tight fast semicircle that held me against the door on my side at a pressure of several Gs and sprawled Penny horizontally across my lap, which was all right.

'Steady, Gilbert,' said Roy in his richest tone.

'Poor me boy! Good me do and thank-ye me get!'

I understood this utterance as a protest, perhaps not unjustified if one cared to look far enough. No time for that now. Penny pulled herself upright before I could assist her, and resettled her hat. She was wearing a mulberry-coloured skirt apparently knocked together out of an old curtain and ample enough to cover another three or four legs besides her own, bicep-height crimson fish-net gloves and a kind of low-cut suede waistcoat above which her breasts showed like the tops of a couple of ostrich eggs. She looked at me and I took in the eyes and skin.

'Your head's better, I see,' she said.

'Yes, thank you. Cleared up in no time.'

'It's left a little mark, but I expect that'll fade away soon. It hardly notices now, as a matter of fact. It's really only because I know where to look that I can see it at all.'

'Oh, good.'

'I'm sorry if I was rude to you that day. I was very depressed about something, and I know I do get rude when I get depressed.'

'I see.'

'Anyway, I'm sorry.'

'That's all right.'

My eyes seemed to want to go on looking at her, but I switched them round until they were looking out of the window. Was she experiencing some fool kick or other, off on some pitiable good trip? Or was I in for a session of the sincerity-sarcasm game, in which A steps up her sincerity to the point where B must declare himself either a moron for going on taking it or a boor for telling her to stuff it? What told against this view was that the game is much better with an audience, and Penny was keeping her voice down, though admittedly she would have had to raise it a good deal to vie with the noise Gilbert was getting out of the engine as he took us hurtling up towards Piccadilly Circus. Perhaps she had simply been apologizing. Then, still quietly, and still in a face-value voice, she asked,

'What have you and him been talking about?'

'Oh, musical stuff. Gossip.'

'He didn't mention Saturday? This coming Saturday?'

'No? What's happening then?'

'Are you free that evening?'

'I can be.' I had a lieder recital and a date with Vivienne, but the one could be missed and the other deferred. 'Why?'

'He told me he was thinking of giving a sort of little dinner-party somewhere. In a restaurant. He wanted me to come, and you, and then this girl.'

The favour! So Gilbert's instincts had not been altogether wrong, and Penny had managed to prevent Roy from putting the proposition to me in his own time. How he had been going to do this with Gilbert within range I could not envisage, but Roy's resources had always been large and varied.

I asked mechanically, 'What girl?'

'She's called Sylvia. You must have met her. She's got long hair.'

'Yes. Indeed she has. When did you meet her?'

'Oh, I've never met her. He told me about her. What's she really like?'

'She's . . . not my kind of person,' I said with an effort.

'Yes, he said she was young. Is she pretty?'

'Not to me. But of course different people—'

'You are going to come to the dinner, though?'

'I don't think so.'

'Oh come on, it'll be fun. You said you were free.'

'*Fun?*' I tried not to sound too airy and gay. 'I can't really see it being much of that, given the . . . given her. But, uh, it would be fun for you, would it, to go out on the town with your dad and his bird and another bloke to make up the number?'

'What's wrong with that?'

I drew in my breath to tell her that if, on grounds of some mouldering old thing like taste, she could see nothing wrong with the proposed outing, I would have to join in with my fellow deacons and churchwardens and not be able to answer her question. Then I held my breath for a moment, realizing, to my vexation or uneasiness or something, that I was no longer sure whether there was much wrong with it after all. Then I let all my breath out at once when the car stopped as dead as if it had run into a brick wall and I bounded forward and hit the top of my forehead against the edge of the back of the seat in which Roy was sitting. The car had not been going very fast, and the line of contact was not as sharp as the lintel of the Vandervane kitchen door had been; nevertheless, the effect felt remarkably similar, and must have looked similar too, at any rate to Penny, who broke out into similar laughter.

I took in facts. The car had run into not a brick wall but the back of a bus, and had dented it somewhat, while itself seeming unharmed. My three fellow-passengers were likewise whole, had no doubt seen the bump coming. Gilbert had his head out of his window, Roy had opened his door, Penny went on laughing without giving any impression of artificiality. Some crossing pedestrians stopped and stared and stayed stopped. We were at the corner of Conduit Street. It was exactly twelve fifteen. A policeman came into view on the far side of the road.

I told Roy I would be in touch, got out of the car and gained the pavement. Lines of stationary traffic stretched unbroken as far as Oxford Circus. I set off at light-infantry speed, opting for arrival at my destination twenty or so minutes late in fair condition rather than something less than a quarter of an hour in a pulp. I negotiated family groups moving at toddlers' pace, ladies with dogs on yard-long leads, arm-in-arm trios, suddenly becalmed old men, a phalanx of schoolchildren, two girls halted in serious conversation, an approaching Sikh with his eyes on an open street plan. What had been chiefly unwelcome about Penny's laughter was that I knew I would be able to see a very good case for it tomorrow without being able to see any particle of that case now. It was the obliteration of this time-lag, not, or not nearly so much, any revelling in others' misfortunes from a safe distance, that made funny stories enjoyable. After my recording I would go along to the George and have a pint of bitter and a round of cheese-and-pickle and a round of ham with too much mustard. Then, at the flat, the new Walter Klien of K.415 and K.467.

I had crossed Oxford Street when I heard my name being called from behind, and it was nobody else but Penny, carrying her hat in her hand. I stopped. Everybody she ran past turned to stare after her. I felt all at once that I had been awake for seven hours, that I had rather liked the rug that had had an accident, that a social diluent ought to have a clause written into his contract saying his duties did not include being put in the wrong about everything from his presence in a club to Mozart's lack of flag-waving sentiment, that I was hot and my head hurt.

She came up, showing less sign of exertion than might have been expected in such a committed idler, but quite enough to draw my eyes to the top of her waistcoat. She must have them propped up, I thought. On supports of some kind. Rolled-up tissue-paper, perhaps.

'Hang on a minute,' she said.

'I can't, I'm due at the BBC. Late already.'

'So? They'll wait.'

'Penny: I have to go.'

A man in overalls coming from behind me barged into her hard enough to swing her half round, but she showed no resentment, as Vivienne or I would have done. 'You coming to the dinner on Saturday?'

'I can't, sorry.'

'What do you mean you can't? You said you were free.'

'I can't, I won't, I'm not going to.'

'Listen, you sixty or something? You go on like you were older than him, twice his age. You're sodding dead, you are.'

I leaned over her. 'I'm not coming because one of the girls who are coming is an exact replica of you and the other one is you. I'd need a good half-hour to go into all the things I object to about you, so I'll just tell you that helping *him* on with this thing of his is being nasty to Kitty, and don't tell me she knows about it and doesn't mind. She's taken you on and she puts up with you, God help her, and I don't want anything to do with someone who thinks it's all right or funny or why-not or groovy or *wild* to behave in that way. Now clear off.'

The clock in the BH foyer stood at twelve thirty-nine when I pushed my way in through the swing door. The producer of the programme I was on, standing by the reception desk, saw me and hurried forward.

'Sorry, Philip. Got hung up.'

'And beaten up, it seems.' He looked at my forehead. 'Are you all right? Good, now not to worry, we've got the studio until one. If you can—'

He looked past my shoulder in muted consternation. It was Penny again.

'I'm sorry I laughed in the car.'

'That's all right. Now just—'

'Help me.'

There is no other injunction like this, in that you have to heed it but cannot, by the fact of its being put, hope to do what it says. I pressed my hand against my head.

'All right. I'll be back here in about twenty minutes, so . . . Or you can telephone me.'

We got through the recording without a single fluff. By the time I had hurried back to the foyer, Penny had gone.

## Three

## The Night of the Favour

Helping Penny became a less daunting prospect as the day advanced and as I considered the possibilities and ethics of stretching it, or confining it, to helping her off with her suede waistcoat, out of her pyjama-top, etc. I felt partly protected on my Vivienne flank by the open and tolerated existence of the other bloke – only partly, so to speak internally: that gnome about the transferability of sauce is far too obviously the result of a consensus of ganders to make any useful impression on the average goose. When it came to Penny herself, matters seemed less clear-cut. The kind of help she might have been asking for ranged presumably from adopting her as my daughter to saying I would come on Saturday after all, with agreeing to be prick-teased by her coming somewhere in the middle, or off to one side. I felt this last as a kind of moral counterpoise to the implications, if any, of throwing a pass at somebody in a state. Yes, and whatever sort of state it might or might not reveal itself to be, it was not that of innocence, in any sense of the term. All this was good self-justifying stuff, and available in fully sufficient quantity to be going on with.

Anyway, when Roy rang me up that same evening, ostensibly to ask if the new rug had arrived (which it had) and if I liked it (which I quite did), and then went on to say casually that he gathered Penny had mentioned to me a very vague sort of thought he had happened to have had about a possible minor jaunt on the approaching Saturday, I agreed that she had, and told him I thought it was rather a good idea.

'A good idea? You didn't say that the last time we discussed it.'

It was no use reminding him that on that occasion I had ended up by saying something to that very effect. I remembered that, although a great one for making other people do what he wanted them to do, he tended to turn suspicious if they showed signs of wanting to do it on their own account. I came back with something about approving only conditionally, in the abstract, and put in a vigilant request for details. This, carrying the bonus of giving him ample scope for mystification, went down a treat. Under pressure, he finally disclosed the name of the pub in Islington where we were to start the evening, and even threw in the time. After that, he said in the tone of a full and inflexible planner, we would see how things went.

'How's Penny?' I asked.

'Penny?' He sounded puzzled. '*Fine*. Why?'

'She didn't seem very fine the last I saw of her.'

He did his comprehending wolf howl. 'Oh-oo. That. That was nothing. You did get the point, I take it? That she thought she'd been rude by laughing when you hit your head and wanted to apologize? I mean you grasped that?'

'Well, yes. Rather drastic, wasn't she being?'

'Nop by her standards, I can assure you. How is the head?'

'Labouring. How's the car?'

'Try smice on it. Oh, it'll be in dock a few days. You seemed so terrified of being late for your bloody recording that Gilbert forgot what the brakes were for. Nobody's fault, really.'

'No. Tell me, how did you join up with Penny again?'

'Gilbert worked out, Gilbert stayed with the car and I just strolled up to the BBC and collected her. We had quite a jolly lunch at the Savoy eventually. Pity you couldn't join us. She kept complaining that you hadn't, incidentally, which Gilbert didn't much care for.'

'What does he think is happening on Saturday evening?'

'Leave that to me. Yes, I don't know what you said to her, but you seem to have made something of an impression. Fine as far's I'm concerned. If you could, you know, reach her in some way it would be a splendid thing for all concerned.'

All concerned, I thought when I had put the telephone down. Like Gilbert, for instance. Like Vivienne. Like the other bloke. Like me. But most of all like Roy. Was what he had said – he had said more in the same strain before ringing off – just a prophylactic against Penny's probable conduct on Saturday, or had he a deeper scheme in train, of the sort I had glimpsed when, in his kitchen that afternoon, he had asked me what I thought of her looks? The real trouble with liars, I decided as I belatedly got Weber out of his drawer, was that there could never be any guarantee against their occasionally telling the truth.

Saturday afternoon found me in reasonably good heart. Earlier that week, Harold Meers had accepted without question, and allowed to appear in his newspaper, a half-sentence of mine in praise of a Bulgarian soprano. I had given Haydn the modified rounds-of-the-kitchen treatment, cunningly laying off by warm praise of the performance and recording, and had sent the review off to *The Record-Player*. The Nonpareil label had commissioned me to do the sleeve-notes for the complete Mozart piano sonatas executed by some Paraguayan newcomer. Vivienne was no problem, having gone more than halfway to meet me, in fact a little further than I really wanted, when I suggested cancelling, rather than putting back, our date for that day. She said it would give her a chance to catch up with her letter-writing, thereby injecting such an authentic note of humdrumness that I almost wished she had told me a lie.

Deciding what to wear took me longer than my usual three seconds. All things considered, the ideal outfit would have been a leather jacket that became the top half of a dinner-suit when turned inside out, a denim dickey over an evening bow, steel-tipped patent-leather pumps, and so on; but I did not possess any of these, and settled on dark everything from shirt to shoes, including a dark neck-scarf, with a little quick-change protective coloration up my sleeve, or rather stuffed into my hip pockets, in the form of two neckties, one psychedelic (a joke present from my sister), the other sane. At half past five I drank a pint of milk to protect my stomach from whatever Roy might have in store for it, transferred my wallet from my right to my left breast-pocket, and got on my way.

A nasty dog-leg journey by Tube, nasty both topologically and as regards the quality of the experience, delivered me at length outside the Angel station. It seemed to me that a newspaper-seller there flinched slightly when I mentioned the name of the pub I sought, but

from a distance it looked harmless enough. I had been rather expecting to find the streets deserted, the buildings uninhabited, having been
quite recently told by a left-wing bassoonist friend and his left-wing
harpist wife that they were among the first people to have moved into
the area. On the contrary, there was every sign of occupancy, and
throngs of young and old passed to and fro, no doubt in transit or
going out for the evening, since at this advanced hour – very nearly
six o'clock – they could scarcely have still been coming home from
work. I moved freely among them and gained the front of the building unmolested.

Close to, it looked less harmless. Its fabric suggested, though not
seriously, only to a fleeting glance or to eyes like mine when unassisted
by glasses, that it was made of variegated planks of wood and strips
of galvanized iron. Here and there archaic war posters, or reproduc-
tions of such, were somehow incorporated into whatever material
composed the exterior. None the less I went in, and found myself in
a small vestibule lit only by a number of signs and arrows: Wipers
Bar, Blighty Bar, Cookhouse, Dug-out. Roy had said something about
below ground, so I chose the last of these. At the foot of a steep
wooden stair with no risers and a rope hand-rail, I beat aside a cling-
ing obstacle that, seen by what illumination there was on its farther
side, proved to be a plastic curtain got up to look like sacking, though
here again the pretence was half-hearted. Two dimly seen couples
crouched in sham-concrete alcoves. Replicas of rifles, gas masks,
grenades hung on the walls. I took in no more of this, but went to
the bar, where I was confronted by a girl in service-dress with medal
ribbons and sergeant's stripes. Just then a wordless yelling, recalling
Ashley Vandervane's but rather lower in pitch and accompanied by
clashes and soggy thumps, burst from several invisible sources. Nevertheless I managed to get myself a Guinness, and went and sat down
on a padded ammunition-box in a corner.

After an hour or so of subjective time, in fact perhaps two minutes,
I was preparing to go and wait in the street, but then Roy and Penny
fought their way past the curtain. Penny was hatless and had boots
on; I could not know what else she might or might not have been
wearing. She settled herself mutely beside me while Roy went to the

bar, and I asked her how she was, cunningly keeping my voice well down to normal volume.

'What? I can't hear with this row.'

I moved much closer to her, close enough for a good noseful of the warm clean smell I had noticed in the car, and repeated my question.

'I'm all right. Why?'

'You didn't ring me up.'

'What about?'

'I don't know. What it was you didn't ring me up about. Because you didn't ring me up.'

'I didn't say I was going to, did I?'

'No, I said you could if you wanted to.'

'What for?'

Most of my brain seemed suddenly to have become unusable, cut off for ever by a massive haemorrhage. It occurred to me that these days, after so many precedents in film and TV drama, especially of the strong variety, people left questions unanswered whenever they felt like it, often shrugging their shoulders as well, so I silently shrugged mine. Then I realized that, in the gloom, Penny might mistake this gesture for an outsize nervous tremor, or even miss it altogether. Accordingly, I muttered for a few seconds. Penny did not pursue the topic. No doubt I had been inept, either in reminding her too early about the helping project, or in assuming she remembered having mentioned it in the first place. There was nothing like the society of youth for making one feel young: about fourteen, in fact, and an abnormally blush-prone, naïve and thick fourteen into the bargain. I found myself asking her if she liked this place.

'Sodding wicked,' she said, lighting a cigarette.

'I don't see why they have to have it so dark. And noisy.'

'What?'

Roy turned up at that point, carrying what I could only assume were drinks for himself and his daughter.

'We were just saying how much we hated this pub,' I said.

'Bloody awful, isn't it?' he agreed readily, drinking.

'Why have we come here, then?'

'Just that it's convenient.'

'How do you make that out?'

'For where we're going next.'

'Where's that?'

'Only round the corner.'

'No doubt, but what is it?'

'I think you'll both agree it's fun.'

I hoped very much that this brick wall had been thrown up out of habit, not so as to conceal a prospect so dreadful that any preview of it would send me, or Penny, or both of us haring down the City Road. I pondered the point intermittently while Roy took me more or less bar by bar through the rehearsal of the Mahler Fifth he and the NLSO had been engaged on earlier that day. The other sort of noise that still surrounded us would have made it difficult for him to address Penny as well without continuously shouting his head off, and her hunched-up silhouette told of withdrawal on her own part. After he had described for the second time a passage of arms he had had with the principal double-bass (was he, understandably enough, drunk already?), I broke in to say, not very ardently, but at least loudly,

'You know, I think old Gus must have written out programme notes first and then worked back from them to his score. Sort of, after the strings have failed to reach the moment of reconciliation they had seemed to promise three-quarters of an hour earlier, trumpets and trombones solemnly deliver a message of—'

'Here she is.'

Sylvia approached, wearing what my night vision, eked out by such knowledge as I had of her, suggested was the rig-out of our previous meeting. Roy had risen and seemingly kissed her, and now introduced bird to daughter, gesturing, even gesticulating, in a way that faintly recalled his manner on the rostrum at a moment of drama. Then he and Sylvia went over to the bar. I turned to Penny, feeling by now several decades older than fourteen, but she surprised me by shouting first.

'Where's he taking us, then?'

'No idea.'

'I don't want to go to it.'

'I said I'd no idea where he's taking us.'

'I heard you. I don't want to go to it. Wherever he's taking us. Got it?'

'You mean you'd rather stay here?'

'Don't talk like a bloody fool.'

I found I could whimper to myself really quite powerfully, at a volume that would have carried across, say, the aisle of an Underground train in motion, without seeming to reach Penny's ears. 'What would you like to do?'

She leaned forward to a point at which she could talk audibly at an almost normal pitch. 'I wouldn't like to do anything. There's nothing I'd like to do. Ever. I can't stand it up there with her' – Kitty, I assumed, rather than the domestic or the Furry Barrel – 'and there's nowhere I want to go outside. I can't stand being on my own, and I can't stand being with one person, and I can't stand being with a lot of people. Well, I can stand it, but I always feel I won't be able to another second. I can't think about anything, except about how I feel, and how I feel's always just me thinking about how I feel. I don't mind being asleep.'

She spoke without the flat hostility she had displayed a few moments before, nor was there the least trace of self-pity in her tone. She might have been a television story editor in conference, briskly outlining in the first person a substantial minor character she was proposing to have written into the script. In a brief glow from her cigarette, I saw her looking at me as if she simply felt it was my turn now. I said conversationally,

'Are you on drugs?'

'Not at the moment. You always think they're going to be good, but they're not, not really. Not for me, anyway. It gets like seeing everything in a lot of mirrors, or through funny glass like a migraine, or looking up from the floor, but it's the same thing really. Even when all the things look different, all covered with stuff or turned into lights and things, or even when you can't see or hear anything you're sort of used to, you know it's all there really. Not just it's going to be back when you're back, it's there all the time. Even when you can't just remember what it's like. Of course, I haven't had anything . . .'

I lost her voice under a short *feu de joie* of howitzers intended to lend emphasis to some crux in the performance that raged about us. 'What?'

'Heroin!' she bawled. 'What they call a hard drug, actually, where you—'

'But you haven't taken that.'

'Not so far I haven't.'

'But you're not going to.'

'Why not? Why shouldn't I?'

'Why not! Because it kills you. God almighty.'

'What's wrong with that?'

At this point, the ambient uproar stopped. I stared towards Penny under the momentary illusion that now I should be able to see her better. She broke into laughter as hearty as if I had hit myself on the head a third time.

'Don't you worry, mate,' she said with friendly contempt, 'I don't have any plans for the old needle just at present, thanks all the same. So you can afford to cool it. All safe and sound and wrapped up snug.'

I had still not thought of anything to say when Roy's shape loomed above us.

'All right, chaps? I thought we might move on, if you've no objection.'

At this I found speech. 'Let's go,' I said.

The illumination at the bar was slightly less minimal than elsewhere in the room. By it, as Sylvia took her time about drinking up, I saw a small, hairy young man turn his head and reveal himself to be wearing sunglasses. I moved on reflex, precipitating my frame between him and Roy's line of sight before I had really got started on wondering just how far, given that incident at the corner of St John's Wood Road, Roy would escalate his reaction to a sunglasses-wearer in these surroundings. In moving, I trod on Penny's foot and collided with Sylvia's elbow, not quite causing her glass to spill over.

'Christ, what's the *muhtter* with you?' she asked me, swinging round and spilling her drink without my assistance. 'You pissed already?'

'It wouldn't be that, darling,' said Roy authoritatively. 'Our Duggers is never pissed. Foreign to his whole nature.'

'Yeah, see him letting go.'

'Sorry,' I said. 'I sort of tripped. Sorry, Penny.'

'Easy enough to do in this bloody mausoleum, old lad. Come on, then – off.'

Roy watched me over his shoulder as I weaved behind him, duplicating or trying to anticipate his movements and keeping a mental bearing on the position of the sunglassed young man.

'You're sure you're all right?' He leaned across to push the curtain aside and studied my shift to the relevant flank. 'You seem a bit—'

'Rather stuffy in here.'

'I blame myself. I'd forgotten how crappy it was. No, actually I think they must have made it crappier since I was last here. But the food's nop bad, or wasn't. You used to be able to get quite a good sort of scampi, hamburger and salad kind of a lunch in the Cookhouse,' he said, outlining in a few swift strokes the sort of meal he must have forgotten I knew he hated most.

Hullabaloo was renewed behind us, and more of it came from all sides when we reached ground level. I had expected it to be at least fully dark out of doors, with perhaps even the eastern stars beginning to pale in presage of the dawn, but in fact the sun was still very much about. White-painted caffs and stores selling hooligans' attire were mingled with murky places calling themselves bistros and boutiques. The two girls walked ahead of Roy and me, Penny seemingly looking at passers-by, Sylvia with her eyes fixed on the shop windows.

'You were getting on a treat with young Penny, I saw,' said Roy.

'Yes, okay.' I could not start about Penny now.

'She'll come round in the end, you know. All this drop-out stuff is just a stage. All talk.'

'That sounds a bit authoritarian. What about her new ways of seeing things? Are they all talk?'

'She hasn't got them much. It's more Sylvia who's got them.'

'So Penny isn't really a part of youth?'

'Not in that sense, I'm afraid, no.'

'How can you be sure?'

'Bugger it, she is my daughter.'

'Yes, there is that.'

We had turned a corner and come up to a large black car parked at the kerb. I could see some of the back view of a man in the driving-seat, and caught Roy by the arm.

'That's not Gilbert, is it?'

'Christ no. Pull yourself together, Duggers. It's a car-hire driver and this is a car-hire car. Just for the evening. Makes us more mobile.'

He put me in the rear seat between the two girls and got in front. We moved off. Penny had turned her back on me as far as she could without kneeling up on the seat. I looked at Sylvia, who was smelling of carrots that evening, and said, neutrally I would have thought,

'Do you know where we're going?'

'Why does it bother you so much?'

'What do you mean, bother me?'

'So much. Listen to you. Everything you do, you've got to have done it before. Whatever it is, it's got to be part of a *pluhn*.'

'I simply asked you—'

'You can't, you know, get into things properly if you always know what's coming. You mustn't let it all be like it was the last time. You can't sort of get hold of it properly if that's what you do. It's all got to be something else. You know.'

Roy's head nodded once or twice, in approval or in response to the motion of the car, which was not well sprung. I tried to imagine his private conversations with Sylvia, and then tried not to instead. For the second time in the last couple of months, the possible virtues of Bruckner's Eighth Symphony presented themselves to me. Sylvia went on,

'You're half out of your mind worrying you won't be able to fit everything in together. You call that living? Just making sure today's like yesterday and last week and last year? You're all frozen up. You can't feel. I'd hate to get myself tied up with you, I really would. You wouldn't go anywhere with anyone in case you had to do something you weren't used to.'

Her demonstration of new ways of seeing things closed at that point; after travelling perhaps as much as half a mile, we had apparently arrived. As with Penny in the Dug-out, Sylvia's manner had not matched the content of what she had said: in this case thoughtful, troubled, sympathetic, that of one really concerned to advertise dangers and propound remedies. The total effect, on me at least, was not much improved thereby. Operating at reduced efficiency, I became part of a small crowd or untidy queue moving towards and into the stone porch of a large red-brick building. Posters abounded, some of considerable age and depressive quality.

'Bingo?' I said wonderingly to Penny.

'Use your eyes, chum. Sodding wrestling.'

I wanted to tell her that she must be joking, but could not devise any non-fashionable way of suggesting this, so muttered to myself, not for the first or last time that evening. Our progress slowed, and I looked to see whether Roy would have us red-carpeted through or insist on our democratically standing in line for tickets. I rather predicted the former, since a programme of wrestling, however distinguished and exclusive, would surely not be thought momentous enough to need symbolical atonement in advance. A Tube-bus-and-or-foot journey to Covent Garden and seats in the middle of the grand tier for the first night of a new *Otello*, followed by a champagne supper at the Savoy Grill – that was more the usual scale. However, I was wrong: we shuffled up to the box office two by two. The two I was in consisted of a sulky Penny and me. At the moment when Roy pulled out his wallet, Sylvia announced that she would go no further.

'Load of old cruhp,' she said, pushing her fists into the pockets of the knee-length buttonless waistcoat she wore. 'Mums and dads stuff. A real hitch.'

This plainly disconcerted Roy. Just as plainly, what disconcerted him about it was far less the prospect of argument, change of plan, etc., than his having guessed so wrong about what Sylvia would like to do, in itself such a substantial proportion of her total outlook upon the world. Bearing just then, for some reason, an unfairly close resemblance to an overgrown Claudette Colbert or Jean Arthur in male rig, but with hair let down for the night, he told Sylvia it was great fun and a real gas and things like that, but did it badly. I chipped in on his side, realizing too late that I would have done far better to denounce the sport as immoral, vulgar, new-fangled, never like it was last time. Instead of simply walking away, Sylvia expanded her objections. Those in the queue behind us grew restive; I shared their feelings. A stout woman in a hat like a yellow fez called to us, not very provocatively, to get on or get out of the road. Sylvia took her hands out of her pockets and turned round quickly, her narrow eyes narrowed.

'Shut up, you,' she said through her teeth. 'Just shut up.'

She was asked who she thought she was talking to, who she thought she was, how she dared, and other knotty questions while Roy blathered disconnectedly.

'Let's go, for Christ's sake,' said Penny, 'or we'll have a sodding pitched battle. That stuff in there's all balls, anyway. I've seen them do it on television. Arm-locks and back-hammers and body-slams and the rest of it, with that maple-leafer bloke explaining. The whole thing's rigged beforehand, everybody knows that. Bloody childish. Come on, let's get out. I'm hungry.'

Having shut the yellow-fezzed woman up just by telling her to shut up, a marvel of economy, Sylvia turned back to us in time to catch Penny's last few remarks.

'Okay, okay, *okay*,' she said, sounding on the verge of impatience, but smiling slightly, 'if it means that much to you. But I tell you I'm going to walk out the moment I feel like it.'

The hall carried traces, in bits of plaster moulding, a fretted frieze along the top of one wall and fragmentary, smudged-gilt electroliers nobody had bothered to rip out, of a previous history as variety theatre or archaic picture palace. It was three-quarters full of a sociologist's amalgam of ages, races and classes, with only the elder landed aristocracy perhaps under-represented. We took our seats at the ringside, Penny on my right, Sylvia on my left, Roy on her left. The first bout was announced as an international middleweight contest between a man from Swindon with a German name and a man from Bolton with a Polish name. I found it quite skilful, in that blows sounding like a sack of cement hit with a cricket bat, backhand chops at the windpipe that travelled a full semicircle before making contact, belly-first drops from head height on to an out-thrust knee – all these and more would see the sufferer on his feet, groggy but game, at the count of nine. In between, there was much paraded chivalry, instant desistance from atrocity in response to the bell, handshakes.

'Couple of blue-eyes,' said Roy at the end of the fourth round. When neither girl stirred, I asked him what that meant.

'Good sports. Fair play,' he said vindictively. 'To get the crowd impatient for the dirty stuff that's coming.'

The girls snorted as one, glanced at each other and then away. I wondered where Roy had done his research, and half recollected a magazine article some Sundays previously. The bout continued. Eventually, German or Pole picked up Pole or German, held him extended across his shoulders, whirled round with him a number of times, laid him quite gently on the floor and knelt on him. The bell rang. A man in evening-dress, who had done a lot of talking at the outset, climbed into the ring with a hand-microphone and announced, with the slow pomp of a returning officer declaring the result of a constituency election, that, by an aeroplane-spin followed by a shoulder-press, somebody had gained the single fall necessary to decide the winner. There was moderate cheering, in which Roy joined with a judicious air, as when applauding a fellow-violinist accurate and agile enough, but deficient in warmth of tone. I joined in too, for appearance' sake, then fell to seeing if I could hum (to myself) the openings of all the movements of all the Beethoven string quartets in order before life moved on again.

I was just embarking on the scherzo of the Harp Quartet (op. 74) when what one would have to fight hard against calling an expectant hush descended on the hall. It was broken by yet another variety of wordless yelling coming from one corner. A moment later, accompanied by a rattling of chains and a mixture of growls and shouts, a rather tall and very broad figure was manhandled to the ringside by a knot of men in white T-shirts and cotton trousers, one of them with what looked like a pitchfork at the ready. This concourse was followed by a comparatively ordinary person, platinum-haired and wearing a silver cloak covered in sequins. Each principal climbed into the ring, the one after a lot more growling and chain-rattling and several flourishes of the pitchfork, the other quite readily. The MC appeared too with his microphone. He said, in part, and after declaring that famous scientists were unable to come to an agreement as to this strange creature, and between outbursts of largely ironical booing, and approximately,

'In-nuh the red-duh cornah, at eighteen-nuh stoh-oon-nuh five-vuh pounds . . . the Thing-nguh . . . from-muh Borneo-oo-uh!'

Amid more booing, the Thing's shackles were removed and, with spread arms and legs, he jumped up and down for a time in an unassuming way, but very high in the air. He wore a stylized loin-cloth, or breech-clout, and was certainly as hairy a man as I had ever seen, though the shaggy curtain that hid most of his face looked to me as if it also hid a largely bald pate. I had heard no less than Penny, or anyone else, about the dramaturgic tendency of professional wrestling, and had enjoyed the chains and pitchfork along with the rest of the audience, and yet somehow was pretty thoroughly glad not to be pitted against the Thing. There was a neglectful air about him, a suggestion that he might spontaneously decide to emend, or forget altogether, crucial passages in his assigned role. He was much heavier than his opponent, now named as the Knight of St George and acknowledging cheers from what I took to be the blue corner; still, with his cape discarded he appeared muscular enough.

The bell clanged, the Thing gibbered, shambled over to the Knight and, with the side of his forearm, dealt him a buffet that made him not only start to fall down at once, but get the act of falling over and done with a good deal faster than I would have thought possible. This was followed up, no less promptly, with a head-foremost descent on to the prostrate one's stomach from a hand-stand position. The Knight gave a cry of pain and outrage, which the Thing cut short by stamping on his windpipe. This move was evidently felt to be unseemly, and after it had been repeated a dozen or so times to mounting protests from the audience, the referee took a double handful of the Thing's back hair and pulled, using a raised knee for added leverage. The Thing turned about with disquieting speed, but the referee had had to endure nothing worse than roars and a few of the yard-high jumps when the Knight, now recovered, came at his opponent from the rear, felled him with a kick behind the knee that would have made a tyrannosaurus lurch, and started doing something complicated and awful to his arm. But it seemed no time at all before the Thing hit the Knight very hard on the head with his head and then dropped him on his head.

So it went for the rest of the round and the next two or three: the Thing giving a good deal worse than he got and being generally unsportsmanlike, the referee intervening more rarely and tardily than, on the whole, I felt he should, though vigorously enough once roused to action. During this phase, Roy kept glancing sideways to see how the rest of us were taking it, Sylvia fidgeted grumpily but also seemed watchful, I sat there being glad I was no longer in the Dug-out and not yet in what fearful other environment lay in store, and Penny was immobile and expressionless. Then came the point when the Knight, whose retention of his left leg struck me as miraculous after what it had suffered over the previous few minutes, brought the Thing's head low with a chop to the back of the neck and drove his right knee up into the creature's chin with more force than either had used so far. The Thing left the ground and landed some feet away on the back of his head and one shoulder. The onlookers cheered with patent sincerity, but quietened down in seconds when the Thing, having taken a count of nine, got to his feet and advanced on his adversary without roars or jumps, with (to my eye) every sign of real, as opposed to manufactured, menace. I told myself that the fellow was a more accomplished mime than I had thought. Penny stirred in her seat, so that her shoulder touched my upper-arm.

After a very quick grab, the Thing had the Knight's head in the crook of his left arm and was working on his face with his right hand, elbow rising and falling in the motion of an impatient man using a screwdriver. Loud, prolonged screams came from the Knight; they sounded genuine, but of course they would have had to. I could not see what was going on. The Thing kept turning his man so as to hide his doings from the referee, who ineffectually circled and recircled the rotating pair. The Knight started screaming at a new pitch of realism. The crowd's boos and yells had lost all irony. Upon me there crept a strong and hideous sensation I had experienced to a minor degree once before, at a bullfight in Majorca, my first and last: a blend of physical fear, or dread, and a voluptuous, almost dizzy excitement: I wanted this to stop and to go on. I felt Penny's thigh press against mine and her long, cold hand grip mine in a grasp I knew was one of fear untainted by any excitement.

'It's all right,' I shouted to her. 'Just acting. They're putting it on.'

This view of events became harder to sustain when the Thing forestalled the referee's intervention by picking him up in one hand and throwing him violently on to the corner-post, and when the two seconds and a third man who might have been a wrestler in mufti jumped into the ring and began trying to break up the fight. One of the seconds hit the Thing repeatedly with a wooden stool he had brought with him. All round the hall, people were on their feet shouting in protest, and Sylvia at my left side was on hers shouting to the Thing to gouge the bastard's eyes out, which was when I saw that Roy had after all not entirely miscalculated in deciding to bring his party here. Gouging the Knight's eyes out was just what the Thing, apparently unscathed by the stool and all other efforts, seemed to be getting to work on, with both his outsize hands over the upper part of his opponent's face, though, among the half-dozen shifting bodies, it was still hard to make out what was going on. The excited half of my reactions had vanished; I caught hold of Penny's arm and squeezed it. Then, momentarily but unmistakably, I saw through the crisscross of arms and hands and trunks that the Thing's thumbs were not where I had feared they would be, but resting against the Knight's cheek-bones. I said loudly into Penny's ear,

'It's all right. I just saw. He's not going for his eyes. He's only pretending to. It's all right.'

She turned towards me a face that had lost its colour, an excessively rare condition among the healthy. Her mouth was open and turned down at the corners, and her eyes were unfocused. I pulled her to her feet at exactly the moment at which a woman in the row behind hit Sylvia in the small of the back with the head of her umbrella, but I did not wait to see what would ensue. Instead, I kept hold of Penny's hand and, being bigger and heavier than anybody I encountered, quite easily shouldered a way for us both through the knots of bawling men and women that now occupied much of the aisles.

In the hallway, we found perhaps a dozen other people in varying states of distress. A middle-aged attendant greeted us with an upward nod.

'Fantastic,' he said morosely and amicably. 'Gets 'em every time.

He does this once a month regular, and every time half of 'em think it's real. Half of 'em. All of 'em. Fantastic. Best actor I ever seen, that Thing chap. Beats me he isn't in Shakespeare. Eh? I mean he'd pull in ten times more at Stratford-upon-Avon than what he gets here. Ernie Adams. Comes from just up the road here, you know.'

Roy arrived a minute later accompanied by Sylvia, who objected with some violence to the idea of leaving, but quite soon after it must have become clear to her how clear it was to Roy and me that her prime reason for wanting to stay was Penny's anxiety to go, she dropped these objections, following for once, I thought, a rather old way of seeing things in preference to any of the new ones at her disposal. I got back into the car between the two girls, aware of hunger, thirst, incipient weariness of mind and body, renewed general wonderment at the way Roy was running his life, barely perceptible self-contempt for having fallen victim to the Thing's histrionic talents, and Penny's shape beside me, which seemed at the moment to be more three-dimensional than most human shapes I could recall off-hand.

'What happened back there?' I asked when we were in motion.

'They got a sort of tourniquet on the hairy shag's wimpipe,' said Roy, 'and then disqualified him.'

'Really. I meant about the woman with the umbrella too.'

'I clobbered her,' said Sylvia.

Roy gave a laugh, not one of his rich ones, conveying roughly that girls would be girls, but leaving it uncertain whether he referred to Sylvia's readiness to exaggerate or to hit people. After a pause, Penny asked carelessly,

'Was the other chap all right?'

'Of course he was all right.' Sylvia, leaning forward so as to see Penny properly, spoke in the solicitous tone she had used on me earlier. 'Why shouldn't he have been all right?'

'He sounded as though, you know.'

'Darling, it was all an *uhct*. Surely you could see *thuht*? You said yourself when we went in. You mustn't let yourself get so drawn about everything. It's all different, you see? Let it go on . . .'

The three of us let Sylvia go on while the car hurried south, mainly along side streets. A creditable time after deciding I could stand no more of her on her chosen theme, or on any fresh one, I braved the risk of a second lecture about my having to have done everything before and asked Roy where we were going now.

'Club I belong to.'

'Not Craggs's?'

'Oh, Socialist Gestapo! Do you think I'm off my head?' Receiving no reply, he went on, 'One of those places where there's music and people dance if they want to. You needn't. We eat there too.'

'Oh, good. You mean pop racket.'

'Well, it wouldn't be Stockhausen, would it?'

'A discotheque, in fact.'

Sylvia laughed with incredulous awe, as if I had mentioned Vaux-hall Gardens or a bear pit. Roy explained more kindly that it was always called a club now, and added, to forestall any fear of social mortification on my part, that there were much flashier joints than the one we were bound for.

I thought this might well be true when, somewhere north of the Fulham Road, Sylvia and I descended a staircase lined with green electric bulbs that fizzed and flickered or emitted no light at all. Roy, adopting his riot-squad manner, had taken Penny ahead and told me to follow in one minute – not less. During that minute, Sylvia had suggested that I loosen up and quit worrying, and I had promised to try.

At the foot of the stairs, we went through glass doors into a cubicle where there was nothing obvious to do except hand over money and be given tickets and change, which Roy was doing, or stand about, which Penny and a small dark man were doing. This man came up and kissed Sylvia warmly.

'Hallo,' he said, leaving a perceptible gap where her name might have fitted. 'Good evening, sir. It's nice to have you with us tonight.'

I was at a loss for an answer, but Roy made marshalling gestures and took us through further glass doors into another cubicle. Here there was a wider choice of activities: going out to one of the lavatories, or passing outdoor clothing over a counter, or standing about. Across much of the far wall there stretched an immense wardrobe with mirror doors and with, by the sound of it, a great many people crammed inside. One of two or three additional small dark men who had taken the standing-about option accepted Roy's tickets and opened the wardrobe. As I heard immediately and saw by degrees, it was not a wardrobe, but a large room or complex of rooms with a quantity of conversation therein that, spread out equally, would have been about right for a fair-sized town on a mid-week evening. Roy led the way into it all. My impressions included a semicircular bar off to one side, somebody's navel with a lot of bare skin surrounding it, a stage at the far end with velvet-clad persons moving about on it, two long-haired albinos holding hands on a black-leather sofa, a great many feet I mostly avoided treading on and tripping up over, dark-blue electric bulbs in better repair than the illumination on the staircase and diversified with flashing red and white lights, a dirty middle-aged man in a sort of tracksuit playing a fruit-machine, and what turned out to be a restaurant slightly shielded by glass screens. On arrival here, I felt the apparently bottomless plunge in my well-being start to decelerate, a moment before a fresh dose of wordless yelling, of such impact as to suggest to me momentarily that anything of the kind was altogether new in my experience, broke out from the direction of the stage. Various mechanical noises, chiefly metallic, were being made too. I was sorry for having too hastily rejected those musical works which consist of a stated period of silence under concert conditions. First Bruckner, I thought. Now John Cage. Who next? Nielsen? Busoni? Buxtehude? Yes, listening hard to the works of any or each would almost certainly prove less onerous than having a tooth drilled down to the gum without anaesthetic.

We were taken to a table in the corner farthest from the stage, where the pandemonium was lessened by about one per cent and there were coloured-glass hyacinths. Roy put Sylvia and me on a black-leather banquette against the wall with himself and Penny opposite, no doubt in further pursuance of the fiction that he was there just to be paternal to the rest of us in differing degrees. And yet, in the murk of that restaurant, which approached that of the Dug-out and was emphasized rather than relieved by the strings of fairy-lights on sweet-or liqueur-trolley, I could not believe that anyone beyond arm's length could have recognized him – and, given the noise-level, anyone who did would have forgotten all about it before he had had time even to cry out. And what about it? What about all of it? Now that the favour was actually in progress, was (I trusted to God) a lot more than half over, it had quite lost any plausibility it might once have had. My surroundings encouraged this feeling of remoteness. Perhaps somebody had slipped a hallucinogen into that Guinness and I was having what current little slobberers called a bad trip.

Time went by as if an unlimited fund of it had suddenly been made available. A girl clad in a piece of silk measuring at least eighteen inches from top to bottom appeared through the gloaming and gave out sheets of vellum which I took to be menus. I peered hard at mine, polished my glasses on the paper napkin provided, peered again and made out phrases to do with garnishing and 4 persons and white wine sauce here and there. One day, I foresaw, eaters-out, if any, would need a more than nodding acquaintance with Braille as well as lip-reading. I took advantage of a lull in the yelling to order soup, steak and beer, my only utterance, as distinct from renewed mutters and whimpers, for quite some time. Roy and Sylvia, their foreheads almost touching across the table, were conversing in amorous roars and howls like creatures of legend, incomprehensibly to me for the most part, but still audibly; Penny was too far away, in all senses, for any sort of chat between us to be feasible: it would have been like trying to borrow money down an ear-trumpet. My steak came, and surprised me, or would have done had I still been open to surprise, by being excellent. While I was eating it, Roy broke off his tender thunderings to remonstrate with Penny for not having ordered anything and to try again to persuade her to do so. As he talked near her ear, he poured himself out some more Scotch from what had been the full bottle that had furnished his aperitifs and now, without a break, had become the source of his table wine. She shook her head and gestured to the titbits plate she had emptied of olives and radishes immediately on sitting down. Sylvia turned to me. I noticed how nearly circular her face was.

'I can't *stuhnd* all these put-ons. She made her point at the wrestling. So she's sensitive. She wants us to sign a paper?'

'Perhaps she's just not hungry.'

'Ah, bugger awff.' (This piece of accentual grandeur, coupled with a large part of what she had said and done that evening, made me strongly suspect she was a peer's daughter.) 'If you're really not hungry you get a plateful and then you just don't eat it. That's what you do, you see?' She leaned diagonally across the table and hooted at Penny, 'We're sold, Snow White. You feel absolutely frightful. O-*kay*. Now let's get on to the next thing.'

Penny looked down at her lap and shook her head again. I moved up to Sylvia.

'What makes you such a howling bitch?'

'I expect it's the same thing as makes you a top-heavy red-haired four-eyes who's never had anything to come up to being tossed off by the Captain of Boats and impotent and likes bloody symphonies and fugues and the first variation comes before the statement of the theme and give me a decent glass of British beer and dash it all Carruthers I don't know what young people are coming to these days and a scrounger and an old woman and a failure and a hanger-on and a prig and terrified and a shower and a brisk rub-down every morning and you can't throw yourself away on a little trollop like that Roy you must think of your wife Roy old boy old boy and I'll come along but I don't say I approve and bloody dead. Please delete the items in the above that do not apply. If any.'

This was delivered at top speed and without solicitude of any kind. Her upper lip was thinned to vanishing point and remained so while she stared silently at me. I found myself much impressed by the width of her vocabulary and social grasp. Roy had probably missed much of her text, but he would have caught her tone, face and so on.

'Penny,' he called to her rebukingly – 'oh, balls, *Sylvia*. Cool it, now.'

Sylvia did two or three of her suppressed-sneeze laughs.

'I don't like fugues,' I said, and might have gone on to tell her I considered the fugue the most boring artistic innovation before the adult Western if I had not been nearly sure I had once said so to Roy, if her harangue had not cowed me a little, and other ifs.

When Penny stood up, I started thinking immediately about how best to separate two girls in a combat that could have rivalled that between the Thing and the Knight, but she only told me to come and dance.

I shook my head. 'I can't.'

'Oh yes you can. Come on.'

Half a minute later we were on a small dance floor below the stage. This was now quite bare of velvet-suited performers, but noises of the same general character and equal volume were being provided by a gramophone record. Everybody in sight was five or ten years younger than I. The majority of couples were performing at rather than with each other, making rope-climbing or gunshot-dodging motions with an air of dedication, as if all this were only by way of prelude to some vaster ordeal they must ultimately share. Before I had fully grasped how much I wanted not to join in any of it, Penny took me into a corner, put my arms round her and hers round me, and began rubbing the whole of the front of herself against me. She moved roughly in the tempo of the prevailing noises, but made no other concession to circumstance. Within a short time, and in direct defiance of everything I was saying to myself, we were both aware of a concrete result. Penny released me and stepped aside.

'Right,' she said. 'Let's go.'

I turned my back on everybody except her. 'I'm not going anywhere until you've given me a short account of the habitat, diet and main domestic uses of the Bactrian camel. And how do you mean?'

'I wanted to thank you, and so I wanted to give you something, and there's only one thing I've got that you might want, but I had to make sure you wanted it. But what's this camel thing?'

'The dromedary will do just as well. In fact I'm not sure it isn't the same as the Bactrian camel. I asked you anyway before, that time up at your place.'

'I made you then. I was depressed that day. You mean you want to think about camels for a bit.'

'Thank me for what?'

'At the wrestling. And not liking her.'

The Bactrian camel (or dromedary), though selected very much at random, was having its effect. I said, 'That's not much, not liking her. I can't imagine anybody who would.'

'He does. So he makes out.'

'He's special.'

'He's special all right. Can you go now?'

'Just about. But we'll have to see this through before we take off.'

See it through we did; take off I thought we never would. In the end, however, after a space of time sufficient for a performance of *Die Meistersinger*, uncut and with supper interval, all four of us stood on the pavement in Park Lane and looked out for taxis – the hired car had been dismissed, presumably to make Roy feel better about security. He worried me severely with his parade of initial incomprehension, dawning comprehension, careful consideration and final approbation when I said I thought I would take Penny off and deliver her wherever she wanted to go. Surely the whole concept of the favour could not have been evolved simply to get me off with her? The answer was that on theoretical grounds it most assuredly could, but that few people who were not canonization timber would have deliberately arranged such an evening just for another's benefit. A taxi came and he and Sylvia moved towards it. I thanked him and said good night, and he said good night and told me he would ring me in the morning. Neither girl spoke nor looked at anybody.

Penny's and my taxi ride took place, after a couple of unanswered remarks from me, in total silence; in fact I was given a booster shot of the back-turning stuff I had had earlier. I foresaw trouble at the flat, but when we reached the bedroom she started undressing with the speed and conviction of someone about to go to the rescue of a swimmer in difficulties. I still foresaw the untoward – request for oddities, indifference with simulated ecstasy or just plain, last-moment refusal – but, again, all went merrily. Although the breasts were rather less hard than they looked, not having been sprayed with quick-drying cement, they were hard, and in the other sense soft. Everything else was good, too, and went on being so. I made no attempt not to compare her with Vivienne, and thought I felt or saw a difference in bodily behaviour: Vivienne (memory told me from a long way off) was unrestrained and unselfconscious, and Penny was those too, but there was an added beauty in her movements that nobody could acquire or intend. I kissed her ear and her temple and started murmuring.

'Darling, you are the most—'

She moved away. 'Listen, I don't want any of that. Stuff that. I don't want any thanks, thanks.'

'Sorry. Think of it as just a habit. One a lot of people have. It wasn't just thanks. Not that there's much wrong with just thanks that I can see.'

'I can. Anyway, I don't want any of it. Letting you talk soft isn't in the contract. If you try and do it again, talk soft I mean, I'm sleeping on the sofa or whatever you've got. Oh, and by the way, mate, so's you won't go and get any wrong ideas, this is it. Until breakfast I'm at your disposal, and then not any more. No phone calls, no letters, no flowers by request. Nothing about you personally, just how it is. Would you like a cup of tea?'

'I'll get it. You don't know where the things are.'

'I'll find them. Have you got a bath-robe or something? Not a good one. I always spill things down me.'

Twenty minutes later I was in the sitting-room, playing the Weber bassoon concerto very quietly to myself on the hi-fi, when Penny came in wearing an old corduroy topcoat of mine (the best I had been able to do in the way of a bath-robe) and carrying a tray with a good deal more on it than tea for two.

'I should have thought you'd had enough row for one evening.'

'Row, yes. That's why I put this on. Do you mind?'

'As long as you don't tell me about it. I hope it's all right, I found some sardines and some other junk and I made some toast. I couldn't eat at that club place. You know, her. Would you like some?'

'No thanks. Just tea.'

'He used to take me to hear things at concerts and play me bits on the gramophone and tell me about them till I could scream. Now he does it to his birds. Perhaps he always has. I felt quite sorry for her. In a way. Get those trombones, aren't they thrilling? Get the way he brings back the first subject of the first movement. Get the fingering in this passage. Get him going into 6/8 time. Get stuffed.'

Having given me my tea, she settled down on the couch with the tray beside her and began eating; quietly, I thought. I pulled down my copy of *Music Ho!* and pretended to read it, so that if she wanted to listen to Weber she could do so without fear of being spotted in the act. I found myself sympathizing with Roy and his tendency to tell birds about trombones. It was faintly comic, and yet not undignified, that he still tried to share or give art, still had not arrived at the sad fact that to listen to a musical work can never be other than a solitary experience. Then, at the start of the middle section of the concerto's slow movement, I noticed that Penny's gentle chewing of her toast had stopped in mid-mouthful. A glance round the edge of my glasses showed her sitting quite still with a half-eaten slice in her hand. Something I took at first to be a tear, but which soon turned out to be a blob of marmalade, fell on to the corduroy coat. The bassoon returned to its opening melody and munching began again. Nothing being more strongly inherited than musical talent, I felt I knew that, if Roy and Penny's mother and Penny and everybody had been born twenty years earlier, Penny would now be near the front of the first violins in a decent orchestra, if not in a string quartet. Anyway, even the back desk of the seconds in some grimy provincial city would be a better place for her than anywhere she was likely to find herself in twenty years' time. These thoughts ruffled me.

The record ended. It was ten minutes to three. My eyelids felt like tattered canvas, but Penny sat on and looked at the floor. I said experimentally,

'Curious evening, one way and another.'

'Sodding grotesque.'

'Why did you come?'

'Why did you? I wanted not to be in the house. And I wanted to talk. To try and explain. I didn't but I wanted to then.'

'Explain now.'

'You can't. I can't. I couldn't.'

'Why don't you go and live with your mother for a bit?'

She lit a cigarette. 'I screwed it up with her. I thought it was her fault, the divorce. It was his really, of course, but I didn't know then.

And anyway her husband won't have me in the house. He's an estate agent.'

'Why don't you and Gilbert go off somewhere?'

'No thanks. I'd be gone on at all the time. It's bad enough when there are other people around. And I'd worry if I wasn't there.'

'What about?'

'For instance you know he's talking of going off with this little slag for good, do you?'

'Oh, God. He can't.' I felt as if I had been told my dinner had been poisoned. Questions formed in my mind and disintegrated again. 'He's off his rocker,' I said finally. 'Does Kitty know?'

'I haven't seen her. He only mentioned it the other day. But he'll leak it, the way he always does, and then we'll be off. And when we've all had plenty of that, he'll move out, I reckon.'

'That's the time for you to go too, isn't it? Or earlier. Anywhere at all. Abroad. Drop out properly. You'd be mad to say around up there, with Kitty doing her stuff from morning to night.'

'She'd come and find me. And there's Ashley, and Chris. He'll go berserk when he finds out. Burn the place down. He hates him. He won't mind much really, the thing itself, but he'll have an excuse then, see. And I don't want to not know what's going on. That's what I didn't like about last time. Keeping it from the children. A bloody scream, that was.'

I said nothing. She moved on the couch so that everything about her was pointing directly at me.

'He takes a bit of notice of you. Will you try and stop him?'

If I had not still been disconcerted by her news, and had not perhaps been suffering from her ability to take any number of years off my emotional age, I might have prevented myself from saying, 'So that was the help you wanted.'

'You and me tonight was nothing to do with that,' she said angrily. 'That was separate. I told you it's not going to happen again. Not after I go. And that wasn't to show you it was separate. It all just is.'

'I'm sorry.' I took in what flushing had done for the whites and irises of her eyes. 'I'd like to help about everything. Take you on.'

'Nobody gets to take me on. Sorry. I told you it isn't you. I quite like you. You're a bit pompous, but you're all right really.' Her faint grin at this reminded me of our reintroduction six or seven weeks before. Then she went urgent again. 'Will you talk to him?'

'I don't know what good you think it'll do. You know what he's—'

'But will you?'

'Yes. Yes, I will. I'll have to. I was going to anyway. I'll tell him.'

'Thanks.'

Penny got up, turned her back, and looked down in the general direction of the tray. I could not think of anything to say that had not been vetoed in advance. After over a minute she shifted half round towards me.

'I'd like to be asleep now.'

# Four

## Great Wag

'How can a Japanese write music?' asked Harold Meers. 'I mean real music, not bloody pots and pans.'

'No trouble. I mean, of course it's trouble, but not any—'

'Totally alien culture, food, drink, dress, art, ways of thought, the whole lot.'

'Originally, no doubt, but there's been a certain amount of Western music in Japan for quite some time now, and in any case he's—'

'You can't change a whole culture overnight.'

'Possibly not, but this chap went to the USA in 1950, when he was eight, so he must know quite a bit about the West these days. And this concerto of his just is very interesting. Not great, but interesting.'

Harold looked down at my copy. 'You say here he's spent most of his life in California.'

'Yes, I do, don't I?'

'But there must be traces of Nip stuff in his work. Bells and so on.'

'None that I could hear.'

'Perhaps you just weren't listening hard enough,' said Harold with his standard lack of inflection. 'There was something else, too . . . What was this a concerto for?'

'Orchestra, if you mean that sort of for.'

'Yes, yes, but what was the, damn it, the solo instrument?'

'There isn't one. It's a concerto in the sense of—'

'Look, a concerto means there's a soloist. Beethoven, Tchaikovsky, Schubert. Even I know that. Anyway, will you check it?'

'No, Harold,' I said. 'You check it if you want to, and then if I'm wrong you can send my fee to the Musicians' Benevolent Fund.'

'All right, all right.'

Harold went on reading, or at any rate lowered his head again. This morning's going-over had been stern, even on current form. It must have been that he resented the absence of any point he felt he could validly let himself go on: praise of a Cuban viola d'amore virtuoso or North Korean bass-baritone. I began mentally composing my last piece for him, the one after he sacked me, all about the glories of a new Bolivian opera with a white Rhodesian conductor and a mixed cast of Brazilians, Haitians, Spaniards, white South Africans and members of the John Birch Society. I had not got very far with it when the telephone rattled.

'Yes,' said Harold into it. 'Get someone to bring her up, will you?' He rang off and looked in my direction. 'My daughter's collecting me, so we'll have to leave it there. Check with Coates about five thirty as usual. And remember to watch those technical terms.'

I went along to Features and was jostled at its doorway by a small man coming out, white-haired yet wearing a cerise corduroy suit, gamboge Paisley shirt and Goliath-size orange tie. Inside, Coates was talking to Terry Bolsover, the hairy hobbledehoy who wrote for the paper on pop noises: not a bad fellow for all that. I did not join them at once, but remained by the long inner window on to the corridor, intent on a glimpse of whatever sort of person Harold Meers might have for a daughter. And my inquisitiveness was repaid hand over fist, for in less than a minute one of the grey-clad attendants from the ground floor came round the corner from the lift with Sylvia at his side and took her along to Harold's office. She did not see me.

'Jesus Christ,' I said.

'I hear profanity,' said Coates. 'And from a normally restrained source.'

'He's remembered he got an opus number wrong,' said Bolsover.

'Worse than that. I've just seen Miss Meers.'

'It is a shaker,' conceded Coates.

'You want to watch it there,' said Bolsover. 'She's not as nice as she looks, from all you hear.'

'No, she's not. I mean I'm sure she's not.'

I had no trouble now in deciding who Sylvia had reminded me of, that first evening at my flat. My imagination boggled away prestissimo while the other two looked at me with mild curiosity. Then Bolsover said,

'Oh, while you're here, Doug . . . You are a great buddy of this conductor character, Sir Roy Vandervane, aren't you? I haven't got it wrong?'

'No. You haven't got it wrong. What about him?'

I probably looked appalled at this collocation. Coates turned up his curiosity-level for a second before raising a riot of coughing. Bolsover brought from inside his guerilla-style jacket a leaflet printed in white on purple.

'You've probably seen this about the Pigs Out concert on Tuesday,' he said – 'Well, there are these other—'

'Pigs what? – sorry.'

'What you'd call a pop group. They do protest stuff mostly, not really serious, just, you know, I want a girl just like the girl that murdered dear old Dad, all this. But then now and again they reckon they'll show they're proper musicians too, extending the frontiers of art. That's where your pal comes in. I'd have thought you'd be sure to get one. Here.'

I took the purple sheet and read (to put it in plain English) that part of the programme would consist of *Elevations 9*, written by Sir Roy Vandervane and performed by him with the assistance of members of Pigs Out. Every purported fact about Roy, except for his sex and his committal to the cause of youth, was wrong. I suffered an onrush of conscience about having altogether dismissed this work from my mind, an onrush mitigated by the calculation that Roy himself had probably taken my name off the distribution list of the document.

'Is this Pigs lot any good?' I asked, handing it back. 'By the standards of the trade?'

'Not really, no. The lead guitarist's not too bad. But they're in the charts all right. Manager and Press agent are okay.'

'I see. Where do I . . . ?'

'I thought you might, well, ask him if I could have a word with him some time between now and Tuesday. How he came to write it, what pop can learn from classical, where it's all going, this type of stuff. I'd really be grateful if you could just mention it. So if I rang him he'd know who I am.'

'Once you've told him what you do you'd get him for as long as you wanted. But I'll tell him.'

'Thanks, Doug. I really appreciate it.'

Bolsover left. Coates was telephoning. When he had finished, I said to him,

'Albert, could I have a quick word?'

'Any speed you want.'

'Old Vandervane. I don't know whether you knew, but Harold's got his knife in him. Just on general grounds.'

'I didn't know that, but I can guess about the grounds. So?'

'I'm . . . I can't quite think how to put this,' – indeed, I could barely think what I was about to put – 'but I suspect Harold may have got something up his sleeve for Vandervane. Some bit of no good he can do him, like a snide para in the Diary or a crack at the foot of the leader. If you see anything like that, or get to hear of it, do you think you could tip me off?'

'Sure, but I couldn't block it, Doug, you realize that.'

'Of course not, but I could warn him or . . . Anyway.'

'Right. You seem kind of jittery or something. If it was anyone else I'd put you down as hungover.'

'Just the sight of Miss Meers,' I said, telling a version of part of the truth. 'Who was that I ran into when I was coming in here?'

'New education correspondent.'

I now had two extra, or extra pressing, reasons for getting hold of Roy, which I had not succeeded in doing since the night of the favour. In the intervening four and a bit days I had not, admittedly, tried as hard as I perhaps might have done. I had telephoned his house three times, finding Kitty at the other end on each occasion, and getting twenty, forty and twenty-five minutes respectively of formless lamentation with a rebuke or two thrown in – why had I let things reach this pass, not let her know before that things had reached this pass? I explained, working under adverse conditions, that I had hoped to exert some influence on Roy and to have something concrete to tell her, but in vain. This was broadly accurate, in that just to report and be told that Sylvia was awful would not have been worth either of our whiles, but I was relieved when she resumed formless lamentation without having asked me just what pass I myself thought things had reached, and so forcing me to lie: nothing but trouble could come of that revelation. As regards what pass things seemed to Kitty to have reached, I was still in doubt, at the end of the combined eighty-five minutes, whether Roy was at the stage of ordering the drink for an elopement reception, starting to drop the occasional complaint that life at home left something to be desired, or in between. Anyway, where was he? Kitty promised, with maximum fervour, to get him to ring me; I left messages at Craggs's, at his agents', at the hall where he was rehearsing Gus Mahler and everywhere else I could think of, with no response. He was lying doggo, no doubt aware that our next meeting would entail my telling him something of how I felt about Sylvia and his invawvement with her.

After leaving the newspaper office, I got through some hock and smoked salmon at El Vino with my colleague on the *Custodian*, went back to my flat and spent the afternoon with my eyes on my Weber notes and typescript and my thoughts on the Roy question. By degrees, I decided that Penny must have been exaggerating, or else I had done so in my own mind. Just talking about going off with that thin-lipped savage might well have been just talk, even though what sounded like just Roy's talk had a way of quitting that state, as a piece of apparently very much just talk about writing a Vietnam demonstrators' marching-song had proved a couple of years earlier: mercifully, it had never caught on. I also decided that it was less important to stop him going off with Sylvia than to stop him performing *Elevations 9*. The latter project was also the more straightforward: breaking his arm on the way to the concert would wrap the whole thing up beyond argument.

At half past five I got through to Coates and found, much to my surprise, that my piece was going into the paper entire. Not only to my surprise: editorial toleration of my existence must indirectly imply, either that Sylvia had not yet said anything about her doings with my friend Vandervane, or that the news had been divulged and welcomed, or that the Martians had landed. I determined to put the whole thing from me until the morning. Vivienne was due at six or thereabouts, as soon after her office closed as transport conditions would allow. I was ready for her in more senses than the usual one or two.

At ten to six my doorbell rang. No head and shoulders were visible through the glass panel downstairs, but Vivienne often moved aside in this situation to look at the flowers and shrubs and such that some forgotten toiler had planted in the small front garden, and on opening the door I really quite narrowly missed embracing Gilbert on the front step.

'May I have a few words with you, please?'

'A few, by all means. I'm expecting someone shortly.'

'Then I can return at any convenient time.'

'No, it's all right. Come on up.'

In the sitting-room, Gilbert refused a drink but accepted a chair, leaving on the piano the two paperbacks he had been carrying; the top one, I saw, was called *Bringers of the Black Dawn*. He was frowning worriedly and his clothes, which had been in noticeably good order on our two previous meetings, had a second-hand look.

'What can I do for you?' I asked.

He shook his head very slowly at this dismayingly facile view of the present occasion. After that, he sighed. When he had quite finished doing so, he said, 'The situation of the Vandervane household has reached the brink of chaos.'

'That's where it's been as long as I can remember. Still . . .'

'In most ways, I must admit, it's none of my concern. Roy's private life is of course his own affair, and the lines on which the family behaves are not my business. However, what I must consider are Penny's interests. It's essential, absolutely essential, that she must leave the house as soon as humanly possible. The tension and the awful feelings there are destroying her.'

'I know what you mean. But I think you'll have a job getting her to go.'

'I've been having such a job for nearly two months now, without any success. At first she was saying there was no money and no place for us to go, which was true, but it was an excuse. Then last week I got the news that the Arts Council will give me a grant to finish my *London Suite*. With good management, it'll be enough for both of us until the book's published. And a friend will lend us his flat for a few weeks, at least. But Penny refuses point-blank to budge.'

'I see. But would you mind coming to the point? As I say, I'm—'

'I need your help.'

'Oh . . .' Sporting spirit, I thought to myself. Christian gentleman. I wanted to dash out into the street before Gwyneth Iqbal from the flat underneath could add herself to the majority of people in the Home Counties currently needing my help. 'What the hell can I do?'

'Believe me, Mr Yandell, if there were any other person I could ask, any whatsoever, I'd ask him. There just isn't. You're the only person I know who might be able to persuade Penny to leave that household.'

'If you can't shift her yourself, I don't see what difference I could make.'

'You're white, Mr Yandell.' Gilbert stated this as a fact, with none of the resentment or scorn that might have been expected of him. 'You and she have grown up in the same culture. Therefore in some ways you know her and understand her better than I can ever hope to do. Perhaps you can think of arguments that I can't think of. You can make an appeal to your mutual heritage. You've known her family. Please try. The poor girl's in a quite desperate state. And I'm desperate myself, too.'

'I don't think she'd even talk to me.'

'I think she would. She enjoyed what took place here last Saturday night.'

'Did she, now? Had you given your permission for that?'

'Not as such. Not specifically. She's a free agent. My only stipulation from her is to answer truthfully any questions I ask her. You see, except in this one admittedly vital matter of our departure I have considerable influence over her. Which . . . I take it you do find her attractive?'

'Yes, I do.'

'I gathered from her that she told you that your association with her, such as it was, must not continue. I think I could influence her to change that decision, within limits. Let's say one or two times.'

'Good God,' I said listlessly. 'That doesn't sound a bit like you. What I know of you.'

'What you know of me isn't much. But up to a point I agree. But I said I was desperate, and desperate men do many strange things. I'm coming towards the end of my tether, Mr Yandell.'

'You've been living at the Vandervanes' too long, Mr Alexander.'

'It's a distressing environment.'

'I meant more than that. All right, I'll talk to Penny, but you'll have to fix everything up yourself. I'm not going to talk her into being talked to.'

'Agreed. Many thanks.'

'If I were you I'd clear out from up there right away, Penny or no Penny.'

The doorbell rang. So, a moment later, did the telephone. I asked Gilbert to let my visitor in as he left and to get in touch with me as soon as he liked. He picked up his books and went. I lifted the receiver. It was Roy.

'Hallo, Duggers, you old sod, how are you?' He spoke with the heartiness-in-depth to be met with in persons laying off at the start of the evening for being fighting-drunk later.

'Fine, thanks. How's Miss Meers?'

'Oh, she's . . . Oh. Who told you?'

'Nobody. I saw her in the office, going along to see her dad.'

'Oh. You haven't – no of course you haven't. Well. Now you know, anyway. We'll talk about it. Duggers, I'm sorry I've been out of the picture, but I've been up to my neck, what with old Gus and the Royal Commission and, uh, Miss Meers herself. Haven't had a bloody minute.'

'What's this Royal Commission?'

'I thought I'd told you about it. Endless discussion, entirely about what'll be discussed at future discussions. You can imagine. The silly old bugger from the—'

'What's it on?'

'On? You mean the Commission. Oh, you know, it's supposed to be dealing with youth problems, crap like that. Load of old rubbish, but somebody's got to—'

'They ought to be able to get a lot of help from you, anyway.'

He gave a rich but rather brief laugh. 'Yes. Look, are you free at lunchtime tomorrow? I thought we might have something to eat and drink and a natter. One or two things on my mind.'

I decided against asking him if Penny was one of the things, on the grounds that to do so would only warn him that she was going to figure prominently on our agenda tomorrow, thus giving him time to prepare his smoke-screens and diversionary sallies. So I said simply that that would be fine and that I would, as requested, turn up at the Queen Alexandra Hall, where he was rehearsing the NLSO, round about twelve fifteen the following day. Perhaps, I reflected as I rang off, it was Roy's system of total permissiveness towards himself that made him such agreeable company; how odd that permissiveness directed elsewhere should have such different results.

Where was Vivienne? Repudiating Gilbert's accusations of white supremacist colonialist fascism on the doorstep? No, here she was, severe and sexy together in her uniform, carrying a canvas bag of the same olive-green colour and with the same airline insignia. In it, I knew, were her overnight things and whatever wondrous clothes she intended to wear later. We exchanged the cousinly kiss that was as much as she allowed herself or me on reunion, even with bed dead ahead. It was a warm evening, but her cheek was cool.

'One of those Pakkies from down below let me in.'

'Actually he's not a Pakky, he's a West Indian, and he was from up here.'

She had taken off her fore-and-aft cap and now took off her jacket, so that I had to concentrate slightly when she said, 'I thought he was a bit black for a Pakky. Friend of yours, is he?'

'Not exactly. He's Roy Vandervane's daughter's boyfriend.'

'Oh, him. Doesn't he mind?'

'Why should he? In fact I'm sure he's all for it.'

'I meant him minding his daughter having a black boyfriend.'

'Yes, I know.' I realized now why I had not simply agreed that Gilbert was a Pakky from down below and left it: because of the pleasure to be got from hearing Vivienne expound her opinions on almost any topic or situation. 'He's very progressive about everything. In favour of racial integration and so on.'

'Why would a white girl want to have a black boy-friend?'

'Why not? But I see what you mean. In this case I think it's because she hoped her father would object.'

'Oh, nobody has a boy-friend because of a thing like that. And anyway, you just said he was all for it.'

'Yes, I know,' I said again, having decided in the interval that there was nothing to prevent my stopping her talking at this point and starting her up again at a later one. 'Would you like a cup of tea?'

Although she must have been expecting it, this made Vivienne blink, if not blush. The question was the first line in what had become a ritual, perhaps puzzling to an outsider, of which the object was to get the pair of us to the brink of bed without the risk of damaging her susceptibilities by some overt word or deed. Now, as laid down, she lifted her head consideringly, narrowed her eyes, said she thought she would wait a little, and walked towards the bedroom with an air of medium-strength curiosity that would have been just right for a home-page journalist on an evening off. This maintained itself, as usual, until I had shut the door after us, and, not as usual, for a moment or two after that. Then it changed out of all recognition. The problem now, if any, was holding her off until there ceased to be any point whatever in holding her off; I surmounted it successfully. What finally ensued went on some minutes over par. This was, by a narrow margin, at her instance rather than mine, as she acknowledged afterwards by apologizing to me. When she pleaded in mitigation that she had been enjoying herself so much that she had not wanted to stop, I forgave her.

Her going-out apparel, when she came to put it on, was something of a disappointment. Most of it consisted of a familiar dress in good taste – dowdy and featureless, in other words, and so forgettable that the eye slid glumly off it at once. As often before, I tried to define its colour, but got no further than locating it in some nameless region between brown and purple. She had tried to liven it up with a shiny green belt, a neck-scarf of a different green, a sort of head-band in a third green, but it would have taken a necklace of shrunken skulls and a nose-ring to do the job effectively. I put on a suit. Over biancos and soda in the sitting-room, she said, in a chatty tone,

'You've got someone else, haven't you?'

'I've had someone else. Saturday night. How did you know?'

'You looked at me before we . . . started. Usually, well, I suppose you must see me, but you don't look. Is she as pretty as me?'

'About the same. I mean she's not at all the same, but she is pretty.'

'Is she as reasonable as me?'

'My God, no.'

'Is she as good as me?' Her eyes flickered towards the bedroom in what was, for her, a flamboyantly lewd gesture.

'I don't think so.' (That felt like a lie, but perhaps I had not made allowance for the first-time excitement of that night.)

'What do you want her for, then?'

'Didn't I look at you on Sunday and yesterday?'

'You may have done; I didn't notice. Perhaps you made sure not to then. What do you want her for?'

'Well . . . People can be no prettier than you and not as good and still be pretty and good. And it was late at night. And she sort of suggested it.'

'She sleeps around a lot, then, does she?'

'I don't know. A bit, I imagine.'

'When are you going to go with her again?'

'I doubt if I ever will,' I said with verbal truth, though I was not above implying a loftier reason for doubt than Penny's fairly certain rejection both of me as I stood, so to speak, and of Gilbert's influence in the matter.

'I suppose she's younger than me.'

'A few years, but it hadn't occurred to me until you mentioned it.'

'Who is she? What is she?'

'She's Roy Vandervane's daughter.'

'Him again. No, not again: still. Phew. Had that black chap come to knock your block off?'

'No, he wanted me to give him a hand with something he's working on.'

'Easy-going sort of type, isn't he?'

'Isn't that what we're all supposed to be round here? What about you and the other bloke? He doesn't sound anywhere near as pretty as me from what you told me about him, in fact you said so yourself, but I quite see he might be a hell of a lot reasonabler and gooder, but anyway whatever he's like you've got him, so it isn't fair for you to start minding what I get up to.'

'Yes it is, it's perfectly fair for me to mind. What wouldn't be fair would be me going on at you, doing things or saying things, anything at all to try to get you to stop going with her. And I haven't, have I? I've been reasonable.'

'Yes, I give you that straight away.'

'Thank you. The other bloke's a bit more reasonable than you and just about as good,' she said, volunteering information for the second time that evening.

'I see. I still can't make out why you mind.'

'If you can't, you can't. Now we're going to forget it. I won't bring it up again and I won't make you think I'm thinking about it even though I'm not bringing it up.'

Unsurprisingly, she kept her word, denying herself even her small-ish mid-week ration of sullenness-cum-preoccupation throughout dinner at Bertorellis' in Charlotte Street, the showing of the nuclear-submarine thriller I had chosen instead of the Hungarian film about the life of Liszt she had thought I must want to see, and the remain-der of the night's events. Nevertheless, I was betting myself I had not heard the end of her part in the Penny question, and put on an inter-nal red alert when she said at breakfast,

'Oh, Doug, have you got anything fixed for Monday?'

I got my diary out. 'Well, half. But I can easily not go. But isn't that the night you go to see your dad?'

'Yes, but I was thinking you might like to come along too. He's often asked about you.'

'Just the three of us?'

'Yes. I was thinking I could come up here about six, and then', she said, looking out of the window, 'we could get on our way about quarter to seven.'

'Fine. I'll look forward to it.'

I won my usual battle to prevent Vivienne washing up the break-fast things, saw her off, washed up the breakfast things, wrote a letter and hung about until three short rings at the doorbell signalled the departure from below of Gwyneth Iqbal, who minded my piano-playing, for the accountants' office where she worked. Accordingly, I sat down at the keyboard at once, although I knew that Fazal Iqbal, who also minded, was still downstairs, and would be for the next hour or so, doing none knew what. But he was tolerant of the piano, because I minded – it seemed to me with better reason – the unsteady wailing, punctuated by explosive clicks, he was in the habit of producing from some apparatus he owned, and I was tolerant about that.

I took myself through the Beethoven op. 109, first piecemeal and then, after a cup of coffee, entire. At the end, I decided that there was something to be said for the Iqbals' point of view. Hands had followed brain with fair efficiency, but brain had been sluggish, lazy, allowing eyes to usurp too much of its function. I decided that my favourite excuse to myself for having failed to become a practising musician, my piano teacher's obstinacy in stopping me from switching to some wind instrument and going for a job in an orchestra, was an excuse and no more. Oh well, bashing piano keys kept one in touch, but in future I had better concentrate on bashing typewriter keys with more elegant and readable results.

By half past eleven I had had enough and left, in the expectation that some royal occasion or sporting event, or one of those mysterious lemming-like impulses that can urge ten thousand extra vehicles into trying to cross central London inside the same hour, would intervene to use up at least the forty-five minutes I had in hand. Not a bloody bit of it, as Roy would have said. As virtually always in this situation, half the people were using the ring road that morning and most of the others had already left for the Channel ports. The drivers of my successive buses performed with dash and intrepidity, scraping through lights in the last instant of the amber, swinging out into the fast lane and rampaging round Marble Arch and Hyde Park Corner as if under notice of dismissal. At two minutes to twelve I was climbing the steps of the Alexandra Hall. In the foyer, a small-headed fellow in uniform came over to bar my way with an air of undifferentiated hostility. Almost at once he recognized me and changed his air to one of differentiated hostility.

'A rehearsal is in progress,' he said.

'So I understood from Sir Roy.'

The man's head seemed to shrink a half hat-size or so. 'There's a round dozen of them in there already, sitting about.'

'I'll have company, then.'

'Name?'

After some Yandell-Randall?-Yandelling, he went through an inner conflict, decided against asking me to submit to a search, and let me pass. I took a seat about a third of the way down the auditorium, as indicated by the acoustics of the hall. Roy, on the rostrum with score and baton, was in shirt-sleeves, both shirt and sleeves flamingo-hued and ruffle-adorned in a mode that might have appealed strongly to Vivienne. The orchestra were giving him their close attention.

'First oboe,' he was saying, 'remember not to take that minim off till the next beat. In the passage in general, the wood-wind balance is much better now, excellent, in fact, but I'd like just a shade more from third and fourth clarinets and a touch less from first flute. Strings, overall, a little more warmth if you can. Try to sing. Oh, I know a lot of silly sods go on about singing, but I'm afraid they're right. I'd use another word if I could, but there ain't one. But don't feel you've got to give it absolutely every bloody ounce at this stage. In these long works you've got to pace yourselves, keep just that little bit in hand, or by the time you get to the finale you'll be drained dry. Right, we'll take the whole of the movement straight through now. Okay, everybody? Fine.'

He drank from a glass that his enemies would have said contained vodka, but which I knew, *Elevations 9* or no *Elevations 9*, Sylvia or no Sylvia, must hold nothing but water. Then he picked up his baton and started them off.

The movement turned out to be the first movement of the First Symphony: a considerable mercy, seeing that it might so easily have been something broad, full, ample, spacious, massive, leisurely and going on for over half an hour from the Second or the Third. Thanks to some paroxysm of curtailment on the composer's part, I was in for little more than fifteen minutes' worth. (It was true that, in a comparable situation, Weber would have gone on half as long and used an orchestra a quarter as big, but then he would have had eight times as much to say.) As the music got into its lubberly stride, I made some attempt to separate it in itself from how it was being interpreted and played, but I had never been very good at this with works on my private never-mind list. At first against my will, I listened to Mahler's enormous talentlessness being rendered by Roy and the NLSO. As they went on, flecks of seeming talent began to insinuate themselves. Factitious fuss turned itself into a sort of gaiety; doodles in the horns and woodwind were almost transformed into rustic charm; blaring and banging acquired a note of near-menace; even that terrible little cuckoo-motif reflected something more than the great man's decision to let the world know how jolly preoccupied he had been in those days with the interval of the perfect fourth.

The ending went off poorly, but that was mostly Mahler, and I could have faulted the 'cellos with a bit of raggedness near the beginning, but all in all it had been a very good performance, approaching the best second-rate, that rare and exalted level to which Roy could decisively lift the orchestra when the concert came and where, I was much relieved to have found, he himself still belonged as he always had. The other listeners – not the crew of rioters at which the microcephalic had seemed to hint, but various attachments of the players – agreed with me. At least, they applauded. So did I.

'Bloody good,' said Roy. 'Thank you, all of you. Very nearly absolutely what I want. Now, it's now getting on for twelve thirty, so we might as well scrub the last half-hour. And everybody's worked bloody hard this morning and the last couple of days, so unless there's a lot of opposition I propose scrubbing this afternoon's session as well. Okay? Ten o'clock Monday, then. Thank you again.'

A couple of minutes later he came up the aisle, buttoning one of his uneasiness-dispensing overcoatish jackets, and greeted me. I suppressed a qualm at his ready cancellation of the afternoon rehearsal, telling myself that I had just now been full of appreciation of the standard already achieved, and had better stop coming over all officious whenever anybody started derelicting my ideas of his duty. No, not anybody. Getting caught up in Roy's affairs meant turning into either his accomplice or his aunt, or both.

We came out on to the steps. The weather had changed in the last day or two, and was making up for lost time with moist grey skies and sudden squalls. Roy's hair rose and swung to and fro in one of these.

'Well, Duggers, I rather think somewhere near. Somewhere close by, if you follow me.'

'Somewhere quiet, too. We've got a lot to discuss.'

'Oh, bugger off,' he temporized. 'I'm not discussing anything until I've got a gill of Scotch inside me. If then.'

'I thought you had some things on your mind.'

'What gave you that idea?'

'You said so over the telephone.'

'Oh, did I? Oh yes. Oh, nothing very much. We've plenty of time. What sort of row did you think we were kicking up back there?'

I gave him my views on the run-through I had heard while we made our way round several corners to somebody's Hostelry and Eating Rooms. Here, the decor turned out to be Vicwardian, not approached in the lukewarm spirit that had shaped the representations at the Islington pub, but carried out with frightening devotion: a bare-plank floor uniformly scattered with a thin layer of sawdust, engraved-glass panels and mirrors at the bar, tables with (perhaps) marble tops and the rest of them made of (perhaps) ancient sewing-machine stands. A whiskered waiter in a plum-coloured velvet waistcoat and ticking trousers took our order: a lager for me and two large whiskies for Roy.

'Well, glad you approve, old lad,' he said, drinking. 'I thought they soundig good myself, but when you get to my age, you know, you keep wondering if you can still tell. I could do with a bit of encouragement.'

'Maybe. What you certainly need is a lot of discouragement. *Elevations* 9 and Pigs Out and all that jazz. No, Roy, I've seen the programme and everything. What the hell are you playing at? A bloke like you. When you ought to be—'

'Oh, erosion of personal freedom! I do wish you'd try and fight your way out of this box you're in about everything stopping when Brahms died. You can't pretend—'

'No, it stopped with Schoenberg and serial technique, that's to say apart from the characters who've managed to—'

'Don't let's start that, Duggers.'

'All right, sorry. But look. What is the point, what do you think is the point, of you getting mixed up in all this pop . . . rubbish? Doing your own thing is a phrase I seem to have heard, or did it go out with wing collars and Frank Sinatra? Anyway, your thing is music. What their thing is I don't know and I don't want to know, but I do know it isn't music. Now. Why do you, of all people, how could you justify trying to mix them up? How are we all supposed to react to it? If we're supposed to think it's just a laugh, then we won't. Everybody you care about won't. Whose opinion you care about. Or ought to care about. I just can't . . .'

'Let strine put it this way. Life's changing, changing pretty fast, so fast you just can't say where things are going to go. All right, let's agree, just for the sake of argument, that the whole pop bit's pretty ropy musically. But what's musically? That's changing too. You've got to look beyond these bloody categories we've all been brought up with. Under late capitalism, there's bound to be—'

'To hell with late capitalism.' I felt we had reached an important point, one that had been slopping about in the recesses of my mind for some time – reached it a good deal earlier than was opportune, but reached it we had. 'All I think you're really trying to do is arse-creep youth.'

Roy gave a laugh of full, authentic richness; anybody could make any sort of personal attack on him, which had always been one of the nicest and most disastrous things in his nature. 'Arse-creep. By Jove, Mr Yandell, sir, you do show an uncommon gift for a racy phrase. Well yes, there is that, and it seems to me quite reasonable in a way, because there are things I can get from youth I can't get anywhere else.'

I felt my face turn very tired all over.

'No, I'm not only thinking of the stuff about new ways of seeing I told you about,' he said, showing what were, for him, stupendous powers of intuition and memory. 'If you work it just right, with a bit of luck they'll give you something you really start to want when you get to my time of life. Shut up, I'm talking about uncritical admiration. A very rewarding thing to have, I can assure you.'

'The Furry Barrel will give you plenty of that. I should have thought you'd prefer the critical kind. Or let's call it reasoned appreciation.'

'That's good too, and I know I get it from you and one or two other people, and I'm bloody grateful, believe me, and remembering it bucks me up no end whenever I start thinking I'm a failed composer and mediocre fiddler ending up as a hack conductor, but you see, Duggers, old lad, the point is, through no fault of your own you don't happen to be ten girls of nineteen or twenty and their boy-friends.'

'Eh? Where do the boy-friends come into it?'

'Well, they sort of eke the chicks out. A girl might give me a lot of bear-oil because she wants to screw me because I'm on the telly, or because I'm a sir, or because she thinks she can twist a platinum bracelet out of me, though there's not much of that around these days, as a matter of interest, now none of them can tell platinum from plastic. Christ . . . Oh yes, the boyfriends don't want to screw me, so that puts it on a broad impartial basis. Makes it look like hero-worship. I know it isn't that really, but I enjoy it all going on. That's why I arse-creep youth. Mind you, I go for their attitudes and the rest of it as well. Quite a bit, anyway.'

After a pause, I said, 'What about Sylvia? Does she give you uncritical admiration?'

'Much more than you might think from the way she behaves on occasions like the other night. No, actually she doesn't, not a lot. Hardly at all. I don't really know why she . . . I think she just likes old men. Some of them do, you know. Still, it's a good thing, her not making with the uncritical admiration. Does something to stop it all going to my head.'

'Roy, I must talk to you about her.'

'What about? What about her?'

At this very point, some unseen master of timing set in motion a record or tape of a piano playing, at top speed and chock-full volume, a dance song of the 'twenties, impeccably in period by prevailing standards, and not exhaustively offensive, but a distraction for one whose ears had hardly stopped ringing after their ordeal of a few evenings ago. Roy beat me to the door by a yard or two. So how did he manage to stand up to the assault of pop in full caterwaul? – which must be substantially grosser to his senses than to mine or to those of almost anybody else not yet adult when the first bawls began. New ways of hearing? No, such could not exist. Not on the scale required, anyway.

Outside, I said, 'Where are we off to now?' I could sense that I said it rather pettishly. I was not sure I could stand another Roy-directed mystery tour, even a diurnal one.

'Pick up Sylvia in some boutique or other,' he replied briskly, 'and then a spot of lunch at the Bolognese. Joint off Knightsbridge.'

'Oh, God.'

'Pull yourself together, Duggers. Be a man. You can face it. Or if you find you can't, then you can scream and run away. Not that I can see why. She likes you. Thinks you're a great wag.'

'How can you tell?'

'I quite see you might say she's got a funny way of showing it, but then you don't know how she performs when she's really taken against a sod. And you were going on about wanting to talk to me.'

'So I was.' Curiosity had already overcome whatever opposition I might have been able to find grounds for. 'Fine.' I noticed we had started walking at some speed, and added, without much curiosity, 'Where's your car?'

'Laid up,' said Roy, briskly again, but with a different kind of briskness. This kind told me at once that his car was being used, or had been burnt down to the axles, by somebody he was not for the moment inclined to have me discuss with him: Gilbert, or Penny, or Chris, or Kitty, or Ashley. Somebody somewhere in his circle.

We picked up a taxi. Roy, instead of taking his place beside me in the back seat, thrust down one of the folding affairs in the partition that separated us from the driver and threw himself youthfully upon it, perhaps in the hope of suggesting a cultural frontiersman's indifference to comfort. I asked him,

'Are you inviting me out to a jolly lunch, or do you still feel you need me for camouflage? Because I thought you were just about ready to tear off the mask and stand in the full glare of publicity.'

'How did you come by that idea?'

'Penny. But we'll get on to her in a minute. Are you thinking of leaving Kitty and setting up with Sylvia?'

'Yes, old lad, between ourselves I rather am.'

'You're off your head.'

'Yes, so everybody seems to feel. I suppose there really might be something in the idea.'

'She's terrible.'

'I think I see what you mean. There are times when I almost feel it too. Things you couldn't know about. For instance, she won't do anything.'

'Anything? I thought there was very little she—'

'Like cooking or preparing food or tidying up, making beds, all that. The first day I spent with her in her flat, there wasn't any food in it, just some milk that had gone off and some very quiet biscuits. You could bend them to and fro like wax. Well, we couldn't go out, you understand, because of being seen, so it ended up with me having to – ended up? Started, with me going out and buying steak and vegetables and stuff. And a bottle of Scotch, I may add. When I brought it all back she wouldn't do anything to it. Any of it. I was going to have to start from scratch on the potatoes. Fuck that. So I went out again and bought some sandwiches and made-up potato salad and cole-slaw, and then I had to wash up plates and knives and forks for us to eat them with and take the lot to her in bed.'

'How does she manage when you're not there?'

'Her flat-mate does it or she goes out. She won't starve, in case you're worrying.'

'And you want to go and live with someone like that.'

'Oh yes. In all other, in most other respects it was a bloody marvellous day. I can get someone in to shop and cook and the rest of it when we're out in the open. In fact, it's the thought of that as much as anything that's weighed with me over going off with her.'

'I see.' I also saw that my line of attack up to now was effectively blocked. 'I suppose you've given some thought to the Harold Meers angle. He had it in for you before this ever came up. When he finds out you're proposing to live with his daughter – if he doesn't know already – he's going to hit the roof.'

'He can beat a timp-roll on it with his balls for all I care. What can he do? Get whoever does the John Evelyn column to put something in about which recently knighted veteran conductor is buggering about with which teenage daughter of which prominent Fleet Street figure? If he pisses on me he's pissing on her too, and himself. And going by the dog-doesn't-eat-dog principle, that'll keep the rest of the Press quiet too. I ought to have thought of that months ago.'

'He'll come up with something.'

'He can't touch my sex life, or my professional life unless he sacks you, and whoever he got instead would still only be the music chap writing in the . . . Sorry, Duggers, I mean you count because you're you, but the paper doesn't in itself, do you follow? Harold bloody Meers doesn't scare me.'

'Well, he does me.' I was going to have to switch again. 'Anyway, Press or no Press, the news'll get round soon enough. Won't you mind everybody who knows you and millions who don't thinking you're rather a charlie? Undignified? A bit of a joke? Even youth?'

'Yes, I expect I will. Not much, though. Partly because I shan't look all that much of a charlie. Film stars and people are going off with much younger girls all the time and nobody gives a shit. Or hadn't you noticed that?'

'I didn't only mean the age thing. You're proposing to do something that's really awful. What about Kitty? And what about Penny? And what about Chris? And what about Ashley?'

'Ashley's a problem, I agree. There'll have to be some sharing arrangement worked out there. And don't think I haven't thought about the others, too.'

'That's exactly what I do think, seeing that you're intending to leave regardless of all of them. Why can't you just stay put officially and see a lot of Sylvia on the side?'

'No. I've had enough of that. So's she.'

The taxi was moving up Grosvenor Gardens, more and more slowly as the traffic thickened towards Hyde Park Corner. Ahead, rattlings and crashings came into earshot from where something was being pulled down or put up or excavated. I would soon, yet again, have to start shouting, but we were nearing boutique-land and my chance would be gone.

'If you've had enough of it, then pack it in. And how do you mean, had enough? You talk as if you've spent the last couple of years fighting in the jungle. What you've had getting on for enough of, no doubt, is making other people's lives a misery while you're watching. I'm sure Kitty goes on at you all the time about why don't you shoot her and have done with it and so on. There's a straightforward answer to that, of course, to do with her going on just the same when the butcher forgets to send the dog's meat. But now and then perhaps it crosses your mind that crying out before you're hurt doesn't actually guarantee permanent protection against being hurt, and that without you Kitty really would be done for – there'd be nobody left in the world for her apart from Ashley, who's a little monster, thanks largely to the insane way you let him do as he likes all the time, because if you tried to stop him you wouldn't be so popular with him, and you couldn't have that, could you? Penny and Chris both despise you for the way you go on in general, but that doesn't mean to say they don't love you, or couldn't be made to again, but if you go off with Sylvia they'll never forgive you. I mean that literally. Do you understand what I'm saying?'

I had had some trouble competing with the noise outside, but Roy had taken in every word, his eyes never leaving my face, his head nodding in thought at irregular intervals. Something struck me about his posture on the folding seat; it was uncomfortable, almost studiedly awkward, that of a man perched on a hard chair or a stool while the man talking to him leant back against padded upholstery. That was why he had chosen the seat in the first place, to advertise his humility, put himself physically in the position of somebody being lectured at by a superior, be seen to be paying close attention – none of it possible with him beside me. My job here, perhaps not only here, was to dish out his medicine and watch him taking it like a man. He had planned to be helped to feel how deeply he was affected by the case against what he wanted to do before going off and doing it anyway. And now, for the moment at least, I saw the basic motive of all the favour business: to see to it that I got a good, solid, continuous six or seven hours of Sylvia and so could act as a key prosecution witness in the show-trial of his integrity, with Penny thrown in not, or not simply, as a lure to me but as a reassurance to him that, even at a time of such crisis for himself, he was thinking of her, trying to get her off with dependable, concerned old Duggers.

I hardly listened at first when he said,

'I understand it all right. The whole thing's an agony, you must know that. I'll just have to live with the Kitty part of it. In a way I feel worse about the kids, Penny and Chris. But they've got their lives to live. There's not so much left of mine, so they won't have to go on never forgiving me indefinitely. With luck I'll make sixty. Fine with me. I'm not interested in living out my span in an odour of sanctity, beloved husband and father, approval of my own conscience – all of which it's a bloody sight too late for anyhow – and no girls or whisky or careering around in my own inimitable irresponsible way. I'll take criticism from chaps who've been in my situation and chosen differently. No one else.'

I was listening now, but could find nothing to say, except for a possible query about the role of late capitalism in the present quandary, and rejected that. The taxi had turned off at St George's Hospital. Roy lit a cigarette and said,

'Anyway, let's have a jolly lunch.'

'Yes, let's. Do you mind if I go up and see Kitty tomorrow?'

'Not a bit. I wish you would.'

'I will, then. When are you and Sylvia thinking of taking off?'

'Not for a couple of months. After I've done Gus and she's over eighteen. Uh, Duggers, could you do me a small favour? Only take a minute.'

'Sure.'

'Nearly opposite this place there's a man's shop.' His eye held mine in a pleading look. 'Could you just nip in there and buy me a pair of underpants? Medium size, sort of boxer's shorts pattern. Or anything they've got that'll do. Nothing fancy.'

Forewarned, I neither sermonized nor laughed, and a couple of minutes later was standing in the shop, which was filled with loud pop noises, of all things. The lad who had served me peered through his fringe out of the window as he gave me my change.

'That's Sir Roy Vandervane over there, isn't it?'

'Is it?'

'Yeah, he often hangs round here. After the birds, see. My sister was at a party once he was at. Five minutes' chat-up and then boof!'

'Boof?'

He gestured outwards and upwards at crotch height.

'I see. How extraordinary. Thanks. Goodbye.'

I crossed the street making faces at Roy, who glanced to and fro in alarm.

'What's the matter?'

'Which way?'

'Along here. What's up?'

'Come on. Bloke in the shop recognized you.'

'Did he really? What of it?'

The pants changed hands like missile blueprints between two secret agents of the meaner sort, such as get sprayed with napalm from a passing car in the pre-titles sequence. When this was done, I said,

'I don't know. I don't know what of it.'

'That's better. All part of the fun, old lad. It ought to tone you up.'

'What? I only went on like that because of the way you—'

'I agree that things like pancy-curity can get me down, but when they tone me up, they tone me up. No, you come in too. Do you good. Broaden your mind.'

Uncouth minstrelsy enveloped me again when I crossed the threshold of what I supposed was the boutique. A single room about the size of a squash court, but with a low ceiling, was illuminated by a faint daylight glow through thick curtains and by some objects that might have been electric-toaster elements fixed to the walls at head height. By their aid I was able to pick out a shirt-collar, a belt-buckle here, a leg, the back of a head there. Roy was going to have to find Sylvia by touch and smell, touch rather than smell, for a rehoboam of deodorant would hardly have been too much to neutralize the miasma of surrounding bodies. It was very hot, too. I stayed near the door, enduring virtually continuous jostling for the sake of not missing Roy on his way out. Time went by. I recognized my present state, a milder but authentic version of that attained over long stretches of the night of the favour, as what a child experiences when his elders take him round a museum or on a conducted tour of a great house: a fusion of boredom and discomfort into some third thing, a solipsistic despair, a progressive and apparently irreversible loss of belief in anything not here and not now, in tea, homework, television, school, cricket, holidays – this place is hell, in fact. To give myself something to do, I started concentrating on trying not to breathe.

Roy became distinguishable, with what must be Sylvia at his side. At the doorway, I saw against the daylight a figure confront Roy and apparently deliver a series of quick punches on the front and sides of his trunk; but he passed on unscathed. When my turn came, the exercise turned out to be a search, expertly and not uncivilly conducted. This precaution, which struck me as unusual in itself, could surely, I thought, have been rendered much easier, if not unnecessary, by switching on a light or two. Then I realized that potential new customers at a place like that would simply turn back at the threshold if their chances of stealing something were to be so visibly hampered.

'At least they didn't have pop in the Black Hole of Calcutta,' said Roy as we moved off.

'Oh, I thought you liked it,' I said.

'When it's a decent group. That wasn't.'

Sylvia, whose black jerkin, black thigh-boots and extended waist-belt of chains hung with padlock-sized pendants (or whatever) made her look like a gaoler in an advanced musical of the 'fifties, said nothing.

She went on saying nothing while we made our way to and established ourselves in the restaurant, and while Roy went away for a couple of minutes, presumably to switch pants. I looked round the room. Its layout and decor, its furniture, even what the waitresses were wearing, seemed indefinably original, strange, almost exotic. It was some moments before I saw that the place was got up as a restaurant, with tables and chairs, people ordering drinks and food and being served with them, others handing over money and receiving change. An odd environment for Roy, I thought. Perhaps he was making a trip in reverse, an expedition to the old world, as a white man gone native might travel into town to see if there were still such things as shops and buses.

The issue was never raised. Nor was much else. Roy asked what I was up to and I told him about the Haydn symphonies and the Mozart sonatas, then about Terry Bolsover's desire for an interview with him. The last interested him more than the other two combined. I asked him what he was up to, and he told me about having had to turn down a commission to write the music for a film about Richard II.

'Why?' I asked.

'Oh, you know, some right-wing shag had written the scream-play. Glorifying the monarchy and so on.'

'Oh, I see.'

Throughout this and such, Sylvia remained silent, vocally at least, though she clanked and rattled whenever she moved at a volume far outdoing Vivienne's charm bracelet. The waitress brought our main course and went away with an awkward, rolling gait. Sylvia watched her go and, speaking for the first time that day in my presence, said,

'Why does that girl walk in that bloody silly way?'

'She's got something wrong with her hip,' said Roy. 'TB, I think. She's the proprietor's daughter. I know them here.'

Sylvia ate spaghetti and went on with her mouth full, 'Why doesn't he do something about it?'

'He has, but there's not a hell of a lot you can do in cases like that, apparently.'

'He must make a puhcket out of this dump. You can see it's had nothing spent on it for ten years.' She was chewing and swallowing like somebody on an eating marathon; perhaps the flat-mate had failed to furnish breakfast. 'Why doesn't he lay out a few quid on his daughter's hip or whatever it is?'

Roy said casually, 'He's laid out all he has on operations in this country, Switzerland and America and is still heavily in debt because of it.'

This might have seemed to settle the matter, but Sylvia did not think so. She ate some more and said, 'He's been done, then, hasn't he? Why couldn't he have the sense to find a proper doctor somewhere? He probably didn't try. Just wanted to fling the cuhsh around so as to feel good.'

I recognized a fully fledged case of that moral vandalism which, in slightly different spheres, could take the form of beating up old ladies because nobody beats up old ladies, shooting at firemen fighting a fire because nobody shoots at firemen fighting a fire. And something else besides. All the more clearly for its distance from the present topic, I saw the root of Sylvia's attraction for Roy, that of the agent for the spectator who would act likewise if he dared, the bomb-thrower for the liberal too decent and cowardly and fastidious and old and late-capitalistic to countenance the existence of bombs. And/or.

With no more said, Sylvia finished her spaghetti, got up and left. I looked at Roy.

'She's young,' he said.

'Roy, forget all this side of it. It's not really important. You can behave like a selfish idiot for the rest of your life and it won't really matter. What Roy Vandervane does as husband and father and screwer and the rest of it concerns Roy Vandervane and a small circle and will be all over and done with in fifty years. What Roy Vandervane does as musician concerns music, and that'll go on much longer. For God's sake drop this *Elevations 9* rubbish and concentrate on Gus. That's your job. What you're meant to do.'

'So music's more important than sex. For Christ's sake, Duggers . . .'

'I think it may well be. I think I'd rather be a monk in a world with music than a full-time stallion in a world without it. I like sex too and I haven't gone into the whole thing enough to be sure about the monk and stallion business, but that's not the point. The point is that music's more important than Roy Vandervane's sex life.'

'Ole lad, with the best will in the world I can't see what's so cosmically disastrous about this little *Elevations 9* caper. You talk as if—'

'What's happened to the other eight elevations?'

'Oh, they're not real. I mean there aren't any. There's a Beatles track – well, that wouldn't interest you. Then it's a sort of pun. You know, elevation, and nine inches.'

'I take it you'll be explaining that to the audience on the night. Or demonstrating it, perhaps.'

'Of course. But I still don't see why it's so—'

'You're bringing – you, a well-known figure with a lot of prestige and rightly so, are helping to bring that very important stuff, music, into disrepute. It's having a hard enough time as it is, what with Cage and Boulez and the rest of them. You're coming at it from the rear. I'd say there's quite a good chance that the time and the mood are right for what you're doing to catch on in a way that the idea of music with jazz sauce never has after dozens of tries. And if your rubbish does catch on, you'll have harmed music.'

'Oh, priceless jewel of melody! It's just a stunt, a romp. I do wish you could see things from that angle once in a way.'

'A romp that'll harm music. All right, perhaps I am being a bit hysterical about it catching on. But you'll certainly be helping to make music look like just another fun thing and now thing, like these clothes they all wear and theatre in the nude and flower power and environmental art and First War stuff. And that's a disgraceful thing to do. On your part above all. Because you know better. You can say what you like about uncritical admiration, you'll get plenty of that out of it, I'm sure, but all your colleagues and all your real friends will despise you. Including me. Especially me.'

Grimly, Roy poured himself more wine and looked at me; I shook my head. Then he looked at me again, with a twisted smile I had not seen before but recognized without trouble. He was taking a second dose of his medicine, being helped to feel bad about what he had unalterably made up his mind to do.

'I think I will have some wine after all,' I said.

He poured it with renewed grimness.

'Has she just gone off?'

'Oh no,' he said. 'She never just goes off. Not without letting you know in full that that's what she's doing. Here she is now.'

'Let's go,' said Sylvia, arriving.

'Sit down and have some coffee,' said Roy.

'Let's go.' She sent him a grimace that spelt bed in an unattractive script.

He got up. I said this one was mine and pulled out my wallet, but he said it would be put on his account and I could do the next one. On our way out, Sylvia jogged the elbow of a man in a chair next to the aisle, spilling his coffee on to an open packet of cigarettes on the table, and Roy apologized to him. A light rain was falling as we walked up into Knightsbridge, Sylvia setting a brisk pace. The traffic was heavy.

'We'll never get a taxi in this,' said Sylvia.

'I'll be off and find a bus,' I said.

'There's one,' she said, pointing.

She meant not a bus, but a free taxi, and sure enough one could be intermittently seen approaching slowly on our side of the road. Roy waved to it. So, at the same moment, did a small brown man, perhaps an Indian, standing nearer to it than ourselves. Just then the traffic accelerated, and the taxi, ignoring the Indian (who gazed after it in astonishment), swept forward and stopped beside us. The driver was a young black man with long side-whiskers. Roy said to him,

'Why didn't you stop for that chap back there?'

'I don't know, guv,' the man said in cockney. 'Perhaps I liked the look of you better.'

'But he was coloured.'

'Well, you were here first, weren't you? I mean it's your island, mate.'

'Turn round and go back and pick him up.'

'Look, I can't turn here, mate. Do you want me or don't you?'

'Get in, you stupid bugger,' said Sylvia. 'I'm in a hurry if you're not.'

'I refuse—'

As if we had been carefully rehearsing half the morning, Sylvia kicked Roy in the shins, I grabbed him, arms and all, round the middle, she opened the taxi door, I bundled him up and in, she followed and the taxi shot away.

'So long,' she called out of the window, waving. 'Thanks a lot. See you.'

# Five

## Absolute Rock

Roy's car made a quick recovery from its bout of indisposition, as I found the next morning when I telephoned and spoke to Gilbert, who told me, with mild but unconcealed satisfaction, that its owner had taken it to London and that therefore I would have to walk from the Underground station. Asked if there were taxis, he told me in the same vein that there was a taxi office at the top of the station approach, but that in his experience it was always shut. His experience proved a true guide. I set out on foot through the town, expecting a cloudburst at any moment, but the heavens, though no less grey than before, kept their moisture to themselves. The people in the streets looked quite normal, even the younger ones. I found this disproportionately reassuring, and found further, on self-scrutiny, that my subconscious had been harbouring a panic-ridden fantasy in which the whole place had, since my last visit, become a sort of Roytown, with pavements and roadway full of youth smoking pot, twanging guitars, rejecting out-moded ways of thought and calling 'Christian gentleman, man!' to one another. But if any of this was happening, it was hidden from sight.

I turned off at a garage and car show-room full of Bentleys and Rolls-Royces, made my way along the side of a gloomy green with patches of standing water, and traversed an area where almshouses round the church gave place to establishments that had their names done in reflectors at headlight height and metal statuary on top of their gateposts. This was more like Roytown in fact. When I approached the Vandervane residence I thought I saw Gilbert standing at an upper window, but there was nobody there on a second glance. In the courtyard, as before, I heard from the kitchen the Furry

Barrel's barks and growls; in the hall she appeared, recognized me and submitted to flattery, snorting a good deal in a well-born way. Kitty came out from somewhere and embraced me. After we had moved to the drawing-room she said, quite temperately by her standards,

'It was sweet of you to come, Douglas dear.'

'Oh, it's good to get out for a bit. How are you?'

She gave me a brave, jerky smile that irritated me and made me feel sorry for her. 'Oh . . . you know,' she said with an affectation of affected lightness. 'One carries on. One has no alternative. Would you like a beer or something?'

'No thanks. You have something.'

'I've got something.'

She had and no mistake: a tall tumblerful of what was no doubt her favourite fearful gin and water, somehow giving the impression of not being the first of its line. Her clothes and general appearance, like the state of the room, indicated slovenliness, but a slovenliness done with tremendous artistic restraint: her dressing-gown, or dressing-gown dress, was old, moderately torn, and clean; her make-up, though ill applied, had at least been applied that day; used crockery, brimming ashtrays, vases of decaying flowers and naked gramophone records lay about, yet the clock, a vulnerable one with its glass dome, showed the right time and the carpet seemed free of gross or recent stains. She and the place had gone to rack and a piece or so, no further for the moment.

Kitty had followed my glance. 'The cleaning ladies have stopped coming and I can't seem to get any other ones. I seem to have used up all the ones round here. Gilbert's marvellous, but he can't do everything.'

'He and Penny are still here, then?' I asked experimentally.

'Oh yes. Here at this very minute. They're always here. I thought you knew that.'

'How's Ashley?'

'He's at school.'

'Really. How's he getting on there?'

'Getting on?' She seemed puzzled.

'Sorry, I just . . .'

'He goes there most days now. Much better than he used to be. We've got a new system. Every day he goes, he gets a surprise when he comes home.'

'What sort of surprise?'

'Something nice, of course. Something it's fun for him to play with.'

'You mean like a trench mortar or a flame-thrower or a—'

'There are no militaristic toys in this house, Douglas.'

'Sorry, I should have known. Whose idea was the surprise thing?'

'His.'

I gave an understanding grunt instead of any of the several sorts of yell that suggested themselves to me. Apart from a faint show of indignation over the militaristic toys, she had stuck to her cinematic war-widow style, behaving with such wonderful control that nobody except everybody would have dreamt for a single moment, etc. I told myself we were going to have to start some time.

'What's the latest?'

She went light again. 'Oh, haven't you heard? I thought everybody knew. My husband is leaving me. He's decided to run away with a younger woman.'

'Mightn't it just be the Bayreuth stage? You know, a halfway kind of—'

'No, it's gone beyond that. It's a luxury he's learnt to do without.'

'He'll be back. He won't be able to stand her for long. Nobody could.'

'Then he'll move on. Find someone with the same . . . attractions. He won't be back. It's not his way, my dear Douglas. Oh, don't think I'm bitter. I've moved beyond all that long ago. He's human, God knows, like the rest of us. And it's human to choose any sort of path into the future rather than face the long road back to what you've left behind. Do you mind if we go out of doors? I'm beginning to find the atmosphere of the place oppresses me.'

I was beginning to find the same thing in a smaller way, and myself lifted the sash of the central window, under which we ducked in turn. The day had lightened a little. As Kitty and I strolled on to the lawn, the Furry Barrel approached at a fast gallop from the corner by the ruins of the greenhouse, an old sandal in her jaws. This she dropped nearby and savaged briefly to the accompaniment of falsetto growls and snarls; after that, barking now, she went off at top speed towards a bank of rhododendrons, alerted by some creature or movement of foliage. I noticed that parts of the lawn were bald.

'It's the stuff off the cedars,' said Kitty. 'Needles or whatever they call them. Anyway, they kill the grass. Nothing you can do about it.'

'Do you manage to get anybody in to garden?'

'Not really. Christopher does a bit of mowing because he likes going on the motor-mower. And Roy got a gang of students in a couple of times, but they pulled up a lot of real plants as well as weeds. Still, it doesn't matter now, does it? It's the next owner's headache.'

'God, you're not selling the place already, are you? Supposing—'

'I've got to get out. Oh, because too much has happened here. Too many words said that can't be taken back or forgotten. Too many tears. No, it's my own decision. He'd let me stay for ever if I wanted to. As I say, he's human.'

I thought that last bit showed a sense of continuity of an altogether higher dramatic order than the general level of style being attained, and nodded soberly. Just then, a small group of people came out from behind a shaggy box hedge and moved off towards the lower lawn. I recognized Christopher Vandervane and Ruth Ericson. Of the other two, both young men unknown to me, one carried a camera and some kindred device slung over his shoulder. Kitty and I halted near an enormous display of roses and thistles very impartially mingled, like a cover illustration for a book on Anglo-Scotch relations.

'What's going to happen to him?' I nodded over at Christopher.

'I don't know. Same with Penny. One thing's certain: neither of them'll take a word of advice from anybody.'

'Or be told to do anything by anybody.'

'You can't tell them; it's just not on.' She laboriously fitted each hand into the opposite cuff of her dressing-gown, looked up at me, waited, and said, 'There's nothing left for me any more, Douglas, my dear. Nothing at all, anywhere.'

'You've got Ashley.'

'I can't do anything with Ashley. It's bad enough with Roy there. I shall have to try and find someone to live in and deal with him. That'll give me something to occupy my mind all right. But no more than that. I haven't a lover and I don't think I want one, after everything. There's nothing I know how to do, like playing music or writing or acting or even being a secretary or typing. All I had was Roy and Roy's world. And now . . . that's all gone. I'm nothing. Nothing.'

'You mustn't talk like that.'

Perhaps my words came out in a rhythm I had not consciously intended. At any rate, her gaze, which had been appropriately wide and unfocused, suddenly sharpened. 'That's what Roy says. Do you believe me at all, Douglas? When I try and tell you how I feel?'

'Of course I do,' I said as stoutly as I could, with no idea whether or how much I meant it.

'Perhaps you do. Roy's the same. I think you both do in a way, but it's sort of how I say it you don't really believe. Or you don't like it, the way I say it. It's too much like how I say things when I'm only tired and cross or late for something. I know I do go on an awful lot. I ought to have always said just I feel bloody fed up and bugger it and what a bastard, and then I'd have been all right now with this when it came along, and you'd both have believed me. But it's too late for that. You see, Douglas, you can't ever allow for how bad things can really get until they do.'

'I understand,' I said, and kissed her cheek.

'Thank you.' She clung to me for a moment. 'You are good. You're so good.'

'I'm not good at all. I've done nothing to help you. I haven't been able to find out anything that's made any difference, and as for trying to stop him, or even slow him down, well, I have tried a bit, I suppose, but even—'

'There's nothing to be done. It's all over. Surely you feel that.'

'I don't know what I feel.'

'But I'll just have to accept it. Whatever sort of experience that may turn out to be. Anyway, it's something I'll be facing alone, I know that much. There's no other way. You've managed to make me feel it's possible, even for someone like me. You've reassured me that I exist.'

Perhaps (I thought without much rancour, but with disappointment) I would have done more good, on balance, by trying to erode her faith in her own existence. At the same time I felt ashamed of my connivings with Roy. 'I wish there were something practical I could do,' I said.

Immediately her expression changed again. 'Actually there is a tiny favour you could do me if you would.'

'A tiny what?'

'It won't take you two minutes. Just a little telephone call. To the flat where this girl is supposed to live, to make sure I've got the right place. Just to see if she's there. Only take you a second, Douglas. You did say you understood.'

She gazed at me with the first faint glimmerings of reproach, not so faint that they obscured the nearness of a vast army of reproach all ready to be swung into action. I realized that there were some people who could use painful insight into themselves as merely one more lever on others, along with abuse, threats, hysteria and God knew what else. Kitty and I turned simultaneously towards the house.

'How did you get hold of the number?' I asked, picking at random from the glutton's plateful of questions in front of me.

'I got Gilbert to get it out of Roy. In case there were emergencies was what he told him, I think.'

'What sort of emergencies?'

'I left all that to him.'

'Why can't he make this telephone call?'

'He wouldn't do it. That would be meddling.'

'Wasn't getting hold of the number meddling?'

'No, I had a right to know it. Him ringing it up would be him meddling.'

'What do you want me to say?'

'Oh, anything, it doesn't matter. Just so I know she lives there. You know her voice, don't you?'

'Yes.'

'That's another reason why Gilbert wouldn't do, you see.'

'Supposing she isn't there? I mean she could live there and still not be there at the moment, couldn't she?'

'Then you try later.'

'Supposing she is there?'

'Then I'll know she's there. That she lives there. Then I can do things like writing her a letter and telling her what I think of her.'

'So you know her name. So why can't you just ring up and ask her if it's her? And you can't write a letter to a telephone number. And she wouldn't read it, anyway.'

'Oh yes she would. That just shows how little you know about women. She'd read it until she knew it damn near by heart and then she'd throw it away and pretend she'd never heard of it. Or even keep it hidden somewhere. And she'd probably ring off straight away if she heard a woman's voice at this end, so I'd never be sure.'

'This one isn't like most women, and what's the good of a letter?'

'Don't you believe it, my dear. We're all like most women. Gilbert got hold of the address for me – don't ask me how.'

'Having access to a telephone directory and knowing the alphabet would be a help, I should imagine.'

'The number isn't listed, Douglas. But Gilbert managed to find out the address just the same; he is wonderful, you know. And you're not to be like that.'

'Sorry,' I said, giving the telephone itself an unfriendly glance, for we stood now in the hall. 'What's the number?'

She produced it with a gunman's speed and deftness from a pocket of her dressing-gown, rather abandoning any implication that our common progress towards this point had been roundabout or accidental.

'What shall I say?'

'I told you, anything. Just so you're sure it's her.'

'Yes, I see that, I've got that. I wondered if you had any suggestions.'

'Say anything you like.'

'Yes, that's it, that's what I'll do. Of course. I'll say anything I like.'

I reached for the instrument. She faced me with joined hands in a mannish posture, like a fairly undevout man at a burial service, in fact. Discarding any hope of her removal, indeed preferring to have her under my eye rather than at the end of another extension, I dialled. The chances against getting through were surely enormous, considering the odds-on likelihood of connection with the speaking clock or a kosher butcher in the Bronx, no connection at all, precipitation into a duologue between psychiatrist and patient, and so on, added to other hefty contingencies such as non-payment of bill at the far end, absence of Sylvia and flat-mate, absorption of Sylvia in new ways of doing something or other. Nevertheless, not much to my surprise after all, the distant receiver was lifted after a couple of rings and loutish tweedledee burst upon my eardrums. A female voice said something.

'Is Fred there?' I asked.

'What? For Christ's sake why don't you speak up, muhn?'

'Is Fred there?'

'Ah, piss awff.'

I put the handset back and said to Kitty, 'That's her.'

'Thank you, Douglas dear. Now I must get a move on. I'll go and get dressed. You find Gilbert and tell him to have a taxi waiting outside the Two Brewers in an hour's time. You and I can walk to it. You don't mind a pub lunch, do you? It's very good there, actually. They make all their own soups and things. We don't want Chris and Penny and the rest of them round our necks, do we? Then I've got one or two things I want to do in Town, and the chap can drop you wherever you want to be. I'll be quite quick.'

I felt like shaking my head as if I had just been thoroughly hit on it, but refrained. 'Gilbert said you could never get taxis round here.'

'He can get one if he wants one. Make sure you tell him it's for me.'

She went away and up the curve of the staircase before I could ask her how to set about finding Gilbert; however, he emerged from some doorway within seconds. Wearing a lumpy cardigan and trousers of a baroque sort of tweed, he still bore the rumpled appearance of a couple of days earlier. His manner was reserved. He agreed to summon the taxi as requested, showing a certain impatience here, as with a task hardly calling for his qualities of generalship. After a pause, he said,

'Perhaps you might be so kind and go and see Penny now. I've told her you're here. You'll find her upstairs, in the second room to the left. I can't say how grateful I'll be.'

'If she makes any move to throw me out I'll let myself be thrown out.'

'She won't.'

Nor did she. Looking, in her flowing crimson robes, pale yellow kerchief and plain sandals, really remarkably like an illustration in a Victorian bible, she stood with her back to a window that gave a view of the common and a distant line of trees. I had been half expecting to encounter her weltering on an unmade bed among reefer butts and empty Coke bottles, and the neatness of everything was a mild surprise, until I remembered that Gilbert lived in here too. Neatness, in fact, was scarcely the word: the place had the bare yet not under-furnished appearance of a vacant hotel bedroom, and Penny might have arrived in it moments before, a few yards ahead of her luggage.

'Hallo,' I said. 'How are you?'

'Fine.'

The eyes could hardly have been bluer than usual, but seemed wider than usual. They stayed on mine while, in a swirl of draperies, she moved across to the bed and began pulling the coverlet off it.

I spoke without weighing my words. 'What's the idea?'

'Oh, Christ, chum. This is eh bed and I am eh girl and you are eh man and we are eh-lone too-gether. What could be the idea?'

'Are we? Alone, I mean. With Gilbert and Kitty and God knows who round the house, I don't feel very alone.'

'There's a bolt on that door. But of course Regulation 82(c) of the By Jove and Great Scott Society states, No gentleman shall lay a finger on a lady if the lady should presume to have the effrontery to make the first move.'

'You made the first move the other night and I laid a bit more than a finger on you that time.'

'What is it, then? Why are we having an argument?'

'Gilbert put you up to this,' I said, marvelling idly at how petulant and unconvinced I sounded.

'So what do you care? If you don't want me you just say. Go on.'

She had let go of the coverlet the moment I asked her what the idea was, and was standing half turned away from me, apparently looking out of the window towards the trees. I reviewed the children-of-Israel get-up, especially its top half, which would have done as much or as little for the thorax of a ten-year-old, a stripper or a great-grandmother, and saw why she had chosen to wear it, and found the explanation for my strange failure to have already hauled it off her or bored my way through it. Again I spoke without thought.

'That makes two of us. Oh, God, what am I saying? Forget it if you can. God. I mean, just for the moment, you don't feel like it any more than I do, just for the moment. Tell Gilbert I said I was having conscience trouble about my girl. He'll understand that.'

'You know, I never really feel like it, not it on its own. But I don't sort of feel not like it all the time either, really. But it's not that I don't care one way or the other.'

'You like a proper reason.'

She stepped forward, kissed me and laid her head against my shoulder, leaning prudently forward to keep the rest of herself out of contact with the rest of me. Both of us sighed deeply. I felt as if I had just sat through a complete performance of *La Traviata* compressed into one and a half minutes. I heard a jet passing somewhere high overhead, and then the Furry Barrel protesting against the violation of her air space. Penny sighed again and turned away. Could I ask her whether Gilbert had actually said to her, 'Now, when he comes, you go to bed with him, you see', and whether she had indeed said to him, 'Yes, Gilbert; well and good, Gilbert'? No. A pity. A pity that the more interesting a question became, the more absolutely one was assumed not to need to ask it. I tried answering this one in my mind. Of course that was what had happened. That sounded quite certain, obvious, solid as iron, plain as the nose on my face. Of course that was not what had happened. That sounded exactly the same. But how could it?

'Shall we get the talking done?' asked Penny. 'There's that as well, isn't there?'

'Oh, yes. I was supposed to try to get you to leave here and go into a flat somewhere.'

'Oh, that one. He put you up to that, didn't he?'

'No, he didn't. Gilbert did.'

'Never mind, I'm staying here.'

'You're mad. There's nothing but unhappiness in this house and it's just going to go on and on. No it isn't just going to go on and on, it's going to get worse. More violent and more . . . awful. Do what Gilbert says. He's the only one round here you can trust.'

'Don't you believe it, mate. Anyway, you're wasting your time. Like everyone else. I'm not leaving, not this side of next Christmas. He wants me to go.'

'He. People can be right for the wrong reasons.'

'Not him.'

'And they're not all wrong reasons, for God's sake. He really does want to spare you as much as he can of all this; you've got to give him that. He doesn't want to chuck you out.'

'I'd like to see him try.'

'Yes, I think you would.'

She looked hard at me and turned farther away. I said to her back, 'Penny, I wish you'd let me—'

'Like I told you, nobody takes me on. Did you talk to him? You know.'

'Yes, I tried to . . .'

'But you didn't get anywhere.'

'No.'

'I had to ask you to try, though, didn't I? I'll make out, don't you worry. The next time you come I'll be much better. Not so depressed. I'm going to take myself on.'

I had been outside in the courtyard for less than a minute when Gilbert, alerted perhaps by his own closed-circuit television system, came through the porch and joined me. The diffidence of his manner struck me afresh.

'So you made no headway. I'm deducing as much from the shortness of the time you spent with her.'

'I'm afraid you're right,' I said, hoping it would be an hour or two before I would have to issue yet another communiqué announcing breakdown of talks.

'I can see now that it was a shot in the dark. But one feels one must have tried everything. I'm sure you understand.'

'Of course.' As an understander of this and that, now, I reflected, there was a tremendous lot to be said for me. 'I'm sorry I couldn't do any good.'

'Don't reproach yourself. The whole thing's a classical Freudian case of a girl seeking her father. Roy's opted out of performing that role, and I'm unfitted for it by nature. Debarred from it, in fact. Each man can only fulfil one or at the most two of the aspects in which he's dealing with a woman, like a husband, a brother, a friend and so on and so forth. I can only be a lover and at times a friend.'

'Yes, I see.'

He seemed uninhibited enough by now. Almost companionably, we sauntered over to a corner of the yard from which the barn, surmounted by an archaic weather-vane, could be glimpsed. The current ill wind would at any rate blow clean away any chance of the structure's being turned into a music laboratory. I speculated whether Kitty, Ashley, Christopher, Ruth, Penny and Gilbert could continue to exist here, visualized the house physically collapsing from neglect, fire or the weight of encroaching vegetation. Not even Gilbert, I felt, could stave off something of the sort.

'What are you going to do?' I asked him.

His face flickered with distress or vexation. 'What can anyone do? I shall continue to try, I suppose. But there comes a time when the will to try begins to disappear. You can't make your whole life out of being unselfish.'

'No indeed. But I hope you'll hang on here long enough to see her through the next few weeks or however long it's going to take.'

He was about to reply when I heard the porch door shut. Kitty had appeared, all dolled up in a bottle-green trouser-suit with frilly damson-coloured shirt, long gloves and what might have been a slightly undersized beach-umbrella, not to speak of well-applied artifices above the neck. I took all this in, marvelling at the promptitude with which it had been assembled, while she instructed Gilbert about Ashley's homecoming, the Furry Barrel's tea and such matters. She did so briskly and without self-consciousness, or with only as much as was appropriate, and inevitable, in a woman being efficient to a male audience. Neither then, nor during our walk to the pub (past, among other buildings, an old people's home from which old people stared resentfully out at us), nor while we lunched among horse-brasses and shopkeepers, nor on the taxi journey through Hendon, Swiss Cottage and farther did she relapse into paraded bravery. She came out with sound forgettable stuff about Christopher's tribulations at his university, the Common Market, whether she ought to take up Ouspenskyism again and when was I going to bring this new girl of mine along for her to meet. I was tempted to regard the impeccable smoothness of this part as further evidence of earlier insincerity, until I saw that what I was really doing was refusing to give her credit or sympathy however she might behave: not a very nice response from a supposed friend. So I started trying harder, but had hardly done more than start when she started acting like somebody summoning up courage for something.

'What is it, Kitty?'

'Douglas dear, please don't think I've gone off my head, but could I possibly ask you to do me one more teeny favour?'

'What is it? I mean of course I will.'

'I know you're tremendously reliable and careful and dependable, but I would feel just that bit easier in my silly old mind if you could have the patience to ring that number again and make absolutely certain that it is, you know, her at the other end. So that I can be sure my letter gets to her, you see.'

'Oh. Yes. Yes, all right.'

Two minutes later, in a telephone box somewhere on the edge of Bayswater, I went through the Fred routine a second time, with the same results as before. Ringing off, I noticed that the call-box telephone and the distant telephone were on the same exchange, a feat of observation that would have been no feat at all in those primeval days when exchanges had had letters instead of figures and so immediately advertised their whereabouts. This, and other matters, set me thinking. Back in the taxi, I said to Kitty,

'She's there all right. And I'm coming with you.'

'Please yourself, my dear, but there's no more to do there than at any other dressmaker's.'

'She may not be on her own, and even if she is you could probably do with a bit of support.'

'At my dressmaker's?'

'You should have put in some work on your dressmaker earlier. A witness might come in handy. How far away is it?'

'Two streets down. You are brilliant to have worked it out.'

'What are you thinking of doing exactly?' I asked when she had spoken to the driver.

'Well, I want to have a look at her is the first thing. Find out what sort of creature it is that's doing this to us all. And then just try to tell her what she is doing, make her see – you know what Roy is, he could have told her I'm running about with a millionaire or anything. If I could make her see . . .'

'Having a look at her you'll probably manage, but I wouldn't bank on getting through much of the rest. But good luck, anyway.'

Ideas of Sylvia and of squalor had become so firmly linked in my mind that nothing about her immediate neighbourhood could have surprised me: a razor-fight in full swing in the street outside, children crapping and giving themselves fixes on the steps, recumbent meths-drinkers cluttering up the threshold. In the event the pair of us walked unhindered along a passage abounding in potted greenery and entered a lift.

'Flat 6,' said Kitty, consulting a scrap of paper and pressing a knob. 'Gilbert is marvellous, you know. He ought to be some colossally high-powered secretary kind of person, not fooling about with . . . Still, I'm sure he's good at that too and I expect he enjoys it.'

She looked charged up: pink-cheeked and square-shouldered, genu-inely intent on whatever was to come. When we got out of the lift, she marched straight to the relevant doorway and pushed the bell-push with a flourish. Ruffianly ululation sounded faintly from within, then, after quite a short interval, sprang into grievous volume as the door opened. Sylvia looked dully out at us.

'Hallo, Sylvia,' I said briskly, moving forward with my hand on Kitty's elbow – 'I was just passing so I thought I'd drop up as they say and see how you were getting on and while I was about it I saw no reason why I shouldn't give you a chance to meet someone you must have heard a lot about. Lady Vandervane.'

First score to the goodies: I had driven both females before me into what could with some reason be called a sitting-room, in that evidence of its use for eating, sleeping, and other personal activities and states, though present, was on the whole minor, random. It might also have served as a music-room, if indeed the gramophone, loud enough at this range to drown out anything much short of a piercing scream, had not certainly been wired up to reject actual music. Rather to my surprise, Sylvia went and turned off the amplifier.

'What do you want?' she asked.

As Kitty, using what was for her a measured tone, began to go through the themes she had just outlined to me, Sylvia sat down on the arm of a couch. This, like much of the other furniture, looked new and battered at the same time, as if somebody wearing football boots had set about it immediately after its delivery. I also took in some posters (including a large and well-produced one of a bare bottom), a cardboard box holding perhaps a hundred light-bulbs, a pie-dish full of pennies and threepenny bits, and an overall version of the smell I had noticed the first time I met Sylvia. Nothing else, apart from the long, multi-buttoned house-coat kind of garment she was wearing. It looked fairly clean.

'I'm appealing to you.' Kitty had got into her stride by now. 'It's all I can do. I've nothing to fight with, no bribe to offer. I can only ask you to realize the unhappiness you'll be bringing four people who've never hurt you.'

'Which are they?'

'Roy's two children, our own child, and myself.'

'You aren't including him, then.'

'That's not for me to say.'

'No, that's right. Well, from the way he talks about his life at home, I can't see he gives a sod for any of you, so I don't see why I should.'

'That's not true,' I said. 'He—'

'Please, Douglas,' said Kitty, and Sylvia said, 'Belt up.' Both spoke absently and without turning their heads.

'And don't come on so strong, Lady Vandervane. Don't try and queen it over me. You're not on camera now, you know. Just talk ordinary, if you can. What else have you got?'

Kitty toned down the queening straight away. 'All right, I suppose there's no reason why you should care about me, but think of the children.'

'I am. I've met one of them, and you can put her through a mincing-machine for all I care. The others I've never even seen, so screw them too.'

'If you can't see it or feel it, I can't make you.'

'No, that's right. Actually I can see it fairly well, and I can even feel it a bit, but not enough to make any odds.'

'Not even about a child of six whose father's going off and leaving him?'

'Well, he'll still have you, of course. And he'll need you more after Roy's gone, so that'll help you use up some of your time, won't it?'

With a fully advertised but (I thought) laudable effort, Kitty kept her temper at this. 'Can't I even ask you to go on . . . being with Roy, see as much as you like of him, but not go off with him, not take him away?'

'Sure you can ask. Why not?'

'I beg you, I implore you to think about it. I shared Roy with his first wife for two years, and believe me it's not so bad. You could—'

'That was because you knew you were winning,' said Sylvia in a reasonable tone. 'If he doesn't come away with me now, that'd mean I'm losing, and I don't like doing that. I'm not having that.'

'*Please.*' Kitty was crying and clasping her hands on the crook of her umbrella, making me afraid she might go down on her knees. 'He could live with you and just come and see us at week-ends. Say every other week-end. Surely that's not much to ask. Could you . . . could you think about it?'

'Yeah. I'll think about it.'

'Oh, thank you, thank you.'

'You're welcome, you're welcome. Right, I've thought about it. The answer's no.'

Sylvia laughed when she said this. As was easy enough for anybody who had met her for more than a few minutes, I had been expecting something of the sort, but the reality was quite enough to make me swear inwardly not to do any laughing in company for a bit without first thinking over how it would sound. Kitty started back as if struck, or like somebody well used to meeting the phrase in print.

'Do you love him?' she asked loudly.

'Yeah.' Sylvia considered. 'Yeah, I think so. I don't know much about loving people, never had a lot to do with it, but . . . Yeah.'

'You're not . . . capable of loving!'

'Maybe I'm not – you could have a point there. But then maybe I am too. But anyway, it doesn't matter, that side of it, does it? Whatever I'm like he prefers me to you, and that's why he's leaving you and going off with me, and that's all there is to it. He wants to and I want to, so that's what we'll do.'

The renewed reasonableness of Sylvia's behaviour looked and sounded real, just that touch more real than Kitty's style could ever have encompassed. An impartial witness of their exchanges would probably have been sympathizing with Sylvia most of the time, provided he was ignorant of English. This qualification dwindled slightly in importance when Kitty said, with maximum voice and face and body,

'It's all so unbelievable. Now that I know the sort of person you are, I'm quite frankly incredulous. What could any man of the remotest intelligence or taste or discrimination see in you?'

'Oh, for God's sake let's go,' I said.

'Oh, that's easy,' said Sylvia. 'I'll show you.'

She drew the house-coat over her head and dumped it on the couch. Underneath she was wearing a brassiere and short knickers, not quite as clean as the coat, and these too she quickly removed. Kitty showed genuine consternation. I have no idea what I showed. Only one thing about Sylvia's body was clear to me: I could have no views on its beauty or health or likeness or unlikeness to others, because it was surmounted by Sylvia's head and face and because it belonged to Sylvia, but I could see (perhaps simply was aware) that it was a young body. For all I knew, Kitty's might carry no signs of age and even be better at all points, properly considered; still, I was quite clear in my mind that nothing of that sort could be of the least help to her now. At the same time, I felt a kind of surge of theoretical homosexuality pass through me.

'That's what he sees in me,' said Sylvia. 'Now get out of here, you old *buhg*, before I go hard on you.'

She advanced on Kitty, who swung her umbrella; a mistake, for any umbrella, though a potentially dangerous lance, is an ineffective club. Sylvia easily fended off the blow, and the two closed with each other. I came out of my lethargy, or put away my distaste for the prospect of touching Sylvia, and moved to intervene. She brought her knee up into my crotch, upon which I retired from the conflict for perhaps half a minute, listening vaguely to sounds of struggle and to cries of outrage from Kitty. Then somebody fell over; I looked up by degrees to see Kitty mostly flat on her back with Sylvia kneeling on some of her. So matters rested for a few more seconds, until Sylvia, whose head had been moving this way and that, evidently caught sight of what I made out as a fat lump of abstract sculpture, about the size of a human skull and done in some veined stone, a yard or so away from her on a low table. She swayed about on her knees as she tried to reach it without allowing Kitty freedom to move. I straightened myself, stepped forward and grasped Sylvia's forearm in both hands. After a quick, vigorous pull and turn I released her, remembering even in that moment having noticed both the wrestler with the German name and the Thing from Borneo use this move with telling effect on the night of the favour. Sylvia did a brief sidelong dash across the room and hit the wall. She was starting to climb to her feet from where she had fallen when, having grabbed Kitty and her umbrella, I got the two of us out of the room and then the flat. The lift was waiting.

'Are you all right?'

'Yes.' I shut the inner gate and pressed the ground-floor button. 'Very nearly. What about you?'

'I don't know. How do I look?'

She spoke dreamily. Her clothes were disordered but apparently undamaged; her hair was in modified madwoman's style; there were shallow parallel grazes across her forehead with a little blood, already drying; a large red patch and a small red patch stood out on her left cheek. I put my hands on hers, which were gripping the umbrella.

'You look as though you've been in a bit of a fight. Nothing out of the way. What would you sort of like to happen now? Cup of tea? Do you want to go to a Ladies?'

'Just the car.'

We went to the car. Inside it, Kitty sat back and sighed repeatedly while I held her hand and reflected that, for the second time that day, I had experienced a good deal in a short space, more so than could be rendered by any mere operatic image: the best of Dracula, Franken-stein highlights were fair approximations. After a couple of minutes, Kitty started putting herself in order. Her movements were lethargic. Normally she would be off like a whippet at the first distant shimmers of a shiny nose.

'That girl's mad,' she muttered. 'Stark, staring raving mad.'

'She certainly behaved very oddly.'

'Imagine her . . . stripping off like that.'

'Yes, extraordinary.'

'What could she have thought she was doing?'

'I know.'

'You do realize she'd have killed me if you hadn't pulled her off, don't you, Douglas?'

'Oh, I doubt it.'

'I tell you she'd gone crazy. She was berserk. She'd have bashed my head in if she'd had the chance.'

I went on doubting it, but inwardly, and without great conviction or interest. Inwardly too, I assured myself that, however loathsome the episode in that flat and however boring Kitty's appraisals of it, I must endure until she had had the chance to talk herself back to normal (or somewhere near one of her norms) as she worked on her face and hair. This she finally began to do, her voice strengthening and hands recovering assurance until she was very largely the Kitty of half an hour earlier in both appearance and manner. The manner part of this impressed me as odd at first. To be in even moderately good spirits so soon after the failure (however predictable) of a last hope, with a whacking physical and emotional humiliation thrown in, surely showed abnormal powers of recovery, especially for a woman like Kitty. Then it occurred to me that she had at any rate done something, struck a blow, survived an encounter with a naked madwoman, given herself something to think about, taken action after a long spell of inaction: and before a longer one. It further occurred to me that very few men would take her on while that meant taking Ashley on as well, and that she would not be free of him until he was twenty or so (if ever), and that by then she would be nearly sixty. I wished that Ashley would meet with a fatal but painless, or not too painful, accident. Something of that sort, not necessarily on that scale, would do Roy no harm, either.

'Where can I drop you, Douglas dear?'

'I thought my flat, if it's not too far out of your way.'

'No, it's right on my way.' She again spoke to the driver.

'On your way where?'

'Home. Or rather to the house I live in.'

The buoying-up effect of the Sylvia exploit had passed, at any rate for the time being. I got the cinematic war-widow all the way to Maida Vale. Her last words to me were,

'Dearest Douglas, I wish I could thank you enough for being such a tower of strength, such an absolute rock. I know it's too ghastly for you, but do come up and see me again soon. Meanwhile, you're not to worry about me. I'll be . . . I'll be fine. Really and truly, I promise you. Strange, the way one finds strength in oneself one didn't know was there.'

I heard my telephone ringing as I climbed the stairs, and climbed faster, failing to find strength in myself that I could pretty well have sworn was there. I picked up the handset and said my name. A huge cough came down the wire.

'Albert,' I said. 'How are you?'

'Terrible,' replied Coates. 'Look, Doug, that business you asked me to keep an eye on.'

'The old maestro.'

'That's the one. Well, nothing definite as yet, but your and my favourite shit has asked for all the griff about him.'

'Griff?'

'Christ, the file, the clippings, the stuff from what you'd probably call the morgue. My guess would be that your chum's booked as the first and probably the last of a controversial new series of profiles, Half-Witted Cunts of Our Time. I can't see what else it could be.'

'Thanks, Albert. Would you let me know if you get anything more definite?'

'Delighted. Anyway, see you Thursday.'

'Yes, I suppose so.'

## Six

## Christian Gentleman

The next morning, Sunday, I telephoned the Vandervane house to see how Kitty was. Or so I would have put it if challenged. An unassessed portion of my motive was the same old irresistible (and averagely vulgar) curiosity. Very much as on an earlier occasion, I got Gilbert and wordless yelling at the same time, then Gilbert on his own.

'Kitty's in bed,' he told me. 'Sleeping.'

'Don't disturb her. Is she all right?'

'Naturally she's not all right. Would you seriously expect her to be all right?'

'I was just asking. I meant is she ill or anything.'

'That's tantamount to a meaningless query. Perhaps you'd care to give me a concise definition of illness.'

'I'll drop everything and work on it. Look, Mr Alexander, I simply don't care how righteous you are, or how learned and sophisticated either. If you can bring yourself to tell Kitty I telephoned, that's fine. If not—'

'I'm sorry, Mr Yandell, I'm being affected by the atmosphere of strain under which we're all living. Of course I'll deliver your message. Hold on, please.'

Sounds like an argument in a deep dungeon reached my ear; I assumed Gilbert had put his hand over the mouthpiece. Then Roy came on the line.

'Hi, you old bastard, how goes it? In particular, how are your balls? I hear they took a knock yesterday. Very nasty,' – a sound pre-emptive approach, this, treating the whole episode as worthy of nothing more than brotherly concern for me dressed up as jocularity.

'They seem to be holding up all right, thanks. How are yours?'

'Aching rather in a metaphorical way. Gus is beginning to shag me out. I've got the bloody choirs coming in next week to rehearse the Eighth. If you had any conception . . .'

He talked at some length about his involvement with Mahler, then asked for and perhaps listened to information about Terry Bolsover, whose interview with him must be impending. With this behind us, he said rapidly,

'Oh, by the way, Duggers . . .'

Thus forewarned of the approach of his reason for talking to me, I started getting my diary out.

'. . . I was wondering if you were doing anything tomorrow lunch-time.'

'What I am not doing is going anywhere with you and Sylvia.'

'Oh, nothing like that.' He laughed slightly. 'The point is, old lad, your pal Harold Meers wants to have a little chat with me. He seemed very keen to pim me down: rang me up last night and pressured me into this date tomorrow. Into agreeing to it provisionally, that is. So I could make sure you were free first. Anyway, are you? I was just going to ring when—'

'Yes, I am, but where do I come into this? He's not going to want me there. He'd sooner—'

'I know it's a lot to ask, but I would very much like to have some-one along to bat for my side. Outnumber him. Christ knows what he's got up his sleeve.'

'Yes, Harold needs a bit of outnumbering. But I don't see why he should—'

'That fits in with what I hear of him. No, actually, when I said I'd probably be bringing a friend he said more or less the more the merrier. Funny sort of sod. I suppose he just saw he wanted to talk to me and I didn't want to talk to him, so being on a whichever it is market I imagine I could have insisted on bringing the World Cup soccer team along without him being able to—'

'He'd have drawn the line a long way short of that, however keen he is to see you. Unless you agreed in advance to pick up the bill.'

'Near bugger, eh? That's worth knowing. Be fun watching him trying to buy me off with thirty quid and his stamp album.'

'I don't think that'll be his approach. And I was going to say he'll probably draw the line at me too. Still, if I just turn up . . .'

'Oh, I told him it was you and he sounded as pleased as Punch. Punch with a hangover, perhaps, but manful as hell. By all means and all that.'

'Strange. I thought he hated the sight of me. But then he probably doesn't care for the sight of anybody much.'

'There again his daughter goes along with you. It would do you good to hear her on the subject. Draw the two of you together.'

'Has she got any ideas on what he's up to?'

'I haven't been able to get her to discuss it seriously. At all, in fact. Anyway, I'm meeting him at the Retrenchment Club at one o'clock. If you pitch up at Craggs's about twelve thirty we can have a fortifying noggin of something and walk down. Okay?'

I said it would be, rang off, and did my best to dismiss from my mind the consideration that Roy ought not to cut tomorrow morning's rehearsal short by the fifty or so minutes necessary for him to be able to keep his rendezvous with me. Failing in the attempt, I went back to where Vivienne was sitting up in bed reading the *Observer*. She wore a white nightdress that would have done very well for Norma in Bellini's opera, granted a rather traditionally conceived production, and a woollen jacket in pink and green, with hanging bobbles, that would have done very well for nobody but her. As soon as I appeared, she picked up and drank from a cup of (by now, surely, no better than) lukewarm coffee. She meant by this to stress the fact that she was finishing a leisurely breakfast and studying the latest news in what merely happened to be a bedroom, just as her attire proclaimed that she was doing these things in what was quite incidentally a bed. So much was her standard practice. But then, with a preoccupied yet antagonistic air, her eyes making wide sweeps over the print, she said,

'Did you get hold of your friend?'

'No. And she isn't my friend.' Out of what had seemed prudence, wanting to get my story in before (say) the irruption of Sylvia in talkative mood, I had divulged something of the previous day's events and the run-up to them – a positively Royesque misjudgement that all my insistence on Kitty's age, not-my-cup-of-teaness and down-stagey goings-on had done little to retrieve. 'Well, she is a friend, of course, but not in the way you mean, as I keep telling you.'

'Who were you on to all that time, then?'

'Only old Roy.'

'What's he up to now?'

'Nothing in particular. He asked me to lunch with him tomorrow.'

'You're not going?'

'Of course I'm going. Why shouldn't I?'

'But you said you were coming with me to see my father in the evening.'

'I still am. That's in the evening.'

'H'm,' she very nearly literally said.

'What do you mean, h'm? I'll be on the spot when you turn up here, sober, undrugged, and unimpaired by any form of sexual indulgence.'

To this, she said nothing in a marked manner, but differently marked from the one she had been using for the last three-quarters of a minute. I picked up the *Sunday Times* magazine section and started reading about poverty and oppression in British Honduras. Vivienne was reading on with equal attention, for after a few moments she said,

'Doug, what's a . . . ? I can't even pronounce it. Something about . . .'

I dropped Honduras and went over to her. My more direct route being blocked by her breakfast tray and the chair it rested on, I made my approach via my side of the bed. Our shoulders touched.

'Where?'

'Here.'

She was holding the paper in a rather awkward position, low down and close to her, so that I had to lean some way across to get a view of the paragraph she was pointing to. As I did so, I noticed at close range, but in adequate focus, that the front of the bed-jacket had fallen apart and that a nipple was protruding from inside the Norma-style nightdress.

'A psephologist is a man who knows about elections,' I said, stumbling a little over the last word and taking off my glasses.

'Oh, darling . . .'

The remainder of the day passed pleasantly enough. No further mention of my friend was made, a reticence I did my bit to sustain by not asking after the other bloke. We parted after confirming arrangements for the following evening. I began the week's work with Weber, with actual physical addition to the words I had already written about him. After two hours and not quite a page of that, I switched to filling in some of the background – some of its remoter, mistier sections – that I might need for my sleeve-notes on the Mozart sonatas. Midday came at last; I put my books back on the shelves and made off.

There was a lot of sun in Maida Vale and down Edgware Road. It shone on girls by the hundred, girls with prominent bosoms, prominent hips, prominent faces. A man like Coates would have said (I was nearly sure I had heard him say) that the fine weather brought them out, dismissing the knottier question of where they were the rest of the time. I knew better. Today's contingent, at any rate, had been brought out by Roy, and not just in the sense that the always close connection between the subject of Roy and the subject of girls had sharpened my eyes; perhaps not in that sense at all, for I had noticed no sudden corresponding increase in the number of anti-American demonstrations or advertisements for Scotch. Most likely what was at work on me was nothing more than the usual tonic effect of going to see Roy. How unfair, I reflected as I walked along Piccadilly, that that sort of effect should so often be absent, if not actually inverted, when it came to meeting far worthier persons. But surely divine mercy was in operation too: except where music was concerned, no one in quest of worth would ever go anywhere near Roy.

I reached Craggs's. While I waited for the porter to finish doing something to a telephone switchboard at the far side of his emplacement, my eye fell on a notice saying that the Wine Committee had acquired a number of bottles of Dom Perignon 1959 and was in a position to offer them to members at £4 each; limit, 1 doz. per member. Below was a column of signatures of those wishing to avail themselves of the opportunity, with the quantity desired, and Roy Vandervane's name – 1 doz. – led all the rest. I found something incongruous in this placing, but only until I realized that I was not, after

all, looking at the correspondence page of a newspaper, where alpha-
betical arrangement saw to it that Roy seldom came higher than last
but one of a number attacking exploitation of immigrant labour in
California or proposed increases in the price of school meals.

In due time, I found Roy in the *Punch* and *Who Was Who* nook with
an opened bottle of champagne (not the Dom Perignon) and two
glasses in front of him. He was wearing what could have been called
a suit if the jacket had had visible pockets, and the tendency of his
hair to seem an inch longer every time I saw him had been checked,
if not reversed. Was this show of conventionality put on to conciliate
Harold? Full morning-dress, with grey topper, white spats and ebony
walking-stick, would hardly be adequate for that job.

Roy looked ill at ease, though not gloomy. When we were drinking
he asked me if I had any ideas on what Harold might have in store
for him. I told him roughly what Coates had told me two days earlier
(and had had nothing to add to when rung up an hour before).

'Does he really think I give a fart what a rag like that – sorry,
Duggers – says about me? He must be losing his touch, if he ever had
one.'

'He had and has one. What dirt can he dig up?'

'Well . . . the previous divorce, and one or two episodes since, I
suppose. But that's all water under the bloody bridge. The only bit
that could embarrass me is the Sylvia bit, and as I said the other day
that's the one thing he can't use. Unless he's gone off his head, of
course.'

'That is a possibility, yes. We'll have to see.'

'All a load of ballocks. Come the first week in September she can
vote – not a right I can see her exercising much, admittedly – and she
can marry who she likes,' he said, pouring me more champagne with
a casual and yet intent air.

'You're the one who's off his head, talking of saying things the
other day. She can't marry you whatever—'

'Because I'm married to someone else, remember? as the Yanks
say. I do wish they wouldn't, don't you? Kitty's agreed to a divorce if
I ask her for one, with full co-operation, naturally, because that makes
me seem more of a shit. QC buddy of mine tells me that means you

can squeeze the whole thing into about four months. And there's a change in the law coming along that'll cut it down to half that. Anyway . . .'

'Yes, anyway. Say you do marry her, what about Girl, 20? What about wanting to get away from normal, decent, God-fearing sex? What about ringing up the paraffin man? What about going down?'

'Yes, I know. But it'll take—'

'It won't hold her to you – you realize that? If she wants to be off she'll be off whether she's married to you or not.'

'There I disagree. It'll take her some time to get browned off with being Lady Vandervane and wife of controversial musician and maverick political figure Roy Vandervane. Without knowing she's going to have that, she'd be away tomorrow. As it is, I think I can probably reckon on a couple of years and that's a bloody long time when you get to my age. Not after it's over; it'll seem like about six weeks then; but from here it looks a lot, I can assure you.'

'Oh, good. But what about Girl, 20?'

'There is that. You get that. But as regards the going-down side of life, it'll have to be Girl, 50 if the point comes up. I couldn't take Girl much under that. I love Sylvia, but one of her's enough.'

'Is it worth all the mess, for a couple of years?'

'How would I know?'

'She's terrible.'

'Yes, I know that. You should have been in the pub the other evening, one of these places where they keep a bloody great tower of pennies on the counter for the blind or something. About ten thousand of the buggers, I imagine, colossally heavy, but she managed to knock most of them off on to the floor. Ankle-deep, and over a surprisingly wide area, too.'

'You mean on purpose.'

'Well, it's hard to say. On purpose or not on purpose doesn't come in much when you're dealing with her. She did tell me afterwards that one of the chaps behind the bar said something about her to the other one.'

'What?'

'She couldn't hear what, but she could tell it was about her.'

'And uncomplimentary.'

'Or complimentary, as the case may be.'

'You're going about with her openly these days, then?'

'More or less. There doesn't seem much point in not. In a way there never was, I suppose, but a couple of months ago I didn't really know what turn things were going to take. Not really. Part of getting older, Duggers, old lad, is doing more and more of those things which we do not want to do, and leaving undum more and more of those things which we want to do. Because there are fewer and fewer people round the place to do them with.'

Roy poured the rest of the champagne. I visualized the wedding reception, to which he would invite me, and which I would attend, and at which he would be wearing either morning-dress (probably minus white spats) or a boiler-suit, according to mood, and in the course of which Lady Vandervane II would perform the ceremony of cutting the cake before pelting the guests with it and setting about them with the knife. The picture depressed me, to the point at which I could not find the energy to administer the supplementary verbal drubbing Roy probably felt he ought to have. After two or three minutes of silence we drained our glasses and left, still in silence.

Outside, I started to turn down the hill in the direction of the Retrenchment Club, but Roy prevented me.

'I've got the car here,' he said.

'Just as quick to walk, surely.'

'I don't like leaving it where it is. May need to make a quick getaway, too.'

The real reason for this trifling change of plan came into view (without for the moment defining itself) when I saw, pasted inside the rear window of the car, a printed strip saying SUPPORT RHODESIA and next to it a fairly efficiently hand-lettered one saying AND SOUTH AFRICAN APARTHEID. I decided immediately that it would be more rewarding to allow the explanation to emerge rather than to demand it on the spot; I could always ask later if necessary. While Roy was taking out his keys, I noticed the same exhortation on the windscreen. He got in, unlocked the nearside door and put on his head a bowler hat that had been lying on the passenger's seat. I still held my peace.

We left the alley in which the car had been parked at perhaps forty miles an hour, causing a van and a taxi to brake violently. Roy blew his horn and shouted and shook his fist at them. He did more of the same when we reached the corner of Piccadilly just as the amber light appeared under the red, and lowered his window to shout and shake his fist to better effect as we swept past a knot of pedestrians who, far from making any move to cross in front of him, showed every sign of being prepared to remain indefinitely where they were. Hooting steadily, he changed lanes several times, and with some risk, as we covered the short stretch along to Duke Street. Here he resumed his policy towards pedestrians, stepped it up, rather, while we negotiated the turn at a speed that gave him the opportunity of singling out individuals for abuse. None of them showed the least irritation or disquiet at these onslaughts, only incomprehension. Between times, I could sense Roy glancing at me as I sat beside him displaying lively interest in everything around me except what he was doing. When the Jermyn Street lights halted us, I studied the goods in the windows of Fortnum & Mason's and Roy blew his horn. He stopped doing that at the sight of a nearby policeman, who approached, ran his eye over the windscreen sticker (with a hint of distaste, I thought), and spoke in at Roy's open window.

'Would you pull into the kerb, please, sir?'

I foresaw a confrontation with the forces of repression being substituted for my lunch, but Roy did as he was told in silence.

'You seemed to be getting a little impatient, sir.'

'Yes, I'm sorry, officer, but I was in a great hurry for a most urgent appointment.'

'These signal lights, like all others that I know of, are operated by a combination of mechanical and electrical systems, and are unaffected by the sound of any horn. May I see your driving licence, sir?'

Roy handed it over without a word. The policeman inspected it at length, and also meditatively, as though he would remember this moment all his life, before passing it back.

'I thought I recognized you, Sir Roy. I've seen you several times on television. Now you realize you've been infringing police regulations?'

'Yes, officer, I do realize that, and I'm very sorry.'

'All right, you can get on your way now, but I'd recommend

refraining from excessive use of the horn in future. After all, it's not what one would call good driving manners, is it, sir?'

'No, officer. Thank you.'

We drove off at a sedate speed. When we were coming down into St James's Square, Roy removed his bowler and said,

'Bloody fascist.'

'Why didn't you tell him so?'

'He only let me go because he approved of these bloody slogans.'

'Cock, and why didn't you tell him he was a bloody fascist?'

'Only this lunch. I would have at any other time. No, I suppose I wouldn't, would I? It's this respect for authority that's dinned into us until it becomes a reflex. Conditioned response.'

'And cowardice.'

'Yes, a bit of that, too. Anyway, it isn't time yet for challenging the system direct. This sort of tactic' – he gestured – 'pays off much better as things are.'

'Tactic?'

'Oh, socialist camp! The negative demonstration. You pretend to be one of the other side behaving crappily, or rather behaving as they actually would if they felt strong enough. Not a new idea, but I think I'm the first in the field with this particular application. I'm going to bring it up with the Anti-Racialiss Solidarity Executive. Just having the thing parked here in the middle of Clubland, saying what it says, will make some people angry in a useful way.'

He had parked the thing within a few yards of the space it had occupied the last time we had met in Craggs's, the day Penny had asked to be helped. Helped. What an idea. As we walked towards Pall Mall, I said,

'I should have thought most of the people using this square would be more likely to be cheered up by seeing that somebody powerful enough to own that sort of car agrees with them.'

'People like that don't notice anything unless it's rammed in front of their noses. Often not even then.'

'Oh, I see.'

'And you probably wouldn't know, but you don't have to be all that powerful to own that sort of car.'

The uncharacteristic malice here showed that I had registered a hit. Good. Well, goodish. Was Roy going off his head in more than a manner of speaking? As if in answer to my thought (or rather, I was sure, actually and quite non-uncharacteristically and reassuringly in answer to it) he burst into one of his bursts of offensive song while we were crossing the road.

> 'Thah cawl shuh-eeds ahv eveneeng thahr mahn-tahl wahr uh-
> spraddeeng,
> Ahnd Mayoree, ahl smoileeng, wahs uh-leestneeng tah me . . .'

This, being delivered *molto largamente*, lasted until we were well on to the far pavement, and excited the interest of an eminent Soviet-ologist who was coming down the steps of the Voyagers' Club. Roy waved to him, deriving added power by grasping the forearm of the waving hand with the free hand and shaking it violently.

'Another bloody fascist,' he said to me jocularly, or in some way that half explained song and wave, perhaps also negative demonstra-tion, possibly much more, as exercises designed to work off anxiety, divert it, outface it. 'Think how many fascists and bastards in general', he added in similar vein on the threshold of the Retrenchment, 'have passed through these portals.'

'I thought fascists and bastards in general were interchangeable.'

'You did? You're coming on. Right. That champagne at Craggs's is bloody good stuff. Lead on to the fascist and bastard in general of the day.'

We had entered a room several times the size of the house I occu-pied half of, opulent, classical and also strongly ecclesiastical in feeling, like an early Christian emperor's orgy chamber. Soberly dressed men in twos and threes straggled across a marble floor to a battered tin cart from which drinks were unhurriedly being dispensed. Roy led the way to the rear of this queue.

'Hadn't we better inquire for him?' I asked.

'Bugger that. This was his idea. Let him find us.'

He did when we were about halfway to the drinks cart. First he and Roy, then he and I, nodded at each other. Harold's second nod led without a break into a glance at his watch.

'Time's getting on,' he said. 'This confounded insistence on ice in everything. A lot of stuff piled up. Do you mind if we have a drink at the table?'

'No, I'd like that,' said Roy. 'But I'd like one here first as well, if I may.'

Harold turned to me. 'What about you?'

He was mistaken if he thought Roy would bow to an adverse casting vote, as also if he expected me to declare against my principal in the smallest particular. 'I must say I'd rather like one, too.'

'You mean here as well as at the table?'

'Yes, if that's all right.'

After another, slower nod, Harold walked briskly away and out of one of the corners of the room.

'Well played, Duggers. First round to us.'

'Do you think it's a good idea to annoy him unnecessarily?'

'Yes. And anyway this is necessarily.'

We got our drinks, but it was a technical triumph only. Harold came back as they were handed us, declined one himself, paid, and stood in silence rather more than a yard off. Although Roy defended stoutly by gossiping to me about musicians and others Harold would not have known even by name, the three of us were in the dining-room after a bare ten minutes. A good half of it was occupied by a central table covered from edge to edge with dishes of cold food that not only were clearly untouched but seemed also inviolable, as at some metropolitan form of harvest festival. We skirted all this and sat down in a corner under a full-length portrait of a duke or other nobleman who, whether or not he had been a fascist, certainly looked the nonpareil of a bastard in general. Menus were before us, and an order pad, complete with carbon paper and uncapped ballpoint pen, lay ready at Harold's side. He led off without hesitation, wrote minutely on the pad and muttered (for publication, so to speak, rather than to himself),

'Tomato salad. Steak and kidney pie. Marrow and French beans.'

I noticed that all these items appeared on the clipped-in sheet on which the set lunch, a remarkably cheap package as it appeared to me, was laid out. I said I would have the same, and Harold wrote accordingly. Roy was finding it more difficult to come to a decision, frowning and cocking his head in a style he might have learnt from his wife. Finally he said,

'Tomato salad . . . yes. Then . . . I think duckling and orange sauce. And a green salad.'

'Three tomato salads,' Harold made an emendation on the pad. 'Duckling and . . . Where do you see that?'

'Over here,' said Roy with some force, hitting his finger at the à la carte section of the menu.

'Oh. Oh, over there. Duckling,' said Harold, in the tone, abruptly assumed, of a fanatical vegetarian. He made no move to write.

Roy swept his hand across his front as if cutting off a final chord. 'Could I change my mind?'

'By all means.'

'I'd like a whole lobster, please, cold, and stuffed with, uh, a portion of caviare. And a green salad, as I said.'

'All I'm thinking of is the time. It wouldn't be lined up like uh, for instance, the steak and kidney pie.'

'They'll be lined up separately, the lobster and the caviare, and there's no need for the chaps in the kitchen to do the actual stuffing. Get the doings brought to me and I'll stuff it myself.'

Harold gave up at that point. He took Roy's request for a preludial double champagne cocktail without overt demur, and made only a token stand by recommending the carafe Chablis. Roy said he found cheap white wines gave him acidity, and chose something with a long name from the wine list. All this Harold received with continuing absence of both good and bad grace, in fact with his habitual lack of reaction to events, reinforced, I fancied, with an unpropitious confidence in whatever weapon he had devised against Roy. The food and drink arrived with a speed that told either of unusual efficiency or of a long history of browbeating on Harold's part. While Roy was ladling out his caviare, Harold gave him a look that answered for me the slightly difficult question why the parties were facing each other here rather than somewhere private. If Roy proved to be restrained by his surroundings from acting up, losing his temper, perhaps physically assaulting his much weaker adversary, well and good; if not, there were very few places where any such misbehaviour would damage Roy more severely than in the crowded dining-room of the Retrenchment Club. Against my inclination, my respect for Harold rose: he knew how false were Roy's claims to despise the kind of society represented by what lay around us. He poured wine; then, with his eyes still on Roy, he took from his breast pocket a folded sheaf of typescript he did not at once open.

'Let's come to the point. You're an unsuitable companion for my daughter and would be a more than unsuitable husband to her. I propose to end the one relationship and prevent the other. For reasons I won't go into, my daughter's beyond my control. As recently perhaps as ten years ago, before the final disintegration of family ties and the whole network of duties and obedience and so on that went with them, I could have stopped this nonsense by stopping her. But now, wherever I sent her she'd break out and go back to you. Thanks to what you and your kind have done. The only place she'd be safe, that's to say comparatively safe, though God knows what with all the nitwitted boohooing about society being to blame and we mustn't brutalize the poor dears they seem to be able to walk out whenever they . . .'

Harold pulled himself up. 'I did seriously consider prison for her. Possession of marijuana. Nothing to it. But even if she didn't get away with a ten-bob fine and being told not to do it again for a week or two, if it wouldn't inconvenience her too much . . . Anyway, she'd have involved you. Medium-sized scandal. That would have injured you, which was a bloody good idea, but then the whole thing would have been out in the open and I'd have lost any hold on either of you. Therefore—'

'I don't get all this about my unsuitability,' said Roy with his mouth full. 'I can support her a bloody sight better than any of the little – any of the youngsters she was running round with when I met her. The age business doesn't matter. You're letting your dislike of my politics interfere with Sylvia's happiness, and that's—'

'I detest your politics, or rather the half-baked mess you call your politics. In the swim and bugger the facts. Sell the country to the Russians. That's nothing to do with it. You're the exact opposite of what my daughter needs. Firmness, common-sense, stability, self-discipline, patience. You're—'

'Save it. What's this point you said you were coming to?'

'I have here a draft of a feature article about you which I shall publish in my newspaper if I ever hear of your having any dealings with my daughter after the lapse of forty-eight hours from this moment. Let me give you some idea of the contents.' Harold unfolded the typescript. 'The Generation Gap.'

'Oh, Christ on a bloody great bicycle,' said Roy, forking in lobster.

'Leading figures of today as seen by their sons.'

Roy stopped chewing.

'I Love Me is Father's Slogan, says Chris Vandervane, 20, son of, well, we know all about that. Brief run-through of your musical attainments and the political stuff. Deadpan. Nothing snide. No need for it in view of what comes later. We do rather stress your involvement with the cause of youth, understanding of it, sympathy with it. But so would you. Before we go on, the lawyers have been over it. They're a little unhappy with I think it's three phrases, but this is only a first draft. You can take it from me that the final version will be writ-proof. Well, then we go on to your house, and its present occupants, Penny Vandervane, 23, who shares a room with West Indian writer Godfrey Alexander, 24 . . .'

'Gilbert,' said Roy. 'Can I have a brandy?'

Harold made a correction on the typescript. 'Thank you. A brandy. Yes. Yes, certainly. Later, in the coffee-room. Don't you want cheese or a pudding?'

'No thanks. Just a brandy.'

At the door, Roy and I waited while Harold thoroughly counted his change at the pay-desk.

'It's a try-on, Duggers. He wouldn't have the nerve.'

'I hope you're right. I think he would have the nerve if it came to it.'

'Lot of bloody nonsense.'

'Which we've got to pay very close attention to.'

'Little shit.'

The coffee-room was not crowded, but there were quite enough people about to deter Roy from any kind of outburst: not that he seemed so inclined in the least. We found another corner, with, this time, the life-sized statue of a long-defunct prime minister towering over us. It was done in a kind of stone that made its subject seem not so much a man as a man coated from head to foot in whitewash. Coffee arrived, also a large glass holding perhaps a tablespoonful of brandy. Roy simply drained it.

'Now,' said Harold, lighting a knobbly cheroot and reopening the typescript. 'In a way, it's not surprising my father goes for youth, because that's what he's like himself. Not grown up. He's like a kid of ten or even less. I don't know what he's like with his music, I don't know anything about that and I don't want to know, but in everything else all he ever thinks about is getting his own way. He's like little Ashley, that's my half-brother, he's six and absolutely diabolical. If you don't give him what he wants straight away he screams the place down, because nobody's tried to bring him up. Nothing in it for my father, you see. He just gives him expensive toys all the time to keep him quiet.

'Interviewer: How does all this affect the other members of the household?

'My sister thinks the same way as I do. He's always let us do exactly as we like, and we liked that until we realized it was all just less trouble for him. We don't get on much with our stepmother, but you can't really blame her. She's half out of her – no, that bit's cut. He, my father hangs around young people to make himself feel young and feel he's up with the trends. He tries to talk like them and it's pathetic. He thinks they think he's one of them, but they're just waiting for him to go. He thinks they like having him around because he's famous, but they don't take any notice of that. And all these politics, it's just showing off. How can you care about peasants in Vietnam when you give parties with champagne and a couple of blokes in white coats going round pouring it? I don't see that makes you any better than the rich people in Spain and Greece and these places. I asked him about that once and he said it was different, it was the society we lived in and he had a position to keep up. It's always different when he does it. I think rich people ought to mind their own business and leave it to students and workers to get on with changing society and the rest of it.

'Interviewer: You're almost saying you'd have found a stern Victorian parent more to your taste.

'No, I'm not saying that. I'm not in favour of that either. Those sort of people did a lot of harm by building up capitalism and the power structure. But they were doing it for the Empire and the ruling class and their religion, not just for themselves. Not all of it.

'Well, that's the core of the thing. Not very coherent or well expressed, but I think that gives it a certain—'

'You can't print that, Harold,' I said. 'Your lawyers must be—'

'Nobody asked for your view.'

'How much are you paying him to put his name to that?' asked Roy.

'Oh, we haven't discussed a fee yet. Welcomed the chance of getting it off his chest was how he put it.'

'I'll take that along,' said Roy, putting out his hand. He noticed it was shaking and lowered it to the table.

Harold gave him the typescript. 'Yes, you'll want to think it over. I've plenty of copies at the office. Time's getting on. One warning. I was never more serious in my life. Good afternoon to you.'

'It's malicious,' I said to Roy outside.

'Yes, that struck me, too.'

'I mean in the legal sense. It is a try-on. He can't hit you with that.'

'He already has.'

I refrained from telling him he would get over it. Whether he would get over the actual publication of the article was perhaps another matter. Whether Harold would publish it as threatened was yet another. In one important sense he was free to do so: the proprietor of the paper, an elderly and ailing peer, had been living in Malta for five years and for the last two or more of these, according to Coates, had confined his daily reading to *The Times*. Harold was one of the very few men I had ever met with the outlook and temperament to face without hesitation the row, the publicity, the dismissal and the loss of prospects that surely must, or probably would, or easily might follow the performance of what he promised. In fact, the only other man of such a calibre I could think of for the moment was Roy.

Turning up towards the square, Roy glanced to his left, had a proper look and gave a harsh yell like a man in a film taking a spear through the chest. I saw Harold's slight figure, neatly clad in its fawn tweed suit, begin to cross the road in our direction. We hurried on.

'Why's that little shit following us?'

'I'm sure he's not,' I said. 'He's probably parked somewhere up here.'

'If I go ahead there'll be no point in him publishing it.'

'Yes there will. Revenge.'

'A moment ago you said it was a try-on.'

'I've had a bit of time to think. Newspapers don't mind libel actions unless they're going to be the people who lose face. This one would be quite a circulation-builder. And imagine the sort of stuff that would be dragged up in court. Assuming you won, you'd be twenty thousand quid or so in pocket, which you don't need anyway, and worse off in every other respect than if you'd just let it go by. As Harold knows very well. He might be positively hoping you would sue.'

'That boy saying all that. Oh, Christ. Old lad, could you come up to Craggs's for some more brandy? Or sit with me while I drink it?'

'Of course.'

A policeman was standing on the pavement by Roy's car. I soon saw that it was the same policeman as earlier. He was about my age, with springy tufts of whisker on each cheek. I also saw, or fancied I saw, that the car sat unnaturally close to the ground.

'I'm afraid you've had a bit of trouble in your absence, Sir Roy. Somebody's been ripping your tyres. With a knife, it looks like.'

He indicated an inch-long slit in the rubber. Over his bowed back Harold came into view, moving on a course that would bring him within fifty feet of where we stood. Roy leaned forward, bent his knees slightly and came up on his toes in the attitude of a man about to spring at another.

'Little bastards!' he roared. 'Scum of the bloody earth! What a lark, eh? What a romp! Ear we are, Sid, ear's a fuyyin grake car blongin to

167

some fuyyin toff – gish your fuyyin knife an ow fuyyin show im! Gawf! Beezh! Hoogh! Oh, how unimprovably witty and trenchant!'

A youthful couple in a peripatetic semi-embrace, the lad wearing one of his auntie's floppy black velours hats with one of her floral silk scarves looped round the crown, the girl in a sort of lead-foil top and patchwork trousers, had come to a halt within earshot. Harold approached the car next but one to Roy's and took out his keys. The policeman nodded sympathetically.

'Most annoying, Sir Roy. But these window stickers of yours, they would constitute what they call a provocation, don't you think? Not that that's any excuse, of course.'

Roy now noticed and glared at Harold, who was having some difficulty with the lock of his car door, wheeled round on the young-sters with a snarl and a yard-long sweep of the arm that (to my relief) got them moving again, and turned back to the policeman.

'And where were you while this little outbreak of high spirits was going on? Checking on meters and illegal parking, no doubt.'

'These days that kind of thing falls within the province of traffic wardens, Sir Roy. I was on my normal rounds, which brought me here only about a minute before you arrived on the scene. It's unfortunate that I came along too late to do anything about this deplorable act of vandalism.'

As he said this, he caught my eye for the first and only time. His demeanour throughout, and his expression now, were not quite incom-patible with full understanding of the negative demonstration, nor with a desire to tease Roy by suggesting that the law had looked impassively on while a well-known foe of authority was having his tyres slashed. In a slightly more wooden tone than before, the policeman added,

'Mind you, this is a rather special area. London Library, Junior Carlton Club. You can never be quite certain of the sort of people you're going to get.'

Harold's car started. At no stage had he paid the least visible atten-tion to our group. Roy looked up and his frame seemed to sag; I knew what he was remembering. Then he said to the policeman,

'Do you want anything? Like a statement in triplicate or a look at my medical history or . . .'

'No, sir. I was only wondering if I could be of some—'

'Well, you can't. Not of any.'

The policeman touched his helmet respectfully, and went.

'What do we do now?' I asked.

'Christ. What do we do. Well, we go back up to Craggs's and get the porter to sort out this bloody shambles. Then we have some brandy, as advertised. Or I do. Though you're very welcome if you feel like it. Actually, if you look at it in the right way, this business with the tyres is very encouraging. I said it would make chaps angry, didn't I? It just shows that even in the most ruling-class areas there's a real spirit of . . . Taxi!'

# Seven

## Copes's Fork

'How old is he, for instance?' I asked Vivienne that evening.

'You know, it's funny, but he'll never say. Never has. But I suppose he must be sixtyish, something like that.'

'And he lives alone.'

'Ever since my mother died, that's nine years ago now. But my brothers and I, we all go and see him every week. Separately, to spread it out for him. He has lunch at the pub and a woman comes in every week-morning and cooks things for him to warm up at night. She cleans the place as well.'

'What does he so to speak do all the time?'

'Well, this job he has with the religious people takes up the mornings and the odd afternoon. Then he likes music. At least he likes Gilbert and Sullivan and Viennese waltzes and the man who wrote *The Merry Widow* and things. Though I suppose that isn't music according to you.'

'Of course it is. A lot of it's very good.'

'On its level. Isn't that what you say?'

I found this an uncharacteristic remark. 'All right, if you like. But why shouldn't it be music at all according to me?'

'Just the way almost everything everybody else thinks is music you don't think is.'

Except in the bedroom of my flat an hour and more earlier, Vivienne had been allowing rather more sullenness-cum-preoccupation to show than was normal for a Monday. I sensed, however, that she had been genuinely trying to reduce its intensity, instead of having it there and letting me take it or leave it. This was new. But the bus we were on, the third in a fearful series, stopped at the stop we wanted before I could take up the point, and I forgot it altogether at the familiar (but always enlivening) sight of her vigorous march along the pavement and the unfamiliar sight of the attractive tobacco-silk trouser-suit she was wearing.

'It's only a couple of minutes' walk from here.'

'What a nice suit that is, Viv. New, isn't it?'

'Yes, I got it today. Do you realize that's the very first time you've ever said you liked any of my clothes?'

'Sorry. I just . . .'

'That's all right.' She took my arm. 'I always feel a bit, you know, hoping everything's going to go off smoothly the first time I bring somebody along. It always does, but you always think it might not.'

Here it would have been natural for me to ask her reason for bringing me along, but, as on all the previous occasions when the problem had come up in my mind, I could think of no way of putting the question that would not seem to carry a why-the-hell initial flavour and a for-God's-sake aftertaste. So I just said, 'Have you ever brought the other bloke along?'

'Who?'

'The other bloke. You know.'

'Oh, not for a long time.'

'A long time before you decided to bring me along, in fact.'

'Yes. He was more – he was keener on the idea than I thought you'd be.'

'I think I see.'

We were walking past a terrace of small houses with thickly hedged front gardens and stained-glass panels in the front doors. Vivienne led me up to one of them and rang the bell.

'I take it he knows we sleep together?' I suddenly asked.

'Oh, I should think so.'

'You should think so?'

'He's never asked, so I haven't told him. About anybody, not just you. But I should think he knows. He must do.'

'Oh, good.'

The door opened and a short, stocky man let us in. He was bald and had a closely cropped beard that (in a phrase that sprang complete and unabridged into my mind) went all the way round his face without him having a moustache. This, coupled with Vivienne's and my exchange of a minute earlier, made me think for an instant that what she had really brought about was a confrontation between me and the other bloke. Then I reproached myself for associating her with such a typically, even grossly, Vandervanean concept. Nevertheless, there turned out to be more than one point during the evening when I was to wonder momentarily whether I was dealing with an actor hired by Roy to coax or bluff me into some new machination of his.

'How do you do, Mr Copes.'

'It's very nice to see you again. But haven't you . . . ? Wasn't there a . . . ?'

He made passes at his chin and jaws, uninformative to the average outsider, but conveying clearly enough to me that it was now in his mind that the image of the other bloke had surfaced, and setting me to wonder in some discomfort how far I really resembled that unknown. Then I remembered Vivienne telling me he was only an inch taller than she, which made him eight inches shorter than me, and cheered up again. Unless there was another bloke . . .

'No, Dad, this is Mr Ee-andell, Douglas Ee-andell,' she was saying in her usual attempt to block off any Randalling on the part of people she introduced me to.

'That's all right, Vivvy, don't you worry, dear. Come on, what are we hanging about here for? Let's find ourselves a glass of something.'

We entered what was clearly a study, with an open roll-top desk, typewriter, postal scales, rows of reference works – or fairly clearly so; the walls were thickly hung with pictures and such of a devotional tendency. I noticed a reproduction of Holman Hunt's *Light of the World*, photographs of the Archbishop of Canterbury, a well-known American evangelist, a Negro divine and somebody who could perhaps have been Samuel Wesley, a lithograph or whatever of Haydn (presumably in his role as composer of *The Creation*), and representations of scrolls, inscriptions and illuminated texts.

Mr Copes waved his hand at parts of this. 'Something for everybody,' he said, making for a card table topped with pink baize on which there stood a silver tray bearing a decanter and three glasses. Briskly, he poured and handed out drinks.

'Not very nice, is it?' he said (to my silent agreement) when we had tasted. 'Cyprus sherry, they call it. A more exact description would be Cyprus raisin tea with some spirits in it. They soak the raisins in a water tank in the sun and either it ferments on its own or they make it ferment – I'm not quite clear which – and then they strain it and put the spirits in it. But perfectly wholesome. You saw what they've been up to today, did you? It was in the paper.'

He soon made it apparent that he was referring, not to the Cyprus sherry-makers, but to the government then in office. Some price-increase or wage-claim had been allowed or met. Mr Copes explained that he took no interest in politics and never had, but that what the country obviously needed was a dictator, a benevolent one, of course, or a reasonably benevolent one, who would surrender his powers the moment the necessary period of martial law came to an end. Asked what that period would have accomplished if all went well, Mr Copes said that unity and decency would have been restored by the fairest possible methods, without the singling-out of any class or group: profiteering tradesmen would be gaoled as readily as strikers and agitators, coloured landlords deported along with coloured tenants, rioting students and rampaging football-supporters shot down side by side in the streets. In the climate of opinion thus engendered, other problems, like abortion and homosexuality, would probably be found to have cleared up of their own accord.

After some minutes of this, Vivienne went out to the kitchen. Mr Copes recharged my glass and said, in the gentle tone he had maintained throughout,

'I must be right in thinking, Mr Yandell, mustn't I, that you and young Vivvy go to bed with each other?'

This query took me off balance. With as much as a throat-clearing by way of prelude, later in the evening, alleviated by Vivienne's presence, if ideas about the imposition of decency by martial law had been less fresh in my mind, it (the query) might have been more manageable. As it was, I found myself saying, if not blurting,

'Oh no. Nothing like that. Not at all.'

'Not at all. In that case there must surely be some other girl, or even girls, among your acquaintance with whom you do go to bed, mustn't there?'

'Oh no. Of course not. No.'

'No. Perhaps you prefer your own sex? I must say, to look at you, I shouldn't have thought—'

'Oh no. Really.'

'Well, then you must without question find relief in the kind of solitary practices they used to warn us against at school, mustn't you?'

'No, I . . . don't go in for any of that.'

'I see. And you've been keeping company with Vivvy for how long?'

'About four months.'

Mr Copes twitched abruptly, as from a small bolt of electricity. 'And you're how old?'

'Thirty-three.'

'Yes. You know, Mr Yandell, I may be very old-fashioned, but I can't help feeling that, as a companion for a healthy, vigorous girl like Vivvy, an apparently equally healthy and vigorous young man who can totally suppress his physical desires over a period of about four months, uh, leaves something to be desired.'

'I can see that,' I said, doing some wistful, tender speculation about how Sylvia might be spending her evening.

'I call it Copes's Fork.' He gave the low, affectionate laugh of somebody watching the antics of a favourite animal. 'Like chess, in a way. Once you've said no to the first question – and the skill, such as it is, all lies in manoeuvring you into saying no at that stage – then your only possible chance of drawing the game is to say yes to the second question and play out time talking about the high plane your feelings for Vivvy are on. There was a fellow once who did that. He worked for a publisher, I think he said. But it's most exceptional. I must grant you, Mr Yandell, you went to your doom with dignity. Evidently you're an easy-going sort of chap. That must be one of the things Vivvy likes about you. She likes easy-going chaps. Do smoke if you want to.

'Over the years, Vivvy must have brought I don't know how many young men along to see me. There was one who was middle-aged, I suppose you'd have called him. Unmarried, naturally. Not divorced, either. Vivvy couldn't have been more than twenty-one or -two at the time. I put my foot down about him. In the first place there was too much of a gap in age, and in the second place I never trust a man who isn't married and a father before he's forty. I had a word with Vivvy and that was that.'

'She just stopped seeing him?'

'She stopped bringing him along to see me, and that means something. I don't think she'd have a great deal of time to see anyone she didn't bring along occasionally. She likes men, doesn't she? We don't discuss these matters, but it didn't take me much thought to work out how she runs her life. There were three possibilities. Either she wasn't going to bed with any of the fellows she brought along, or she was going to bed with some of them and not with others, or she was going to bed with all of them. Now, there've been some fellows she's brought along over periods of a year or more, and most of them have lasted a few months. So if she wasn't going to bed with any of them, she was rustling up an entire string of fellows who were going on going round with her because they were so keen on her conversation. Well, to be able to keep it up for ten years and more, continuously rustling up fellows like that, in quantity, these days, would take a very extraordinary sort of girl. And Vivvy's hardly extraordinary at all. That took me to possibility number two. There, it was harder to be absolutely certain in one's mind, but I noticed that she talked about all the fellows in just the same sort of way and treated them in just the same sort of way when she brought them along. That was pretty well good enough for me. Vivvy tells me your job's to do with music. I'm pretty keen on music myself.'

I had almost stopped feeling uncomfortable since the promulgation of Copes's Fork, thanks to its author's friendly manner, but was relieved on the whole when he started telling me about a performance of *Iolanthe* that he (and I) had recently seen on television. There followed a discussion of the propriety of modernizing the librettos of light operas intended to be topical in their day. Vivienne came back in the middle of it. She gave me a how's-it-going? look, and I gave her an all-right one in return.

'I can't help feeling Gilbert's wit has been rather overrated,' I said to Mr Copes, took a further look from his daughter that suggested I had chosen an unpropitious line, and added quickly, 'but at his best he can be very ingenious and inventive.'

'I'm glad to hear you say that. I know it's fashionable to decry him, but I am rather fond of the old chap. Perhaps it's simply that I'm used to him and know most of him by heart. I should certainly agree that Sullivan is the senior partner, as it were. Well, Vivvy, how's it going? Have your efforts been crowned with success?'

Vivienne seemed to think he was talking about dinner, which did in fact turn out to be ready in the next room. This was a kitchen in the old-fashioned sense, but not in the old-fashioned style: no wall-clock, rocking-chair or cat, nothing much at all, really, and I guessed that Mr Copes ate off a tray in his study when alone. He saw me hesitating to sit down as soon as it occurred to me that I was doing so, and waved his hand.

'Let's get on with it. Unless you'd positively like me to say grace . . . I only say it when some sort of man of God is of the company, and as often as not I don't even say it then. I worked out a sort of rule of thumb years ago. Under about thirty, or these days let's say more like thirty-five, they're not keen on it. Outmoded ritual. I should have thought that a modish ritual or an up-to-date ritual was a contradiction in terms, but that's by the way. Then the middle lot, going up to fifty or so, they rather care for a touch of benedictus benedicat. Above that, it tends to be outmoded ritual again. You've no idea how much I've sometimes wanted to find out why chaps who feel like that feel like that, the older ones, I mean, but I can't help thinking it would be unkind to ask them. I don't know whether I'm making any sense to you.'

'Oh yes,' I said truthfully. 'Perfect sense.'

The soup was out of an opulent packet or authentic tin, the fish pie had been prepared by an expert and warmed up competently enough. Mr Copes poured stout of a brand unfamiliar to me and began to talk about the American and Russian space programmes. It seemed that development of these was altogether too slow and unambitious for his liking, and that our country's failure to have put up a decent orbiting satellite approached a national scandal. He said he realized that such projects cost a lot of money, but, by his reckoning, the outlay necessary to get a manned ship off to Mars and a new drive evolved, whereby the outer planets became reachable in a matter of weeks, could be met by stopping public expenditure on everything else whatever – far more than met: the abolition of income tax, sufficiently urgent on moral grounds, could be carried through at the same time.

'I don't quite see in that case where all the cash would come from,' I said.

'Oh. Taxation. Cars, television, tobacco, drink, all these domestic machines. Anything at all to do with cars. Anything people spend their money on, in fact. Food. That way you'd catch everybody.'

'You'd certainly need a dictator to run a system like that.'

'A dictator. Yes, come to think of it you probably would. As you imply, it isn't a particularly realistic scheme. But what a splendid thing for everybody if it could somehow be put into effect.'

'You mean the advances in knowledge that might be made?'

'Oh no. I don't in the least hold with advances in knowledge. No, it's the idea, the wonder of it all. Tell me, Doug – do you read any of this science-fiction stuff?'

'I know it sounds silly, but I have so much listening to do I hardly get time to read what I've got to read for my work.'

'No, I quite understand, but with respect I think you should make some time to read a few of these stories. They'd show you, much more clearly than I could explain, what I'm trying to get at about wonder and so forth. It's necessary, that sort of feeling, more and more so every year, as people bother less and less with religion. How much do you bother with it?'

Twice might have been coincidence: sex via (or hurtling out of the blue after) dictatorship, religion behind the snatched-off mask of space travel. To be certain I was faced with a full-grown policy, I was going to have to wait until nursery schools had led instantaneously to my income, its sources and amount, or an exchange of views about the fabled lost portion of Atahualpa's ransom had, in the twinkling of an eye, become an inquiry into the incidence of madness in my family. Meanwhile, I must answer the current question, doubly so, for Vivienne, instead of sending her father the now-then-Dad look I had been bank-ing on, had turned in her chair and was sending me a look of genuine, amiable expectation.

'Well, I'm sorry, but I'm afraid I don't bother with it much.'

'Never be sorry or afraid to speak your mind. Don't bother with it much. You mean you don't bother with it at all,' said Mr Copes, almost more gently than I could bear.

'Yes, I'm . . . I suppose I do.'

'But you must think there's something more than just this world,' said Vivienne. 'I know you can have a lot of argument about what. But something. You must.'

'I can't see why.'

'Have you ever tried? To see why?'

Mr Copes frowned for the first time, in puzzlement, not disap-proval. 'But surely the two of you must have gone into these matters together, mustn't you! Having known each other all these months?'

'No, Dad. Never.'

'Never. What an extraordinary state of affairs.'

'It just hasn't happened to come up,' I said, feeling slightly hedged in. 'And I don't think that's all that extraordinary. Not statistically extraordinary, anyhow.'

'Oh, I should have said statistically very extraordinary,' said Mr Copes, 'if you took a conspectus of the last couple of hundred years as opposed to the last couple of dozen. And even over the shorter term my considered guess would be that numbers would tell against you if one were to survey the country as a whole, rather than merely the south-eastern corner of it. I needn't speculate about the rest of the world. But do go on.'

I had no idea how I had come to seem to have started something, let alone what it might be; however, I went on. 'I just lead my life from day to day, like most people, whatever they may say to themselves or one another about it – in fact like everybody I've ever met or heard of, apart from a few prophets and such. Which suggests to me that what you say to yourself and your friends about what you're doing can't be very important.'

'I don't see why not. At all events, it's natural to think and talk about one's life in the whole. I should like to call it human in the most literal sense. It would take a funny sort of soldier never to think or talk about war, wouldn't it? I wonder how many sailors there are who've never thought or talked about the sea.'

'You've got to believe in something.' Vivienne did not look or sound very amiable now. 'Everybody has to.'

Trying to sound light and airy, I said, 'You'll be telling me in a minute it doesn't so much matter what it is as long as it's something.'

'Suppose I did, then? I'm not, but suppose I did?'

'Well, good God, it matters all right if it's fascism or communism or any of those. Or flower power or love-ins or any of—'

'I didn't mean anything soft or anything nasty. I meant something reasonable. I thought you'd have seen that.'

'Okay, sorry, but I still feel—'

Mr Copes broke in. 'Very, very nearly everybody who's ever done anything has believed in something, and by anything I don't mean anything important, I mean anything whatever. Rather in the same way as very, very nearly everybody who's ever done anything whatever has had two arms and two legs. But I seem to have interrupted you again.'

'No you haven't, Mr Copes. I've pretty well run out of things to say about all this. Not that I had very many in the first place.'

One still in stock concerned belief in belief in something reasonable, and just how reasonable the something had to be in order to count as reasonable, but I kept quiet. So, for a short time, did the other two. Then Vivienne said she would see about some coffee, and Mr Copes took me back into his study, where he poured out two glasses of port.

'I know you're not a drinking man, Doug, but that's no excuse for not giving you anything nice at all. This isn't in the least out of the way, but it is port and not port type or port character. Not too bad, is it? Now, while I've got you on your own for a few moments, I wonder if I could intrude on you a little, as it were, and ask you to put my mind at rest about something, if you would.'

He sat down facing me across the hearth, where a green paper fan partly hid the emptiness of the grate, and stared, for quite a few of the few moments he had me on my own, at a point on the opposite wall where there was a fearful reproduction of Guido Reni's sufficiently fearful *Ecce Homo*. When he had accumulated enough spiritual afflatus from this, he said,

'How shall I put it? Is this country heading for a state of complete moral anarchy?'

'Oh, I doubt it,' I said, trying not to fall out of my chair with relief. 'It's not a question I bother about much, quite frankly, but I would have said there's about enough respect for tradition still going, family life, discipline and that kind of thing, to see us all out. Perhaps you've been taking too much notice of the way some people behave in the south-east of England.'

'Well taken. Perhaps I was looking at it in the rather longer term. Have you ever thought of marrying Vivvy? I don't mean have you any sort of intention to – I've no right to ask that and it's none of my business – but simply and literally if you've ever thought of it.'

I had no trouble staying in my chair now. 'Oh. No. I can't honestly say I have. But that's nothing to do with Vivienne, it's to do with me. I just feel – when I look at the mess so many people—'

'With respect, Doug, what an extraordinary number of things you don't think about and haven't got time for. Science fiction. Religion. Whether the country's heading for moral anarchy. Marrying Vivvy or evidently anybody else either. I expect you must find a great deal to occupy you in other ways. Your music and all that. Some men have made music the only really important thing in their lives, I suppose. Bach, Mozart, Mendelssohn. But then they were all . . . Ah, here we are. Well done, Vivvy.'

Vivienne came in and handed round coffee without any kind of look at me. While we drank it, Mr Copes talked about the doings of his sons, politely seeing to it that I could follow the main drift without being encumbered with detail. He passed over some photographs of the senior son and his family, for me to look at while he himself described to Vivienne his visit to them over at Ealing the previous day. I turned through the series of holiday snaps, amusing myself at first by trying to pick out bits of Vivienne and her father from her brother and two small nephews, but finding nothing recognizable.

The maternal strains must have predominated there. Well, why not?

Finally, Mr Copes said he had an archdeacon coming to see him at crack of dawn, and would take the liberty of chucking us out, if he might. This proved within his powers, once I had rejected a return bus-journey in favour of some sort of cab and he had successfully telephoned for one on my behalf. We parted cordially. The sort of cab concerned had no lateral partition, and was also the sort with a driver lacking in geographical knowledge or aptitude, so that what with one thing and another Vivienne and I exchanged no more than a dozen words until we were back in the flat. It was five past eleven. She said she would make some tea. I followed her out into the kitchen.

'Are you cross with me?'

'Yes, a bit. Or I was. I'm getting over it.'

'What about?'

'You didn't think much of my father, did you?'

'Viv, what are you saying? It's quite true he disconcerted me once or twice, but that was just his way. I thought he was a marvellous old character. Most entertaining.'

'Character. Entertaining.' She put the lid back on the electric kettle and slammed the plug into its base. 'That's about it, isn't it?'

'I really don't know what you mean.'

'Where you're concerned. That's as far as it goes. You wouldn't discuss anything with him.'

'Now that is just not true. We covered a hell of a lot of ground and whatever he wanted to discuss I discussed back at him. Except your brothers, admittedly, but there wasn't much in the way of a side for me to take in the discussion about them.'

'You weren't really talking to him, you were getting him to go on saying more things for you to go on thinking what a wonderful old character and incredible old codger and fabulous old buffer and fantastic old gaffer he was. You do the same with me: that's how I noticed.'

'Me think you're an old gaffer? You must be—'

'Not a gaffer, but funny. Zany, screwy, dotty, kooky. Not on purpose, but because I can't help myself, because I was made that way. An oddball, a card, a caution. I've seen you watching me as if I was television. Comic.'

I took the lid off the teapot. 'I do sometimes think you're funny when perhaps you aren't really intending to be, yes. But I never think you're silly or absurd or undignified. And it's part of being fond of somebody: you must know that, surely. Anyone who was never funny except on purpose would be a freak, and a repulsive sort of freak at that, especially if it was a woman. From my point of view. And what about men, from your point of view? You're not going to tell me you've never thought I was funny not on purpose.'

'No.'

I was less whole-heartedly relieved to hear this reply than I had expected, but at once thrust aside the temptation to ask in what circumstances, and to what degree, I was funny not on purpose. 'There you are then.'

'But I don't go round thinking it's the main thing about you.'

'I don't think it's the main thing about you, for God's sake. You know what I think the main thing about you is. Not the only thing, but the main thing.'

'What is it?' She sounded considerably mollified.

I was in the middle of telling her when the kettle boiled. She turned it off with an absent-minded gesture and said conversationally,

'You know, Doug, I sometimes find a cup of tea this time of night keeps me awake. Do you ever find that?'

'Yes, I do sometimes.'

Without looking at me, she started to walk out of the kitchen. 'After all, tea's supposed to perk you up, not sort of slow you down.'

'Yes, quite,' I said, intrigued at this variation on our established cup-of-tea ritual. 'It's the caffeine, you know.'

'Really?'

'Yes, apparently there's more caffeine in a cup of tea than in a cup of coffee. Isn't that interesting?'

'Oh, darling . . .'

Afterwards I went and made some tea, and we both managed to fall asleep before the caffeine had had time to hit us.

# Eight

## Pigs Out

It was the next evening, that of *Elevations 9*. I had arranged to meet Roy for a drink in Craggs's at half past eight and escort him to the concert hall, or rather to the converted tramway depot south of the river which, over the past couple of years, had served as the venue for many an exciting transmedial breakthrough, anti-Establishment manifestation and punch-up. His pre-performance routine, always strict, normally led off with a light early dinner attended by Kitty, two or three of the orchestra with their wives, husbands, etc., and a close friend or so. For more than one reason, this custom was not going to be observed tonight. Nor, as I saw when I arrived and went to join him in his corner, were other familiar prescriptions: a caramel-coloured helping of what I took to be whisky stood at his elbow, replacing, probably as one of a group rather than solo, the single glass of wine to which the routine restricted him. I was relieved (taking one possible view of the matter) to see his violin case within his reach. Here, at any rate, tradition had held: no cloakroom attendant, waiter or functionary of any kind would be allowed to take the thing out of his sight for a moment. At my approach, he got up and pressed a bell-button.

'Hi, Duggers. I suggest champagne. For you, that is. You do like it, don't you. In so far as you like anything one could properly call a drink. What was that about a bite to eat you said you were going to have eaten? Have a sandwich or something.'

'No thanks, I had a sort of high tea at the flat.'

'High tea, Christ. Ham and Russian salad and sweep pickle and tim peaches and plung cake and lots of cups of char. Each to his taste is what I always say.'

He seemed to me fairly drunk already. While he spoke to the waiter, I dallied with the thought of plying him with his own drink to the point at which he would be unable to leave the club, or at least mount the concert platform, then put it aside. We must take off in half an hour or less, and ten times that time of continuous soaking would hardly have been enough to put him under any table I had ever seen in his vicinity.

'How's life?' I asked him when the waiter had gone.

'That's the silliest bloody question I've heard for longer than I care to remember. Life gets lived. That's how life is.'

'How's Sylvia?'

'That's more like it. A bit more like it. She's fine as far as I know, which is virtually no distance at all. I haven't seen her or been in touch with her for . . . But don't exult prematurely, old lad. Temporary arrangement. While we, or more accurately while I go to work on devising some counter-measure to your friend Harold Meers's little stratagem.'

'Any progress?'

'No. None whatever. Very nearly none whatever. To anticipate your next question, everybody else is in very much the condition you might expect them to be. Oh, I've been to work on young Christopher. Offered him anything he cared to name to refuse to let the interview be published. Can you do that, by the way? Stop a chap printing something you've already given him? Buggered if I know. Anyway, we didn't get to that stage. He and I aren't on very good terms these days, to tell you the truth. The others are all okay. Well . . . except Gilbert. Rock of stability normally. He's taken to going off for hours at a time, wandering round those woods that lead off from the common apparently. Nothing there apart from trees and sexual maniacs. You know, I sometimes wonder whether I might not end up as one of those, when Girl, 20 and going down and all the rest of it are as if they'd never been. You could easily find yourself stuck with flashing what was left of your hampton at Girl, 8. Or I suppose by that stage it might even be Boy, 8. No sign of it at the moment, I can assure you, but you never know. I expect it's quite an agreeable sort of life when you get used to it: plenty of fresh air and exercise, and Mother Nature on every hand, and a spot of spying on courting couples thrown in to rekindle memories of long ago. Quite romantic. Not much fun in January, though, I grant you.'

He went on like this until, indeed until after, some champagne, a plate of smoked-salmon sandwiches and another brunette whisky had been delivered to us. I refrained as studiously as I could from studiously refraining from any flicker of reaction when Roy poured the new whisky into the substantial remains of the old, but I must have over- or underdone it, because he stared coldly at me and said,

'Liberation from the tyranny of the bar-line! If I'm not good and pissed when I stand up in front of that lot I'll never get through it.'

'Fair enough. After all, it isn't as if this were a musical occasion.'

'Oh, random noise considered as art!' he half roared, incidentally providing me with further evidence that he was much more hostile to recent offshoots from music when he was off guard or stirred, as now, than when he was soberly lecturing me and others on our duty to keep abreast of new developments. 'I do wish you'd try to . . . Well, it's a totally different sort of audience. Not one of those little . . . Their ears aren't attuned to the kind of nuances in performance you're in the habit of looking for. Or I'm in the habit of looking for. Under other conditions. What does this bugger want, do you suppose?'

This bugger was the glaring hall porter, who came up and told Roy that a Mr Harold Meers wished to speak with him on the telephone. Roy asked me to watch his violin, I said I would, and he hurried out. When he came back, five or six minutes later, I was measurably better informed about who had been who in 1935 than on arrival. He looked puzzled, also drunk.

'What did he want?'

'I never got to him. Somebody took a lot of trouble, when he wasn't coughing his head off, to establish that I really was Sir Roy Vandervane and not his grandmother, and then took a lot more trouble to explain that he was speaking from Mr Meers's private house. He really let that sink in. Then whoever it was said Mr Meers had been called away but would be back in a moment.' Still on his feet, Roy began eating sandwiches at top speed, with gulps of whisky to eke out salivation, and continued to talk. 'Then I got a detailed account of how they'd found out where I was. What did Mr Meers want? He didn't know, but Mr Meers would be along directly to expound in person. I hung on a bit longer and then got fed up and rang off. I suppose it was his way of cheering me up for the concert. Though I can't understand why the bastard didn't speak to me himself. Very odd.'

'Call him back in a few minutes. I've got his private number on me somewhere.'

'Bugger that. I've got a little job to do that nobody else can do for me, and then we ought to be moving. I just hope Sylvia's all right.'

'If it were anything serious there wouldn't have been this mucking about. He was just trying to worry you. Don't let him.'

'I'll try not to.'

The tramway depot might, to all appearance, have seen the back of its last tram no earlier than noon on the day in question, in time for the rails to be ripped up and two inspection pits filled (to all appearance) with tins and broken bottles, but not for even a token assault on the layer of grime that clung to every visible square inch of the roof, its network of supporting girders and the otherwise bare brick walls. These last were partly hidden by broad strips of hessian or sacking hung so as to form a series of curtains along all four sides of the building, whether to mitigate draughts or for acoustic reasons or in the interests of decoration I could not tell, nor did I at any time inquire. The stage, a low wooden platform looking at once unfinished and not far from collapse, was occupied by jerking anthropoid figures with musical instruments or microphones in their grasp, and surrounded in depth by enough electronic equipment to mount a limited thermonuclear strike. Nobody who still retains his sense of hearing, I suppose, can properly claim to have experienced a deafening noise, but that was how I immediately felt like describing what was coming out of the loudspeakers, and was to continue feeling, too, with remarkable persistence, every time it started up again after an interval and now and then while it was simply going on. The element I was trying to breathe seemed not so much gaseous as fluid, or even some rarefied form of gelatin that shuddered constantly under the swipes of immense invisible ping-pong bats. It smelt of tennis shoes, hair and melting insulation, and was fearfully hot.

If the place itself had the look of the hastiest possible adaptation to human occupancy, the audience – five hundred strong? a thousand? – might have been making it their home for weeks. They were not exactly all lying about, standing, strolling, chatting, making mild love, beginning to dance, buying and selling, preparing food, but neither were they all sitting in the rows of unfolded folding seats attending to what they, or some number of them, must have paid money in order to witness. Every few feet were plastic carrier bags, radios, footwear and clothing discarded momentarily or for good, coloured newspapers of strange format, textiles that might have been blankets or stoles or things intermediate, and the already substantial foundations of piles of general litter. Here and there I could make out an ordinary human being: journalist, performer's parent or ill-instructed queer.

A degenerate descendant of Charles II came and took Roy away. My own guide, a girl (so I provisionally decided), escorted me to the end of a row, or lateral straggle, in which I recognized Terry Bolsover, a tremendous visual achievement amid the prevailing hairiness. Near him was a vacant chair.

The person with me articulated quite clearly, and yet without seeming to shout much, 'You can go closer if you like.'

'No thanks,' I bawled, 'I think I can get everything I want from here.'

'Sorry?'

'This'll do.'

Those sitting, sprawling, lying between the aisle and Bolsover made no attempt to move themselves or their belongings out of my path, but showed no vexation when I kicked, trod on, fell over booted foot or bulging string-bag. Bolsover looked up at my approach and made quite a show of checking what would have been an inaudible roar of laughter. I pulled my chair up to his and began wiping steam off my glasses.

'You here for the paper or just giving your pal moral support?' he asked in the same style of utterance as that I had heard a moment earlier: an occupational skill, no doubt, such as foundry workers and warship deck-hands must have to develop. I tried to imitate it when I answered,

'Moral support, yes. I don't know about the paper yet.'

'Eh? Look, hold it until this lot's over. There can't be much more.'
I mimed a question.

'Because he's already pretended to be going to stop and been
carried away into going on twice. Three times is the usual limit for
that one. Here, it's just coming up now.'

I looked at the stage. Sure enough, the young man who had been
making most of the vocal noise, and whose body had so far merely
been making stylized copulatory movements, plainly began to suffer
the effects of some convulsant poison, perhaps conveyed into his
bloodstream by blow-pipe dart: in its way an impressive sight.

'Yeah, this'll be it,' said Bolsover.

It was. What followed it surprised me mildly: hardly a scream, not
a single whistle that I could hear, a small amount of ordinary yelling,
nothing to compare with the pervading loud but fairly steady hubbub,
like that of a cocktail-party on its second drink, that might well have
been going on at much the same level underneath the din from the
stage. I reasoned that no one turns enthusiastic about the maintenance
of his natural environment; as well cheer when water comes out of
a turned tap, give the milkman a standing ovation. When I tried it, I
found I could converse with Bolsover as easily as if we had been in a
record-breaking train.

'Are there any more acts before Roy comes on?'

'Acts? Oh, I get you. No, this bunch do one more, then it's Pigs Out
with their . . . like their latest hit number, you see, Doug. Then your
bloke comes on and does his stuff with them. Did you say you were
writing it up for the paper?'

'Harold wants me to. He says people would think it was interesting
to have two different points of view on the same event. I don't think
I shall want to.'

'There can't be more than about eleven people in England who
read you and read me.'

'There can, I'm afraid. Anyway, I told him something of the sort,
and he said that didn't matter: people would still think it was interesting.'

'I sort of get it. Could I pick your brains a bit on the classical side later? I won't go into it, that's your style, but just so's I don't say pizzi-cato when I mean 7/4 time. I'll do the same for you.'

'Thanks.'

'Nice fellow, old Sir Roy, I thought when I went up to see him. Makes you feel brilliant, doesn't he? There wasn't anything came up he didn't go on as if I knew ten times more about it than he did.'

'Including music?'

'You mean classical? In a kind of way. Like of course he *knew* more, but what would a bloody great genius like me care? Sort of, me witch-doctor, you heap big American scientist with computers and all. Does he always go on like that?'

'No. Only sometimes.'

'There was a parson down the youth club I used to go to . . . Here we go again. Full of piss they are, actually. Not much in them for me, never mind you.'

The ensuing stretch of time recalled to me a night I had once passed in the grip of a fairly severe throat infection. I had had a series of vivid, realistic dreams that each appeared to cover the events of an hour, an afternoon, a whole day, and had awoken again and again in a sweat, frightened or just bewildered, but with the thought that anyhow morning must now be appreciably nearer, to find something like two minutes had elapsed since my last awakening. So, there in the dirty vastness of the tram shed, my mind seemed to be plunging and skid-ding towards and through everything I could remember or imagine, seemed to be when measured against the all but stationary hands of my watch. When I put my fingers in my ears it was worse. I was very relieved when it came to me from somewhere or other that I had felt like this, though less intensely, in the Dug-out at the start of the night of the favour. It had been Penny's arrival that had put an end to that phase.

I had just decided to try to think about her when those on the stage stopped doing what they were doing and began to go away. Hubbub was restored, somewhat louder than before. Next to me, Bolsover had turned preoccupied, once or twice scribbling a couple of lines in a notebook of incongruously neat appearance. What were presum-ably Pigs Out appeared before us one by one. I registered a strong impression that, should the choice arise, I would reject them in favour of a joint Nazi-Soviet tribunal as arbiters of my destiny, then heeded them no more. A man aged between twenty and sixty, wearing a shoulder-length wig that might or might not have been made of fine silver wire and clothes that glittered fiercely all over, spoke over the loudspeakers in tones of clangorous wheedling. Then the noise was back.

Penny. When I tried to think consecutively about her, I found that my mental traction had slipped out of overdrive into bottom gear. It was hard even to remember what she looked like. I worked at it, but every time her image showed signs of clearing and steadying, my surroundings shook it out of focus again. In the end I clutched at a single idea and held on to it: that I would telephone her and try to get her to come down to the flat while Gilbert was on one of his nature rambles. Another thought swam up alongside, to do with something having happened or been said to me recently that had engendered the first thought, but a drum solo put paid to that.

After several false stops, the noise came to an end. The silver-wigged man stepped up and delivered a mixture of misstatements and (to me) unpalatable half- and three-quarter-truths about Roy, who presently came into view carrying his violin case. The ambient hubbub grew, became mildly enthusiastic, but I fancied that some of the enthusiasm had an ironical edge to it. So, it seemed, did Bolsover.

'I don't know why some people come,' he said. 'The bunch who went on first tonight have got a couple of queers on guitars, it's well known. That lot up the front gave them the hell of a time. I don't know why they come.'

'Roy's not queer.'

'No.'

'What is he, then, from their point of view? Old?'

'Yeah,' said Bolsover, implying in the monosyllable that that was only about half the story and that he was not going to tell the other half.

'I see.'

By now, with a grinning jauntiness that made me want to turn my eyes away, Roy had taken his fiddle and bow out of their case, disposed of the case, and shaped up to begin playing without further ado. I had never before known him to reach this stage without careful, even fussy, preparatory tuning. My heart fell. He had stopped caring. Or perhaps – my heart rose again a notch – he had reasoned that, apart from himself, me and any other professional critics who might be present, nobody would notice a disparity of pitch smaller than about a semitone. The hubbub sank to the level one might expect from a soccer crowd just before the appearance of the teams – a solemn hush by the standards prevailing.

Pigs Out squared themselves and played a short series of what they probably thought of as chords, during which the bongoes rattled and thumped. Roy lifted his bow – giving it, I thought, an inquisitive glance – and, as Pigs Out fell silent, brought it down across the violin strings. A faint slithering and squeaking, not altogether unlike that of rats in a cellar, was all that resulted. On the stage, general bafflement followed; elsewhere, heightened hubbub.

'Bum mike,' said Bolsover. 'Bloody bad luck. Still, they can—'

'I don't think it's that. It sounds to me as if someone's doctored his bow. Grease or oil of some sort. Anybody could—'

'Fuck me!' thundered Roy's amplified voice, refuting Bolsover's diagnosis.

The audience loved that. They also loved Roy's hurried production of his spare bow, his equally speedy discovery that it too was unusable, the intervention of the silver-wigged man, and the whole thing. The lot up the front identified by Bolsover loved it most. I could see Roy thinking, and could guess at least one of his thoughts: that it would take much too long to find by telephone some fellow-violinist who was not out at a concert, or just out, and have a bow of his or hers brought to this comparatively remote spot. Then he was struck by a thought I could not guess. Turning away from his microphone as he spoke, he said,

'I wonder if there's a doogher-boogh boogh aboogh.'

The silver-wigged man left the platform at a run. In the ensuing minute or two, the hubbub grew further and became less generally amiable. At one point, Roy turned towards his microphone again, and I was very much afraid he was about to harangue the audience on the repressive tolerance of bourgeois society, or perhaps lead them in some revolutionary community singing, but he changed his mind, followed a style more deeply rooted in him, and stood gazing over everybody's head with admirable impassivity. In the end, the silver-wigged man returned bearing what I recognized as a double-bass bow. Roy took it from him and nodded authoritatively at Pigs Out.

'But Christ,' said Bolsover, 'that thing's only about half the size.'

'He can make a fair shot at it. He's a professional, you see. And anyway, it's not as if—'

*Elevations 9* began again, and this time continued. I devoted myself to the horrible task of listening to everything that was being played: the popping of the bongoes, the wailing of the sitar and the sticky thudding of the bass guitar as well as Roy's *obbligato*. This started off with some passage-work that, while probably exacting enough even for a performer equipped with the right kind of bow, made no demands on the listener – indeed, a contemporary of Brahms could quite safely have gone out for a pee during it. About the time that such a one would have been returning to his seat, however, Pigs Out took on a more subordinate role and the character of the violin part changed. Having calculated (I guessed) that by now, if ever, the audience would be reconciled to the fact and sound of a violin, Roy was going to show off his paces as a transmedial innovator. Or so he might have put it to himself. What he proceeded to play, still cleanly enough to an untrained ear, was a set of variations on his theme in, or not far from, a jazz style that even I knew had faded out thirty years before, round about the end of his student career. I remembered once having had to let him play me half a dozen thoroughly scratched records of some jazz fiddler of that epoch, an American with an Italian name, and thought now that I recognized one or two of the man's turns of phrase. I could have had no better proof, had I wanted one or known any use to put it to, of the total failure of recent or contemporary products of the pop industry to impress themselves on Roy's musical consciousness. Well, that was something.

Perhaps, in their unimaginably cruder way, those about me had come to a roughly similar judgement on what Roy was offering them, perhaps it was just too unfamiliar to be borne. At any rate, a momentary increase in the nearby hubbub distracted my attention from the stage sufficiently to bring it home to me that the central aisle, in which earlier there had been about as much movement to and fro as in a village street on a fairly busy morning, was now more than half full of people shuffling unhurriedly but steadily in one direction: towards the door. I drove my mind back to its business. Some sort of climax evidently approached: the fiddle mounted to a high note and held it, Pigs Out did another series of as it were chords and sustained one that quite closely resembled that of the 6/4 on the dominant – the signal, in the true classical style, that the accompanying forces are about to shut up while the soloist displays his technical skill in a cadenza.

I felt my cheeks burn. Absurdity amounting to outrage – how many of those still inside this abode of muck would recognize the 'wit' and 'piquancy' of this last transmedial stroke, or would fail to jeer at it in the rare event that they did? And what followed was worse: a passage of fast double-stopping into which Roy was putting everything he had, making what must have been troublesome enough with a violin bow, and quite fiendishly difficult with the short and clumsy double-bass bow, sound natural, effortless, easy. Oh God, I thought, how could he not know that this lot positively disliked the idea of the difficult being made to seem easy, seem anything at all, exist in any form – that what they liked was the easy seeming easy?

Without sparing me the trill on the supertonic that classically heralds the return of the accompaniment, Roy was briefly reunited with Pigs Out and brought his composition to a close in something like silence. Distant hubbub marked the departure of the last of the audience, except for a few individuals like Bolsover and myself. *Elevations 9* had been a complete flop. I had devoutly hoped it would be, and yet I found myself overwhelmed with feelings of anticlimax and defeat.

Bolsover lit a cigarette. 'Was it any good from your point of view?'

'No. It was . . . No. Was it any good from yours?'

'No. I'll have to put something about it in my piece, but not much. I might ring you, if that's all right. See you in the office, anyway.'

We got up and began to move along the row of empty seats.

'Right. All the best, Terry.'

'Look, Doug, I should get the maestro away a bit smart if I were you. There's some rather gaunt lads here tonight. I've seen a couple of them round the festivals, turning messy. The maestro's enough out of the ordinary to take their eye.'

'I'd better go and find him, then. Thanks.'

Lights were already being switched off and equipment dismantled when I came upon Roy on the far side of the stage. He, the silver-wigged one and a Pigs Out or so were standing in reflective silence near a low doorway through which (imagination suggested without trouble) overalled men carrying tool-kits had once been accustomed to arrive on errands of repair and maintenance. Roy, violin case in hand, looked round at me with a fixed grin.

'There you are, old lad. I was just saying, it might have been as well if I'd accepted defeat when I had the chance.'

'I suppose it might.'

'Don't worry: I'm not going to ask you what you thought of it. That can keep, among other things. Anyway, the majority view was clear enough.'

'Dead ignorant,' said somebody.

'Lot of sheep,' said somebody else. 'One goes, next thing they've all gone.'

'Let's be off,' I said to Roy.

'Indeed let's. A drink and a chat somewhere or other, I think. Good night, everybody. My sincere thanks and apologies.'

After some handshakes, protests that no apologies were called for, and general Roying, the two of us made our way in near-darkness along the side of the building towards the main entrance, opposite which Roy had parked his car.

'Roy, I want to say I'm sorry about—'

'Don't say anything for now, Duggers, if you don't mind. Not another word until we're clear of this remarkably unwholesome spot.'

We reached the area round the entrance, which was crowded with chatting and dispersing groups. My eye fell immediately on a tall young man in a suede-and-leather jacket who turned briefly to the half-dozen others standing near him and led them across to bar our path.

'Hey, it's Sir Roy Vandervane,' said the leader. 'With his awful old violin. I say, fellows, let's be frightful rotters and take it off him.'

He made a token, indeed balletic, grab in the direction of the case; token or not, I took off my glasses and put them in the top pocket of my coat. Roy did a wriggling shrug.

'Yeah, well I know it ding go,' he said in his worst accent and a matey tone. 'Can't win 'em aw, you know.'

'Let's go, Roy.'

'Still, I thought Pigs Out did okay, din you?'

'Piss off,' said the boy in the jacket. 'Right, let's have it.'

This time he made a real grab for the case, while two of his mates seized Roy by the arms. Two others converged on me. As the leader swung away with the case in his hand, I hit him behind the ear and dropped him to his knees, which caused him inadvertently to slam the case down on the pavement. Somebody's head butted me in the stomach and brought my own head down. A knee came up, missing my face but connecting with my collar-bone hard enough to knock me over. As I fell, I was conscious of a silence spreading outwards round us. Before I could get up, somebody's foot swung at me; I caught it and twisted it and it slipped from my grasp. Another foot struck me in the back, not hard: whoever it was, I reflected, was merely going through the motions of inflicting damage. Now I did get to my feet, and began an inconclusive struggle with probably two people. I could hear panting and scuffling, and the splintering of wood, and then the dreadful sound of what I knew was a human head striking the pavement, and then running feet. I took a kick in the shin and was free. An arm came round my shoulders.

'Are you all right?' asked a frightened voice, that of a young man in a bluish corduroy suit.

'Yes. Thanks.'

Some way off, figures were fast receding into the darkness; at least one of them was a policeman. Nearer at hand were the violin case, its lid half ripped off, and Roy's Stradivarius in half a dozen pieces, held together here and there by its strings. Two girls were bending over Roy himself, who lay still. Voices called in the distance. More people began to arrive.

# Nine

## The Other Bloke

'Now are you sure you're all right?'

'Yes, honestly, Viv, absolutely. Just a couple of bruises.'

'It didn't sound like that in the paper.' Vivienne's voice over the telephone was distrustful, as if she suspected me of covering up a broken back for motives of vanity or financial betterment.

'Well, you know what they're like. All I really am is tired. I had to talk to the police, and then it took them God knows how long at the hospital before they were sure Roy hadn't fractured his skull and I could come home.'

'So he's all right after all, then.' This time, the implication was very roughly that Roy's cranium was of that special hardness commonly found among show-offs, adulterers, etc.

'Well, up to a point. A bang on the head can have all sorts of odd effects. They haven't given him a clean bill of health yet. Comfortable, was all they'd say when I rang them just now. I'm going along there later.'

'When will that be, about?'

'When I've summoned the energy. Probably about eleven. Why?'

'I thought we could have lunch together.'

'Fine. Shall I pick you up at the office?'

It was arranged that I should do so at twelve fifteen, returning her at one fifteen. The less than ideal time and duration of her regular lunch-break had meant that we rarely met in the middle of the day, and I would be seeing her that evening as usual, but I relished the thought of an earlier chance of telling her all about what had happened last night, plus whatever was going to happen at the hospital. Before I went there I had a couple of hours to fill in. This I managed without any trouble at all, shaving at *adagio sostenuto* pace instead of my usual *allegro con brio*, playing the gramophone (only records I had already reviewed, and nothing by Weber or any of his contemporaries, so that the remotest possible suggestion of work was rigorously excluded), falling asleep, and trying to wonder effectively what was going to happen about Roy's Mahler concerts.

The day was hot and hazy. I was sweating while, in the gloomy vestibule of the hospital, I tried to find someone who could tell me who to ask where Roy was. Eventually, after provoking much bafflement and a couple of rebukes, I was confronted by a middle-aged woman in grey who wanted to know if I was a reporter. I said I was not, gave my name, was asked if I were not the one who had been with Sir Roy when he was admitted, agreed that that was the one I was, received directions and climbed a great many stairs.

Roy was in a private room, sitting up in bed with newspapers and wearing what amounted to a lopsided white skull-cap. Otherwise he looked quite normal.

'Good old Duggers.'

'How are you, Roy?'

'Fit as a fiddle, old lad. They . . .' His face went loose. 'Though that's hardly the . . .'

He stopped speaking and drew in his breath. I was afraid he was going to cry, and that, if he did, I would do the same.

'There are others,' I said.

'Not enough others. You probably know four hundred odd were destroyed in the last war. But even if they hadn't been, there still wouldn't be enough. Oh, I'll find one all right, but it won't be the same one. Do you know, I'd had the bloody old thing for nearly twenty-nine years? Played my first concert on it. The Max Bruch warhorse. Anyway, in answer to your kind inquiry, I have five stitches, they say no concussion to speak of, and I should be out some time tomorrow, with a couple of days' rest afterwards. Balls to the last bit – there's Gus to think of. George' – the leader of the NLSO – 'is keeping them at it today and tomorrow, but I'll have to be back waving the stick the morning after that.'

I nodded. Roy grinned at me and shook his head slowly.

'A very neat job, Duggers. What did you use?'

'Butter. Finest New Zealand. I didn't mean it to happen as it did. I thought you'd find out as soon as you started tuning, or earlier. I'm sorry you had—'

'Not at all, it was highly dramatic. A bit of a surprise, though. On reflection, I mean. I hadn't realized you'd follow up your principles quite that far into practice.'

'I felt I had to do something.'

'Most laudable. Did you just sit there in the writing-room and smear away?'

'The Gents.'

'One likes to have the full picture. Well, it seems you were wasting your time.'

'So I saw and heard.'

'No, I mean the critical reception, so to call it. Have you seen the *Orb* this morning? Very quick off the mark.'

I took the folded sheets. 'Violinist-composer Roy Vandervane Blazes New Trail,' announced Barry somebody, and went on to declare that, despite a technical hold-up and an unappreciative audience and never mind about the deplorable scene that followed (see page 3), he considered himself privileged to have been present at the birth of a new this, that and the other which would surely lead to further exciting what-have-you. Before he ended, Barry drew a staggeringly learned comparison with the hostile reception given leading nineteenth-century German composer Ludwig van Beethoven's pioneering First Symphony.

'Terrified of being caught out being square,' I said. 'Like all of them.'

'Except you. Yes, there's a slightly shorter piece in the *Flyer*. Care for a flip-through?'

'No thanks.'

'Your piece comes out on Friday, doesn't it?'

'Yes.'

'So you'll be able to give it mature consideration.'

'Yes.'

'You thought it was piss, didn't you?'

'Yes. Everything about it except your own performance.'

'Thanks.' Roy settled himself back against his pillows. 'So you see it wasn't quite such a flop as we all thought. Mind you, last night taught me quite a bit. The sort of chamber concerto approach was a mistake. The kids got too much of me and not enough of Pigs Out. I'll give them a lot more to do next time. Quartet style, or quintet with a lead guitar added.'

A weary incredulity possessed me. 'Next time?'

'Oh, Spiro Agnew! You don't suppose I'm going to let myself be choked off by one adverse reaction like that, do you? Nobody would ever—'

'I've given up supposing where you're concerned,' I said, advancing on him. 'I can just see you next time, or after next time, when one of them's broken all the bones in your left hand, explaining that the time after that it might be a good idea to introduce a vibraphone and a tenor sax. You learnt a lot last night, did you? You didn't learn the most obvious lesson anybody could possibly have in his whole life. You're just incapable of . . .'

I stopped speaking because somebody else had come into the room. From the flash of white I caught at the corner of my eye, I momentarily took the newcomer for a nurse or other hospital person, but it was Sylvia, wearing a long coat that might once have belonged to an undersized cricket umpire or professional house-painter, though not undersized enough, in the sense that it was still too big for her, or would have been considered so by the vanishing minority of which I suddenly felt myself a member. Her hair had been sprayed with glue while she stood in a wind-tunnel – at that stage I could think of no other explanation for its appearance; her eyelids were dark green. She went straight across to Roy and started what gave every promise of being a long bout of embraces, interspersed with whispers. I moved to the window and saw a block of flats, red brick and stucco with little balconies, on one of which a large white dog hurried to and fro like a tiger in a cage.

'Why's he here?' asked Sylvia behind me.

'Now, Sylvia. Duggers came to see how I am.'

'He's seen, hasn't he?'

'Why's she here?' I asked, turning. 'If you don't mind my putting it like that. I mean I thought Harold had put a stop to things.'

Roy gave a rich laugh and looked up at Sylvia with admiring affection. 'We think we've rather put a stop to him putting a stop, don't we, darling? That ole counter-measure we've been working on, Duggers, there's a better than even chance it's going to pay off, from what I've just heard. Fix everything.'

'Everything?'

'Yes, everything,' said Sylvia. 'Like him and me going off together and there's nothing you can do to stop it, or anybody else.'

'I see.'

With a show of great seriousness and strength of mind, Roy said, 'Go on with what you were saying, Duggers. About last night.'

'There's no point. Not now.'

'Yes there is. I want to hear.'

'You want to be able to tell yourself you listened to every word and you had to admit in fairness I was right in a way but it's just something you'll have to live with, and then you'll forget all about it.'

'Get out,' said Sylvia, who had evidently appreciated my tone, if nothing more. 'Get out of here and out of our lives. You're nothing but a big *druhg*. Nobody wants you around.'

'Shut up,' I said.

She started to move round the bed towards me with something of the same demeanour as when she had been about to grapple with Kitty. I picked up the water-jug from the bedside table.

'If you come near enough I'll pour this all over your head.'

'Ah now, be a *good* darling.'

One appeal or the other took its effect: she sat down on the bed with her back to me. Roy reached out and held her hand.

'Fire away, Duggers.'

'All right. I cannot understand, I will never understand, how you can even consider going on with this youth thing of yours after what happened last night. They didn't want you there; they felt you were out of place. And by God they showed it . . .'

'Oh, for Christ's sake, that was just a gang of bloody hoods. A tiny minority. You get them everywhere. You're not going to tell me they were representative of the whole—'

'Yes I am. In a way. Nobody tried to intervene, did they? They just stood by, because they—'

'People don't intervene. That happens everywhere too.'

'Oh yes they do intervene, at that kind of do. Punch-ups galore. Rival bands of youths, as they say.'

'Duggers, you'll really have to show me your birth certificate to prove you're not sixty-five. Young people don't consist exclusively of rival bands of youths. If there had been a rival band of youths there it had gone home. And Jesus, even if there had been one around it wouldn't have had time to do anything. You're talking complete ballocks.'

'All right, perhaps I am, on that. But the fact remains that that bunch were putting into action what the others were feeling. Partly – I mean not all of them can have felt aggressive towards you, but I bet the vast majority were out of sympathy with you. Last night, I thought they got up and left because they were bored. That too, no doubt, but now I realize the chief thing was that they were embarrassed. At the sight of somebody quite old enough, easily and demonstrably old enough to know better, making an exhibition of himself. Like seeing your auntie doing a strip. It wasn't your scene, dad, and it never will be.'

Sylvia began to speak, but Roy silenced her, perhaps by twisting her wrist. He kept his eyes on me as he had for the last minute, with the artless, total concentration of a man who is thinking about something else. I saw that I had been talking, and was going to go on talking, so that I could tell myself afterwards I had said everything, just as he was going to tell himself he had heard everything, but I went on all the same.

'You know what I honestly expected, after last night? After your piece had failed and you'd been beaten up and had your Strad smashed – which is like having your child maimed. Isn't it, Roy? After that I honestly expected you to swear to have nothing more to do with any of it, no more pop, no more youth, no more new ways of this and that – and then to sneak back to it bit by bit after a month or two. But here you are, twelve hours later, full of horrible plans for more of the same. That's frightening. You're going downhill faster and faster. I only hope you hold up long enough not to disgrace yourself and humiliate the orchestra over the Mahler. After that's over I advise you to retire to one of those places in California where nobody knows anything or notices anything. I'll be off now. Oh . . .'

Remembering, I brought out the half-bottle of Scotch I had been carrying in my coat pocket, and put it on the bedside table.

'Christ, Duggers, that's a handsome gesture, I must say. Thanks a lot.'

'I should hide it if I were you. Well, goodbye. You bloody fool. And good luck. To both of you.'

'Be in touch, old lad.'

Outside, I came to an unfrequented stretch of corridor, stopped, and kicked the wall several times, also hitting it once or twice with my fists. 'Fuck,' I said. 'Shit. Oh, God.' Then I saw and heard a trolley being pushed round a nearby corner, so I made for the stairs, and was soon outside the building in the same hot haze.

I still had nearly three-quarters of an hour in hand before meeting Vivienne, but there was nothing I wanted to do except in the world of theory, like getting drunk or rushing off to a brothel. I walked up through Hyde Park thinking of things I wished I had said to Roy, to do with Kitty and Penny and Ashley and such, and deciding that none of it would have done any good. At Marble Arch I got on a bus, then got off it again on finding there was nothing to distract me from the same cycle of thoughts. Making my way on foot along densely crowded pavements was better from that point of view, if from no other. I reached the airline office at eighteen minutes past twelve, collected Vivienne and took her across the road to a chain eatery of the sort that serves wine by the glass and beer to those devil-may-care few of its customers who want them.

We ate scampi and spinach and I told Vivienne my story, to the later sections of which she responded with what I took to be sullenness-cum-preoccupation, low intensity, preoccupation the more marked of the two. I told myself she had never approved of Roy. Then, over apple pie and cream, she said,

'Doug, I've got something to tell you. I might be going to marry Gilbert.'

A piece of apple fell out of my mouth. I said, 'Who?'

'Gilbert Alexander. That West Indian chap. You know him.'

'Yes, I know him, but I don't know you know him. I mean I didn't know you knew him. How do you know him?'

'I met him on your doorstep.'

'But that was only for a minute.'

'Just long enough for him to say good evening, and would I like to have a drink with him some time, and I said I couldn't then, and he said of course not, but would I write my name and telephone number on a blank page of a book he had with him, and he had his ballpoint out all ready and he just didn't give me time to think why to say no.'

'But this was only last week, last—'

'We're not getting married anything like yet. We're getting engaged.'

'But nobody gets engaged these days.'

'He says where he comes from they do. When they get married at all, that is. And they used to where I came from. I don't suppose they've stopped, either.'

'Does your father know?'

'Yes, I took Gilbert up for a drink yesterday evening. And the opposite to what you might think, he doesn't mind him being black at all.'

'I wasn't thinking anything about that.'

'Oh, Doug, don't be silly, of course you were. If you want to know what I think, the trouble with most black people isn't that they're black. Who could possibly mind that? – unless they were all prejudiced and horrible. It's a lovely colour. Anyway, it's never really black, not jet black. Even if it was, it would probably still be nice. No, what's wrong with a lot of black people is that they're Negroid, with great big lips and spread-out noses and the rest of it. But Gilbert's different: he looks like a dark-brown Englishman. Great.'

'I shouldn't have thought that was enough to get married on the score of.'

'Of course it isn't. What it is, he's my type. The sort of thing I mean, he interferes with my life. He makes me do some things and stops me doing others.'

'The masterful male.'

'Yes, that's right.'

'I thought we'd all managed to get beyond that stage.'

'Well, we all haven't.'

Coffee arrived at that point, and I extracted the bill at the same time. A memory from last night returned, bringing with it an explanation: I had thought about Penny with new resolve because I had unknowingly sensed a basic and (to me) adverse change in Vivienne's life. But I still hardly believed in it.

'It isn't just me wanting to be dominated the whole time,' resumed Vivienne. 'But when you care about someone, you've got to interfere with their life now and then. It's all part of it. I interfere with his over some things. For instance, he's a bit silly about being black, and I don't let him get away with any of that.'

'You sound as if you and he have spent about six months together.'

'It feels rather like that. We did spend the whole of yesterday together.'

'You took the day off? You've never done that before.'

'Not to be with you, no. You never asked me to. And here's more of what I mean. I've got bad taste in clothes and everything, haven't I? Give me an honest answer, Doug. You can now.'

'Yes, you have.'

'But you never told me, because you were being the unmasterful male. Not interfering. Gilbert told me straight away. He went through the whole of my wardrobe and picked out about five things and said I could keep them, but I was never to wear any of the others again. Same with my jewellery and stuff.'

After a moment, I said, 'What does you being engaged mean exactly?'

'Well, I got rid of that chap with the beard right off.'

'And now you're getting rid of me.'

'I hope so. No, Doug, the point is, you know about me liking being shared, because I like a lot of, you know, because I'm a bit . . .'

'Highly sexed.'

'I suppose so. Anyway, Gilbert doesn't approve of that, me being shared, I mean. Decadent, he calls it. He says he'd think the same

whether I was having anything to do with him or not, and I believe
him. And I agree with him, really. So, we're going to be engaged for
three months and if I haven't had to be shared or missed being shared
too much in that time, then we'll get married.'

'I see.' I paused again, then said as genially as possible, 'Of course,
these blokes are supposed to be greatly gifted, aren't they? That would
make up to some extent for . . .'

During our association, Vivienne had done her fair share of laughing, but mostly, I realized, out of high spirits or in response to a
full-grown external joke, at the cinema and so on, not as now. 'Fancy
someone like you thinking there's something in that. Oh, I know a
lot of people do. Girls. Gilbert says quite a lot of stuff's come his way
because they think – you know. If you're interested,' – she blushed
and looked down at her coffee-cup, but with a silent snigger – 'it's just
like yours, only black.'

I counted out money. 'So as far as that's concerned, you could have
got engaged to me instead.'

'Yes, I could, except you never asked me, and I always knew really
you were never going to. I suppose I took you along to see my father
just in case it might make you think of it. Anyway, there's Penny, isn't
there? Gilbert told me all about that. Now he's gone, you can move
in. Or she can with you.'

I considered in silence. Actual moving-in either way round was
surely out of the question; the general prospect of some sort of affair
with Penny struck me as attractive but irrelevant, like the free offer
of a new and prodigious set of hi-fi equipment.

'Gilbert thinks it would be a good idea. He doesn't want her to be
left on her own. He's quite worried about her.'

'But not worried enough to stay with her.'

'Not now, no, but he thinks you might be able to tide her over for
a bit. I must go, Doug.'

In the street, her manner, which had cooled rather in the last
minute, warmed up again. She took my arm.

'Dad's having a few friends and neighbours in for drinks tomorrow
about six, sort of a very informal unofficial engagement-party. I mean
the engagement's unofficial as well as the party. Can you come?'

'Oh, you won't want me there, will you, you and Gilbert?'

'Yes we will. I will, because of you and me, and he will, because he thinks he owes you an apology, he says.'

'What for?'

'Well, he has taken your girl-friend off you, hasn't he?'

I looked into her clear brown eyes and at her firm mouth. 'Yes, he has, hasn't he? But tell him there are no hard feelings.'

We halted on the kerb opposite her office, between pedestrians and hurrying traffic.

'Can you come tomorrow?'

'I'll have to see,' I said. (What I would have to see was whether Penny would be at home and available later the following evening, when attendance at the informal-etc. party would have brought me nearly three-quarters of the way to her on the good old North-Western Line.) 'I'll make it if I possibly can.'

'Mind you do. Don't bother to come across the road with me: let's say goodbye here. I don't mean completely, of course, but – you know.'

'Yes, of course.'

'Thank you for being so sweet about everything.'

'I haven't been sweet at all.'

'Yes you have. Because of what you haven't said and haven't made me feel. You should have heard the way the bloke with the beard went on. Letting him down and letting myself down. I expect you can imagine.'

'Yes, I think I can.'

We embraced and kissed briefly. I could not see her eyes when she turned away, but her mouth had lost its firmness. Her figure, trim in the olive uniform, and strong-looking in a sense that had not struck me before, moved confidently across to the far pavement and, after a final hasty wave at her office doorway, disappeared.

I went back to the flat and wrote my piece for the paper, half of it about a new opera just then going into rehearsal, the other and slightly longer half about *Elevations 9*.

# Ten

## *All Free Now*

'Was it really as bad as you say?' asked Harold.

'Well yes. Even worse, if anything. I haven't gone into the way he used classical conventions to—'

'I hear all the other notices so far have been wildly favourable.'

'Not all. The *Custodian* this morning was very stuffy.'

Harold shifted his gaze from my copy to what appeared to be another sheet of typescript beside it on his desk. 'On this piece of . . . popsical music the kids voted with their feet, and only that noted sense of duty kept me from going along . . . mixture never got to the boil . . . somewhere between three stools. That's young Bolsover.'

'I know; he was—'

'The point of sending the two of you to cover the same event was to get two quite different points of view, and here you are both taking the same line.'

'It isn't the same line. From our quite different points of view, we each decided independently and for our own reasons that there was nothing in it for either of us.'

'A line which runs directly counter to the general verdict. We've talked before about the dangers of eccentricity for its own sake. Independence is one thing, but can't you find a redeeming feature or so? The technique of it, or something like that?'

'You can't talk about technique as if it were . . . No, Harold, and I don't think you'll get Terry to shift either.'

'All right, all right.'

'And you hate him. Roy, I mean.'

'I'm running a newspaper. How is he?'

'He'll be out of hospital some time today.'

'I'm sorry to hear that. They ought to have kicked his head in while they were about it. Still, in general they showed him up for the oaf he is.'

Perhaps for the first time since I had known him, warmth had entered Harold's voice, and, certainly for the first time, he looked me straight in the face. One more mini-mystery seemed cleared up: I had been included in the Retrenchment Club lunch-party not out of indifference but by design, so that I might witness my friend's discomfiture.

'You don't know him,' I said. 'You wouldn't—'

'One thing you can do for me.' Already he was back in his poky little shell. 'I want no further dealings with him, so you tell him he's won. I'll make no further move to interfere.'

I stood and waited, in the substantial hope that Harold's style of oral free-association would see to it that my curiosity was satisfied.

'It was much more damaging than the piece I was threatening to print. The two of them must have got together on it. No newspaper would take it, but *Peeping Tom* isn't a newspaper. You remember what they did to that actor chap last year, and he didn't get a bean out of them. Even if you win, they've nothing to pay you with. And you're fired.'

'Yes, I imagine you are,' I said, taking the last remark as a mildly fanciful description of what happened to you, or how you felt, when you tried to sue *Peeping Tom*.

'No no. *You're . . . fired.*'

'Oh, I see.'

'I'll make out a cheque for four weeks' worth and send it along to you.'

'Thanks. This is the next best thing to getting at Roy himself. Not a very good next best.'

'Better than nothing, and that's only part of it. Just the timing. I don't care for what you write. I was against hiring you in the first place, as you know.'

'No, Harold, I don't know. You told me it was all your idea.'

'Rubbish, you're dreaming. Good morning to you.'

Along in Features, I told Coates and Bolsover my news.

'It's the way he keeps thinking up new ways of being a shit that you can't help taking your hat off to him for,' said Coates.

'So perhaps sacking me as well'd seem a bit tame,' said Bolsover. 'How much actual difference will it make to you?'

'Not an enormous amount. I can more or less walk into a small spot with *Discs and Listening*. And I've got a contact in Brandenburg Records. But it's a bit unsettling.'

'Come over to the Fleece and I'll buy you a beer,' said Coates.

'I owe you one. Several, in fact.'

'I'll join you when I've got my okay,' said Bolsover.

'Did I do all right the other night?' asked Coates in the saloon of the Fleece.

'First-class. You gave me all the time I needed.'

'I kept being afraid he'd think balls to it and hang up. How did your end of it go? – whatever it was.'

'As well as could be expected.'

'That's bloody well, isn't it, as well as that?'

'Looked at in one way, I suppose it is, yes.'

I arrived back at the flat about three, with a good deal of beer and some sausages under my belt, and settled down to play the Brahms-Handel Variations. I performed the piece, after a false start or two, with great dash and depth of feeling, but also with an unusually high proportion of wrong notes. Never mind, I thought to myself as I started to fall asleep on the couch – Schnabel had played plenty of wrong notes in his time. Tea, toast, a bath and change saw me through until five, and a long brisk walk, a ride in the Tube, and a shorter, less brisk walk brought me to the Copes doorstep just after six.

Mr Copes himself, wearing a pink-and-white striped jacket that recalled bygone musical comedies with a campus setting, let me in and took me into his study. Here, a couple of dozen people of high average age and rather crude type-casting stood about with curious-looking drinks in their hands. I caught sight of Gilbert face to face with a gesticulating cleric; then Vivienne came out from behind someone, gave me a cousinly kiss, and introduced me to her (elder) brother and sister-in-law, whom I recognized from having seen their photographs, together with a fat and silent aunt-like figure. Vivienne went away again at once, to be replaced by Mr Copes, who handed me a small tumbler containing what I tried, with some success, not to think of as a urine sample drawn from one gravely ill. He was accompanied by a man who could there and then have sat for a left-wing cartoonist assigned to portray a retired major, and who turned out to be called Major somebody.

'See what you think of it, Doug. It's by way of being a little invention of my own.'

Under the silent gaze of five persons, I forestalled, perhaps by the briefest of margins, actual spotlight and/or side-drum roll, and drank. The fluid was both sweet and bitter without blending or reconciling these qualities to any degree, held a powerful tang of something far removed from any liquor I knew – something like roast chestnuts or camphor – had a bubble or two in it and was slightly warm.

'Interesting,' I said.

'Interesting. That's a terrific postcard word, isn't it? Today we saw all round the folk museum; it was very interesting. Spanish champagne, Angostura, and something else I keep very dark. Yes, I think interesting is just about right. You saw what that fellow from Zambia was saying the other day, did you? Or was it Malawi?'

Since Mr Copes was looking at me, it was I who answered, 'No, I don't think so.'

'Oh yes, I promise you. Our Prime Minister was worse than Mr Hitler. I swear to you. Our Prime Minister.'

'Oh, but he's got to say that,' said the younger Copes. 'Home consumption. You don't want to take it too seriously.'

'And we and the South Africans were plotting to massacre the entire black population of Africa.'

'I only wish it was true,' said the major in a cockney whine so exaggerated as to make even me want to ask the name of his regiment.

'Oh, you're joking,' said the younger Copes.

'I bloody am not joking, mate. They're monkeys, that lot, all of 'em.'

'You're not to mind the major,' said Mr Copes. 'He's a bit of a reactionary. I don't feel we should go any further than just invading them all and turning them back into colonies. They'd thank us for it, you know. I'm thinking entirely of them. Unlike the major here. Would you let your daughter marry a black man, Doug?'

'Yes, if she really wanted to.'

'Ah, now that's the point exactly.'

'I'd have forced mine to if I'd had half a chance,' said the major. 'Teach the cow.'

'There, there, Major.' Mr Copes lifted his glass towards his mouth, then quickly lowered it again. 'Of course, it's a silly question, isn't it? One can't prevent them these days. Still, one can exert various sorts of pressure. I'm not going to. I positively wish my daughter to marry a black man – that black man over there, anyway – and I'll tell you why.'

'Don't you think, Dad, perhaps another time . . . ?'

'As many times as you like. I've told Gilbert all about it already. The whole thing is this. She really wants to, because she's bright enough to have foreseen the difficulties, and because she's always got on very well with me and her brothers and everybody and she's never hankered after any different sort of life and background from the ones she's got. And that means she hasn't decided to do this so as to show me or what the major would call teach me or get her own back on anything. She isn't doing it on purpose, if I make myself clear. That's good enough for me. Now you must excuse me while I go round and top up the beakers.'

Given that every glass in sight was at least three-quarters full, this move seemed unnecessary, but Mr Copes took hold of an earthenware jug and set off. The major's suitably bloodshot eyes flickered at mine. After some slow-motion twitches involving his head and shoulders, he whined,

'Not that I wouldn't rather die than make that fellow feel uncomfortable, you understand. Trouble is, I've had some unfortunate experiences of those people. I remember when I was in—'

With the sense of timing that was better developed in her than in any other girl I had ever known, Vivienne came up at this precise point and took me off to talk to two additional girls who worked in her office. That was all right, but their and her sudden withdrawal in favour of three further aunt-types was less welcome, and the later arrival of the gesticulating cleric, who turned out to gesticulate when listening (or not talking) as well as when talking, did little to mend matters. After some minutes of him, I disengaged myself, said good-bye to Mr Copes, and cornered Vivienne under the portrait of Haydn.

'Viv, I'm off.'

'But you've only just come, and we haven't had a chance . . . All right. I'll see you out. Hang on a second.'

By the time we reached the doorstep, Gilbert had joined us. He showed no traces of the scruffiness I had noticed on our recent encounters: this was the Gilbert of our first meeting, smartly and soberly clad. What with Vivienne beside him in her new trouser-suit, the pair of them looked ready for the taking of a commemorative photograph.

'Vivienne tells me you don't need an apology from me,' he said, 'but also I've good reason to be grateful to you. I wanted to tell you that.'

'Thank you, but there's really no . . .'

'But for you I should never have met her, you see. In addition, you've been kind to my friends the Vandervanes.'

'Not to much effect, I'm afraid.'

'You've been of some comfort to them at various times. If you can help Penny in the least, I'd be still more grateful. Perhaps you could let me know how she is.'

'Yes, of course.'

'You must be sure to come and visit us when we're settled. Good-bye for the present, Douglas.'

'Yes. Goodbye, Gilbert.'

We shook hands; then, without either hurry or hesitation, he turned and went back into the house. Vivienne looked at me in silence, rubbing between finger and thumb a head of lavender she had picked from a clump that grew by the wall.

'Why didn't he bring any of his, uh, pals along this evening?' I asked incuriously.

'Said he couldn't get hold of any of them he could be sure they'd behave themselves in time.' Her tone was as flat as mine had been. 'You know, wouldn't start going on about the colour bar and things. He's changed a lot about all that.'

'Really.'

'Doug . . . when I told you about him yesterday and you didn't make a scene or act up or anything, and I said it was sweet of you . . . Well, it still was sweet of you, but it was because you sort of didn't care all that terrifically, wasn't it? Oh, of course you liked me and everything, and you can see I'm not cross or upset, but I'd just like to know. You weren't so off your head about me that you'd try and stop me going, isn't that right?'

'I was very sorry we were packing up and I still am . . .'

'But.'

'All right, but I don't think people should try to stop people doing what they want to do.'

'Because people always know what they want to do without anyone else saying what they want, the other ones. I thought so.' She broke off another head of lavender. 'You're going off to see Penny now, are you?'

'Yes.'

'Do you think you'll be able to help her like Gilbert said?'

'I don't know.'

'Because you mustn't mind me saying this, Doug, but if you're really going to help somebody in the state she's supposed to be in, or actually if you're really going to help anybody at all, then you've got to really do something about it, take it on, do nothing else for a bit, well, not nothing else, but make it your number one priority until it's cleared up or you realize it absolutely can't be, whatever it is.'

'Gilbert tried to really do something about Penny, and he doesn't seem to have got anywhere.'

'I know, I'm not saying you'll always get somewhere if you really try, I'm saying you won't get anywhere if you don't. And at least he really tried.'

'I'm sure he did.'

'Sorry, but I've been thinking about you a lot, these last few days. Isn't it awful? – I was so relieved you didn't make a scene, and I was disappointed too. That's women for you, isn't it? Off you go now – I must get back to those people. I'll give you a ring, probably in a couple of weeks.'

We performed another cousinly embrace and parted. That point about helping others, or not helping others, had been well taken. At various times, Roy, Kitty, Penny and Gilbert had asked me for help. Amount of help actually given: nil. The sort of help I actually gave was assuring Terry Bolsover by telephone that his piece on *Elevations 9* contained no musical solecisms. On the other hand, or more likely the same hand, I had certainly adhered to my self-proclaimed rule about not stopping blokes doing what they wanted to do. Exception: delaying by two minutes Roy's professional and public degradation.

These and similarly disagreeable reflections occupied me until, alighting at the end of the North-Western Line into a still, clear evening, I started feeling apprehensive, and also mildly excited, at the prospect of seeing Penny. By the time I was passing the pond, over which a hawk hovered, a less mild excitement had driven out apprehension. I made my way past some Yandell-high nettles into the courtyard. A moment later, the Furry Barrel's voice rang out from inside the kitchen.

I entered the house through the glass porch and found Penny hurrying towards me. She wore a plain scarlet cotton dress that negated any concept of style or fashion, and looked both desirable and pleased to see me, though tired. I kissed her, hearing as I did so a curious sound from the direction of the kitchen. It proved to herald the approach of the Furry Barrel, not at her usual canter, but laboriously and on three legs. One hind leg, with what looked like a rubber bandage on it, stuck out at an angle, and there was an arrangement of straps over her rump. She hobbled up, smelt me and wagged her abundant tail.

'What's the matter with her?'

'She's broken something, or dislocated something. I'm not quite clear what it is.'

'But she'll be all right?'

'That leg won't, the vet said. She'll always be more or less on three legs.'

'How did it happen?'

'It was Ashley, apparently. I wasn't here, but he must have given her a kicking. He said she tried to bite him.'

'She'd never bite anybody.'

I stooped down and stroked the dog's silky head, feeling as if something dismal had happened right in the middle of my own life and concerns, something major, something irretrievable, as if I had taken a fatally wrong decision years before and only now seen how much I had lost by it.

'She's quite old,' said Penny consolingly.

'Oh, good.'

'You can't blame Ashley.'

'Oh yes you can. And you can blame his parents even more. Where is he, anyway? He's not here, is he?'

'No: Kitty's taken him away for a few days.'

'With a couple of ex-Royal Marine commandos in attendance.'

'A nurse, and she's gone to stay with a friend who's got a little girl of eight and another nurse. Near Brighton.'

'Four against two. They ought to be able to hold the number of animals crippled at a reasonable level. One a day, perhaps.'

'Calm down. Would you like a drink?'

'Yes. Yes, please. Does Roy know about this?'

'Scotch and water?'

'Yes. Does Roy know?'

'Yes, and he was terrifically upset and gave Ashley a frightful bawling-out.'

'And that was that.'

'Well, you know Daddy and Kitty are dead against hitting kids and so on.'

'So they are. Is there anybody else here? Christopher and his girl?'

'They've gone back to Northampton.'

We had moved along the passage, which was lined with piles of empty cardboard cartons, across the hall, where there was a mound of old newspapers and a much bigger one of apparently discarded toys, and into the drawing-room. Here, surprisingly, everything was in order, though there was no look of disuse. I said something about this to Penny when she came up with my drink.

'I live in here, really,' she said. 'Here and in my bedroom. The rest of the place I've pretty well had to let go. Oh, except for the kitchen. I can just about manage, with only me to look after.'

'Don't you get lonely, on your own in the house?'

'No, not a bit. I love it. I never want to go out: there's so much to do here. I know I should have gone down to see Daddy in hospital, but when I telephoned they said he was doing well, and I suppose it was ghastly of me, but he seemed to be coming out more or less straight away, and I was so busy I just didn't go. You'll have been, I expect?'

'Yes. He's all right, physically at least. Busy doing what?'

'Oh, nothing much.' She gave me an embarrassed half-glance. 'Reading and . . . all that kind of thing.'

I noticed, on a table beside a clean ashtray and a bowl of freshly cut roses, a thin paperback in a format I thought I recognized. I soon saw it was the BBC publication by Denis Matthews on Beethoven's piano sonatas. And, I further saw, the first volume of these sonatas lay on the music-rest of the piano, open at the minuet of No. 1. Immediately – though belatedly enough – I said,

'What's happened?'

'Happened about what?'

'Even the way you talk. And your accent. And the way you stand. Have you fallen in love, or what?'

She laughed: a different laugh, with no edge of sarcasm to it. 'Oh no, nothing like that. That wouldn't be me at all.'

'What is it, then? You seem so self-contained. Happy.'

'Yes, both of those. It's very simple. I've gone on to the hard stuff.'

'You mean the booze.'

'No, Douglas. Hard drugs.'

'Heroin?'

'Don't sound so terrified. Yes, well, that kind of thing. It's not a bit what you think it's like. Surely you can see that just by talking to me.'

'The expectation of life of a heroin addict is about two years. A doctor friend of mine was telling me.'

'That's one of the things that's so nice about it. Nothing's going to last. None of that awful business of getting married and having children and being responsible. Nobody expecting anything of you.'

'What about Beethoven? He lasts.'

'He won't last me. I'll never be good enough. You've got to find out what your limitations are. I've found out mine, and I can arrange my life to fit in with them exactly. Not many people can do that.'

'Penny, go up and pack a suitcase and come down to my flat and let me look after you.'

She laughed again. 'Do you remember me telling you, nobody takes me on? Anyway, I do. That's one thing that hasn't changed. And you couldn't do it. Thank you for asking me, but you wouldn't stick at it, would you? Do you think you could do what Gilbert couldn't do?'

I looked down at the newly swept carpet. 'Does your father know about this?'

'I don't think so. I suppose he'll find out eventually. He won't do anything about it either. Why should he? He's got his own life to lead. You know, Douglas, going off with that girl is going to be the best thing he'll ever have done. For everybody, not just him. We're all free now.'

# PENGUIN MODERN CLASSICS

**ENDING UP**
KINGSLEY AMIS

At Tuppenny-hapenny Cottage in the English countryside, five elderly people live together in rancorous disharmony. Adela Bastable bosses the house, as her brother Bernard passes his days thinking up malicious schemes against the baby-talking Marigold and secret drinker Shorty, while kindly George lays bedridden upstairs. The mismatched quintet keeps their spirits alive by bickering and waiting for grandchildren to visit at Christmas. But the festive season does not herald goodwill to all at Tuppenny-hapenny Cottage. Disaster and chaos, it seems, are just around the corner ...

Told with Amis's piercing wit and humanity, *Ending Up* is a wickedly funny black comedy of the indignities of old age.

'A genuine comic writer, probably the best after P. G. Wodehouse' John Mortimer

'Amis has never done better ... a very funny but also a very serious book' *Observer*

With an Introduction by Helen Dunmore

# Penguin Modern Classics

**ONE FAT ENGLISHMAN**
KINGSLEY AMIS

Brimming with gluttony, booze and lust, Roger Micheldene is loose in America. Supposedly visiting Budweiser University to make deals for his publishing firm in England, Roger instead sets out to offend all he meets and to seduce every woman he encounters. But his American hosts seem made of sterner stuff. Who will be Roger's undoing? Irving Macher, the young author of an annoyingly brilliant first novel? Father Colgate, the priest who suggests that Roger's soul is in torment? Or will it be his married ex-lover Helene? One thing is certain – Roger is heading for a terrible fall.

Outrageously funny and irreverent, *One Fat Englishman* is a devastating satire on Anglo-American relations.

'Few have been as perceptive or funny about bad behaviour as Amis' *Daily Telegraph*

'The leading British comic novelist of his generation ... his aim was deadly accurate' *The Times*

With an Introduction by David Lodge

# Penguin Modern Classics

---

**THE KING'S ENGLISH**
KINGSLEY AMIS

'A terrific book ... learned, robust, aggressive, extremely funny' Sebastian
Faulks

*The King's English* is Kingsley Amis's authoritative and witty guide to the use
and abuse of the English language.

Ascourge of illiteracy and a thorn in the side of pretension, Amis provides
indispensable advice about the linguistic blunders and barbarities that lie in
wait for us, from danglers and four-letter words to jargon, and even Welsh rare-
bit. If you have ever wondered whether it's acceptable to start a sentence with
'and', to boldly split an infinitive, or to cross your sevens in the French style,
Amis has the answer – or a trenchant opinion. By turns reflective, acerbic and
provocative, *The King's English* is for anyone who cares about how the English
language is used.

With an introduction by Martin Amis

# PENGUIN MODERN CLASSICS

**LUCKY JIM**
KINGSLEY AMIS

Jim Dixon has accidentally fallen into a job at one of Britain's new red brick universities. A moderately successful future in the History Department beckons. As long as Jim can survive a madrigal-singing weekend at Professor Welch's, deliver a lecture on 'Merrie England' and resist Christine, the hopelessly desirable girlfriend of Welch's awful son Bertrand.

'A flawless comic novel ... I loved it then, as I do now. It has always made me laugh out loud' Helen Dunmore, *The Times*

'A brilliantly and preposterously funny book' *Guardian*

With an Introduction by David Lodge

# Penguin Modern Classics

**THE SOUND OF TRUMPETS**
JOHN MORTIMER

When a Tory MP is found dead in a swimming pool wearing a leopardskin bikini, the embittered Leslie (now Lord) Titmuss sees the ideal opportunity to re-enter the political arena. All he needs is a puppet, and Terry Flitton – inoffensive New Labourite – is perfect. Along with his beautiful, very PC wife, Terry heads blindly for the Hartscombe and Worsfield South by-election. But is he too busy listening for the sound of victory trumpets to notice that the Tory dinosaur is not quite extinct?

John Mortimer's brilliant follow-up to *Paradise Postponed* and *Titmuss Regained*, *The Sound of Trumpets* is a devilishly witty satire on political ambition, spin and sleaze, and the culmination of a masterly trilogy.

'Delicious … Mortimer in vintage form' *Observer*

'A thumping good plot … Titmuss is one of the writer's finest creations' *Sunday Telegraph*

# Penguin Modern Classics

**A VOYAGE ROUND MY FATHER**
JOHN MORTIMER

In John Mortimer's most famous and highly autobiographical play, a young man looks back on an unconventional childhood and youth overshadowed by his irascible and eccentric father. Sent away to boarding school to be 'prepared for life', he finds teachers deranged by shell shock after the First World War and boys who try to coat their ordinary home lives with romance. As the Second World War begins, the mild-mannered protagonist tries to become a writer, but is compelled to become a barrister like his father – a towering character depicted with affection and exasperation.

Hugely popular since it was first performed, *A Voyage Round My Father* is a sublimely comic drama of warmth, nostalgia and wisdom.

'Generous and humane … Mortimer's fond tribute to his father could hardly be a finer tribute to himself' *Guardian*

'A skilful, witty and touching evocation of his extraordinary parent … a perfect synthesis of reality and art' *Daily Telegraph*

*Contemporary … Provocative … Outrageous …*
*Prophetic … Groundbreaking … Funny … Disturbing …*
*Different … Moving … Revolutionary … Inspiring …*
*Subversive … Life-changing …*

## What makes a modern classic?

At Penguin Classics our mission has always been to make the best
books ever written available to everyone. And that also means
constantly redefining and refreshing exactly what makes a 'classic'.
That's where Modern Classics come in. Since 1961 they have been an
organic, ever-growing and ever-evolving list of books from the last
hundred (or so) years that we believe will continue to be read over and
over again.

They could be books that have inspired political dissent, such as
*Animal Farm*. Some, like *Lolita* or *A Clockwork Orange*, may have
caused shock and outrage. Many have led to great films, from *In Cold
Blood* to *One Flew Over the Cuckoo's Nest*. They have broken down
barriers – whether social, sexual, or, in the case of *Ulysses*, the
boundaries of language itself. And they might – like *Goldfinger* or
*Scoop* – just be pure classic escapism. Whatever the reason, Penguin
Modern Classics continue to inspire, entertain and enlighten millions
of readers everywhere.

'No publisher has had more influence on reading habits than Penguin'
**Independent**

'Penguins provided a crash course in world literature'
**Guardian**

*The best books ever written*

PENGUIN ![penguin logo] CLASSICS

SINCE 1946

Find out more at www.penguinclassics.com